MW00709720

THE TIME OF THE
CRICKET

THE TIME OF THE CRICKET

A NOVEL
WILLIAM D. BLANKENSHIP

DONALD I. FINE, INC.

New York

This book is dedicated to the new generation
Billy and Jessika Blankenship
and
Rachel Volosing

Copyright © 1995 by William D. Blankenship

All rights reserved, including the right of reproduction in whole or in part
in any form. Published in the United States of America by Donald I. Fine,
Inc. and in Canada by General Publishing Company Limited.

Library of Congress Catalogue Card Number: 94-68099

ISBN: 1-55611-430-3

Manufactured in the United States of America

10 9 8 7 6 5 4 3 2 1

Designed by Irving Perkins Associates

This novel is a work of fiction. Names, characters, places and incidents are
either the product of the author's imagination or are used fictitiously. Any
resemblance to actual events, locales, organizations or persons, living or
dead, is entirely coincidental and beyond the intent of either
the author or publisher.

Chapter 1

"Where are we?" Kay Williams asked. "Still in Shinjuku? *Kajima Katana Wadoko desuka?*"

The taxi driver, who wore gloves as sparkling white as a wedding dress, nodded vigorously to indicate he understood the question, though obviously he did not.

Kay had a few words of Japanese. And German and French and Italian and Spanish and Greek. She took pride in the fact that she could make herself understood wherever she stepped off a plane.

Except in Tokyo.

This was her second trip to Tokyo and she still felt lost and unable to communicate. Even though she spoke her few Japanese words with the precision of a speech therapist, most people reacted to her with muted confusion, real or feigned, it didn't matter.

Nevertheless, Kay renewed her conversation with the taxi driver.

"Kajima Katana?" she repeated. "Kajima Sword?" In case the driver knew some English, she added: "Do you know where this place is?"

Another energetic nod, accompanied by a guttural *"Hai!"*,

1

the all-purpose Japanese word that might and often did mean anything.

Kay gave up and peered out the window.

She had expected to have trouble finding Kajima Katana. Her client had warned her that Turo Kajima seemed to detest the telephone and in any case refused to list his number in the Tokyo directory or on his letterhead. Kajima apparently preferred to do business in person and in the Japanese language, though it was said he could speak some English. But only on rare occasions would Kajima do business with Americans or Europeans. He believed that the antique samurai swords that he sold should remain in Japan.

Why then, Kay wondered, had Kajima agreed so readily to sell an important piece . . . a legendary samurai sword once owned by Emperor Meiji . . . to an *American*? Strange. She would discover soon enough that the reason was not just strange but reflected his sense of foreboding and fear . . . a climate she was, all innocently, moving directly into.

For now he just sounded like another of those irascible eccentrics she seemed fated to deal with, like the Stuttgart industrialist who longed to own Hitler's personal P-38 pistol; the wealthy Palm Beach widow who collected garters worn by famous courtesans of history; the Texas real estate developer with a penchant for hand-carved antique penises.

At least this deal with Turo Kajima was, or seemed, fairly straightforward. Complete the negotiation. Make payment. Take possession of the sword. Deliver it to the client in Philadelphia.

Piece of cake, compared to her last acquisition. On that one Kay had spent four long months tracking down the owner of Hitler's P-38 pistol and another three weeks persuading the owner to part with the object. In the end, money talked, the handgun went for one million eight. Not too shabby. And her fee—one hundred and eighty thousand dollars—had made the long search lucrative. The acquisition, though, had been a tough one. At one point she was threatened by a competitor from Berlin, and in the end she closed the deal for the pistol in a hotel suite in Dublin and scooted out a back door two steps ahead of a thug sent to take it away from her.

Now here she was in Tokyo negotiating for still another weapon, not so surprising since weapons with brutal histories were especially prized by antique collectors. She spotted a building they already had passed at least twice and realized the taxi driver was searching for Kajima Katana.

"Tomate, kudasai," she said as clearly as she could.

To her surprise, the driver came to an immediate stop. The meter read three thousand one hundred. Kay took a five thousand yen note from her purse and thrust it into the driver's hand. "Keep the change."

If any English phrase was universal, that should be it. It was. The driver appeared to understand but seemed offended. With utmost dignity he counted out the exact change and passed it to Kay over the seat. What a country . . . where people acted insulted when you offered them a tip. Not a promising omen.

She found herself pressed into the center of the largest crowd she had ever seen on an ordinary city street. Thousands swarmed through the winding, alleylike avenues of Shinjuku with the power of a tidal wave. No one seemed to be just walking. Not the children with schoolbags strapped to their backs. Not the bent elderly women in traditional dress. Not the young office girls giggling with each other on their way back from lunch. Not the serious businessmen in dark suits. None walked, all scurried.

The pressure of the dense jostling crowds made it difficult to concentrate, so she stepped into the doorway of a noodle shop and took out of her purse a Tokyo city map provided by the concierge at the Imperial Hotel. The concierge had circled Shinjuku and apologized for the fact that most Tokyo streets had no names, and that since buildings were not numbered sequentially it didn't help much to have an address.

"Hard to find right building," the concierge said sadly. "Need landmark."

"I only know that I'm looking for an antique shop in Shinjuku called Kajima Katana."

"You know phone number?"

"No, it's not in the English-language Tokyo phone book, and the hotel operator can't find it in the KDD directory. I've never talked to the man, only exchanged letters with him. You say the address doesn't mean anything?"

"To postman only. The number of a Tokyo building says in what year of which emperor, not where it is located. *San-chome. San* means three. *Chome* means neighborhood. That is as close as I can direct you."

"God, what a system."

The concierge looked crushed, as if he personally had caused Kay's problem. "Walk east of railway station. Old section of Shinjuku. That is Shinjuku *san-chome.*"

Which was what Kay was now attempting to do, without much luck.

As she walked east the streets became narrower and still more congested and the noise overpowering. When she stopped to get her bearings she found herself caught between the shrill sales pitch of an old man peddling baked sweet potatoes from a dilapidated truck and the blast of electronic noise from a nearby *pachinko* parlor.

Headache time. She reached into her purse for a tin of aspirin, swallowed two tablets, winced at their bitterness and pressed on.

Now that she was deep into a neighborhood where few westerners were ever seen, she began to attract attention. Not surprisingly. She was a beautiful woman of thirty plus, so slim and fit that people sometimes took her for a pro golfer or dancer. Her face had the elegance of simplicity—a straight nose, high cheekbones, lips that needed no gloss. A few girl-hood freckles were still visible on her cheeks. Her flamboy-ant head of reddish-brown hair, stylish clothes and long tanned legs turned all heads, men and women alike. Espe-cially in Japan, where elegance had been elevated to a kind of religion.

Kay's search through Shinjuku was conducted with her customary attention to detail, one square block at a time in grids of three blocks, gradually working her way eastward. She found Tokyo similar to New York in that particular neighborhoods housed many shops doing the same business. A street of pottery shops. Another lined with boutiques sell-ing designer clothes. On still another narrow street she found enough hair salons to give perms to every woman in the state of Connecticut, which is where she made the home she didn't see very often. There was even a restaurant row along which one could find everything from Japanese *soba* to French cuisine.

She walked on through a section of movie houses and porn shops. Plastered to the front windows of the shops were small color photos of naked Japanese girls, along with their phone numbers. Judging from the outsized proportions of the girls, breast implants were as popular in Tokyo as in the States.

What Kay did not find was an antique shop specializing in Japanese swords.

She had about decided to break off for the nonce her search and return to the quiet opulence of the Imperial for a drink and a bath when something caught her eye. At the end of a street of ragtag apartments and shops stood a gleaming red Mercedes limousine. Kay walked toward the car, pulse quick-ening. Behind the wheel a uniformed chauffeur was reading a *manga*, a two-inch-thick adult comic book full of the kind of *outré* sex and violence that many Japanese men seemed to love so much.

The owner must be inside one of the shops. Which one? Not the shoe-repair shop. Not the grimy toy store with the window full of matchbook cars . . . At which point she spotted a handsome wood carving of a sword fastened above the entrance to the shop closest to the limo. She couldn't read the Kanji pictograph underneath the sword, but it was identical to the Japanese printing on the letterhead of her correspondence from Turo Kajima.

"Got'cha!"

She crossed the street and entered a shop no more than twenty feet wide by thirty feet deep, simply but graciously decorated, with recessed lighting that bathed the interior in soft tones.

Two men were examining a sword. Holding the weapon was a short, heavyset Japanese in a dark suit. His hands were large. They held the sword awkwardly, but apparently with a feeling of reverence.

The other Japanese, taller and older, gray-haired, at least seventy, was dressed in a navy blue blazer, gray slacks, a patterned shirt and knitted tie and Gucci loafers. He looked over the rims of his glasses at Kay.

"*Kanichiwa.*" Then, switching to English, "Please excuse me, I will be with you in a moment."

So Turo Kajima did speak English. A blessing. Kay moved through the shop, relieved to have a few minutes alone to pull her thoughts together.

There were no more than a couple of dozen swords on display. A small stock but obviously select. They were laid out on silk backgrounds of gold or red in glass cases. Beneath each sword was a card on which the weapon's provenance had been written by hand in Japanese. The prices were stated in yen. The least expensive sword was listed at 1.5 million yen, or about fifteen thousand dollars. The most expensive was eight million yen—approximately eighty thousand dollars.

Someone who did not deal in antiques might have been surprised to note that the most expensive sword was the least beautiful. Its wooden handgrip had rotted away decades ago, leaving only the bare steel tang beneath. It did not even have a scabbard.

Though hardly an expert in antique Japanese weapons, Kay understood that the less imposing sword must have been owned either by a shogun or by a member of the Imperial family, thereby increasing its value tenfold over better pre-served swords from the same era.

The customer who had been examining the sword replaced it in its case. After a few words the visitor bowed to Kajima. Kajima bowed in return and the visitor left.

Kajima turned to Kay with a smile. A fixed smile. "I am so sorry you were kept waiting. Oh, please excuse me. I take it for granted you are American. Or French?"

"I'm American."

"Amazing. You are so *chic*, you should be French." He bowed. "I am Turo Kajima, the proprietor of this establish-ment. How may I help you?"

Though well up in years, Kay thought, Turo Kajima was still a handsome man with strong, unlined features, erect posture, and magnetic dark eyes. "I'm Kay Williams and I'm here to complete our negotiations for the sword that be-longed to Emperor Meiji."

"Ah yes, the Meiji sword. . . ."

She couldn't read much from that response. "I hope you were expecting me. Since I didn't have a phone or fax number for you I wrote *and* sent a telegram confirming the date I'd be here and the price we had agreed on." His quiet scrutiny was disturbing. "Our deal for the sword is still on, isn't it?"

"Yes," Kajima answered . . . with a certain melancholy? "The deal is still on, as you put it." He straightened his shoulders and managed to look more cheerful. "But before you examine the sword we must drink tea. My poor shop is so small that I must ask you to come up to my office for that. This way, please."

They went up a narrow flight of steps to an office Spartanly furnished with a desk, two chairs and, in one corner, a low tea table flanked by two cushions. The floor of the office, like the floor of the showroom below, was covered by a traditional Japanese woven mat rather than carpeting.

"Do not worry, my dear. You won't have to squat on the *tatami* mat for your tea. We'll have it right here at my desk."

"I wouldn't mind sitting on the floor."

"I'm afraid that I would." Kajima poured out two cups of hot water from a kettle that sat on a warmer behind his desk and offered Kay a variety of tea bags. "I'm seventy-eight, much too old to sit cross-legged on *tatami*. We would not be able to talk over the sound of my poor old bones creaking away."

Kay doubted that. The man looked very fit, indeed.

They sat across the desk from each other. Kajima sipped his tea and from time to time looked rather directly at Kay's breasts. She wanted to proceed with business but knew that the Japanese preferred to move very deliberately into a negotiation. So she sipped her tea and tried not to be put off by Kajima's direct gaze. He was, after all, she reminded herself, seventy-eight.

"From your letters I see that you have an antique store in the town of Ridgefield, Connecticut. I have never been to Connecticut but I hear that it is a lovely green place with rolling hills and many trees."

"Yes, I do have a shop there, though I'm afraid I don't get to spend much time in Connecticut. The last few years I've specialized in finding and acquiring pieces for serious collectors. I have a manager who runs the shop for me."

Kajima nodded. "I made inquiries and was told you are a modern treasure hunter, wandering the world to unearth rarities for your clients. That sounds very exciting."

"It also can be pretty tiring."

"Yes, I'm sure that's true. But you aren't the kind who stays in one place for long. You're a restless person, I saw that in you immediately. Always on the move. What are you looking for, Miss Williams? I mean besides antiques. A little peace? A man to share your life? Or are you running away from something, I wonder?"

Kay was now annoyed, and somewhat shaken, by Kajima's observations. They were too much on target. "When I find out, I'll let you know."

He wasn't easily deflected. "I was also told how beautiful you are. Even so, my contact in the United States did not do justice to your sexual vitality. So much travel must put a terrible strain on your sexual energies."

Kay wasn't sure she had heard him correctly. "I beg your pardon?"

"Sexual energy is so hard to maintain when one travels a great deal. That is why I seldom venture very far from home these days. My mistress . . . my current mistress . . . is twenty-two. A student at Sophia University here in Tokyo. Swedish girl. Very demanding sexually. No, I do not travel much these days."

Turo Kajima canceled out Kay's simplistic image of Japanese men as drones who thought of nothing except money and careers. If she hadn't wanted the sword so badly she would have gotten up and left.

Instead she changed the subject. "Why do you specialize in swords?"

"When I was a boy, my father kept a samurai sword on the wall of his office. He was a rice merchant. Quite successful. We traveled a great deal, which is how I came to learn French and English.

"However, when I was sixteen my father lost all his money in a bad venture. Disgraced, he took the sword down from his office wall and committed *sepuku*. My father killed himself," he repeated, in case she did not know the Japanese word for ritual suicide.

"How awful." Kay was regretting her choice of a new subject.

"I suppose so. Although to a Japanese *sepuku* seems a rational way of avoiding disgrace. At any rate, my mother was already dead. When my father's debts were disposed of the one thing left to me was the sword he had used to kill himself. So I sold the sword and was amazed at how much it brought. From then on I have made a good living buying and selling Japanese swords. Oh yes, Kajima Katana is an honored name in this business."

"You do have an excellent reputation." One thing Kay knew about Japan was that compliments were coin of the realm.

"Thank you. And you, my dear, have excellent breasts. May I ask . . . do you always wear a brassiere?"

Kay felt her face reddening. Not to mention her gorge rising.

"I know what you are thinking. *Dirty old man* is your American phrase. However, I am convinced that a rich sexual life is the key to longevity, so I give a great deal of time and thought to that activity. I hope you are not offended."

"Mr. Kajima—"

"Kajima-san."

"Kajima-san, I can understand why a twenty-two-year-old Swedish girl would be attracted to you. And yes, I generally wear a brassiere. But not always. For instance, I like to run. I don't sleep much so I run early in the morning and when I run I don't wear a brassiere. Does *that* satisfy your curiosity?"

He smiled and sat back, his tea forgotten. "At what hotel are you staying?"

"The Imperial."

"And so you will probably take your run tomorrow morning in Hibiya park. Do not be surprised if you see me lurking about."

Kay had to laugh while Turo Kajima sat back in his chair and continued to admire her breasts. Yes, he *was* a dirty old man. But at least he had *style*, which seemed to be in short supply world-wide.

"Tell me how you got into the antique business," Kajima said.

It was clear that he wasn't in any rush to get down to business. Kay sipped more tea and gave him a vest-pocket version of her story.

"Seven years ago I went through what we call in the States a messy divorce. I was living in New York City, emotionally wiped out, didn't know what to do with myself, tired of my job evaluating antiques for the St. Michael auction house.

"I drove up to Connecticut one Saturday for lunch, just to get away from the city, and spotted an old farmhouse for sale on Route 35. Kind of a dump, more or less abandoned, needed lots of work, but the basic lines of the house were lovely. I don't know what came over me. I had to have it." Kay shook her head, remembering the power of her desire to own that house. "You could call it an epiphany. I decided I *had* to have that house. *Had* to open my own antique shop. *Had* to fix it up myself, do all the repairs with my own hands.

"And that's how I got started. Quit my job, used money from my 401K plan, that's a retirement savings fund, to buy the place and turn it into an antique shop. For the first two years I barely scraped together a living, had only a few antiques in stock. Then a wealthy collector asked me to look for a Queen Anne table for him. I found it and made more on that one commission than on a normal month's receipts.

"I started to gain a reputation for being able to find and negotiate the sale of rare items, and things have gone pretty well for me ever since. End of story."

"Did you remarry?"

"No."

"Do you have a lover? More than one?"

He had a talent for asking outrageous questions in a way that didn't anger her. Not any more. "None at the moment," she said.

"None? Then there is hope for me." He said it like he meant it.

"I'm sorry to rain on your fantasies, Kajima-san, but taking a new lover isn't on my agenda for this trip. And now I'd really like to examine the sword and conclude our deal."

"Of course . . . I am prepared to complete the sale today." His face abruptly drained of all good humor. "Believe me, Miss Williams, I will be happy to sell you that sword and know that it is out of Japan."

"Why? People told me you don't like to see Japanese swords in the hands of American or European collectors."

"Generally true. The weapons I sell are as much a part of Japan as Mount Fuji. They should remain on our soil." His mouth tightened. "But this particular sword *must* be taken out of Japan. Do not ask the reason. And do not be concerned that I am trying to sell you an antique of dubious provenance. This samurai sword was owned by Emperor Meiji, I assure you. I have had it for years and never thought of selling it, especially to a *gaijin* collector. But . . . there are strange winds blowing through Tokyo today." He looked angry. "Dangerous winds, Miss Williams. And so this particular sword must be taken from these shores. Soon!"

Kay was a bit alarmed by his abrupt ferocity.

He noted that and forced himself to smile. "I'm sorry. First I flirt with you, then I frighten you." He stood up. "Come, let me show you a fascinating piece of Japanese history."

Chapter 2

"SAJI-SAN! REPORT IMMEDIATELY to the office of Superintendent Supervisor Yamato!"

Through bleary eyes Detective Inspector Takeo Saji tried to identify the face behind that grating, officious voice. He knew the voice well. Too well. By its very timbre it always annoyed him. In painful stages the rotund features of Senior Superintendent Tadashi Ueno swam into focus.

"Did you hear me, Saji-san?"

"I hear you, Senior Superintendent." Ueno liked to be addressed by his full title. "Tell me something. What does such an exalted person as the superintendent supervisor want with me?"

Ueno drew himself up to his full height of five feet two. "You will be informed at the proper time."

Ueno didn't know the reason for the summons either, but admitting that would bring him down to the same level as his subordinate. Tak stood up carefully in order to disguise his unsteadiness. "I'll go see what Knuckles wants."

"Don't ever use that term in connection with the superintendent supervisor! Do you understand me?"

13

"Why not? From what I've heard it's a well-earned nick-name."

Ueno regarded Tak Saji uneasily. Tak was, after all, a member of the Central Tokyo Special Crimes Unit and therefore a representative of his office. Ueno did not like what he saw.

"Saji-san, we have the same old problem here. You are not discreet. What's more your shoes are improperly shined and your suit is wrinkled. It is a disgrace."

Ueno might have added that Tak was monumentally hung over but did not. There was no stigma to a hangover. Millions of Japanese men struggle daily with the effects of too much *sake* or *beiru* the night before. Men were born to drink and struggle with hangovers.

"I'll give my shoes a quick brush."

"Very well. But hurry. Yamato-san doesn't like to be kept waiting. And don't let your tongue get away from you!"

It doesn't matter how courteously I speak or how well groomed I am, Tak thought. Yamato despises me. So do you, Ueno. So do most of the people in this building. Nothing will change that. Not ever.

With that gloomy thought Tak went at his own pace through the maze of corridors linking the various headquarters elements of the Tokyo Metropolitan Police Department.

On mornings when the effects of cheap *sake* were especially painful, he hated this building and everyone in it. The building itself was so grimly spartan that it made the Pentagon in Washington look like a Club Med. No attempt had been made to enliven the long drab corridors, except for an occasional poster bearing an exhortation such as: BE OF ONE MIND . . . SERVE YOUR SOCIETY.

I don't belong here, he told himself for perhaps the millionth time. But then, I don't belong anywhere. So does it matter where I go?

The reception area of Yamato's office was a festival of steel desks behind which secretaries worked with quiet intensity.

The duty officer composed a frown as Tak approached. He was young, with front teeth so prominent they dominated not only his face but his personality.

"You took your time. Yamato-san has been waiting for you."

"I was working on an important case." Tak tried to imagine what sort of case that might be. "A matter of vital interest to the security of Japan."

The duty officer instantly dropped his rebuking expression. In every branch of the National Police Agency the security of the country was an overriding issue. In his wildest imaginings the duty officer would not believe a Japanese policeman capable of inventing such a lie. "You may go in."

Tak knocked twice and entered. Yamato's office was one of the largest in the Tokyo Metropolitan Police Department, but also as drab as Tak's own cubbyhole. A large steel desk instead of a small one. Official posters and a massive map of the city covering the walls. Flag of Japan standing in the corner. No family pictures. No mementos. Tak had been in prison cells that reflected more warmth.

"Sir. Detective Inspector Takeo Saji reporting as ordered."

"Come in, Saji-san."

Yamato sat in shirtsleeves with two other men at a long table, a steel table, in front of the huge wall map of Tokyo. The other two were senior police superintendents. Yamato stood up.

Tak gave a curt but respectful bow, which was returned by Yamato.

"I have an important assignment for you."

Several manila folders lay on the table along with black-and-white photos of a face familiar to Tak—Hideki Kohno, chairman of Seisa-ko Securities.

In that moment Tak realized why he had been summoned. The trial. Hideki would be going on trial for fraud in two weeks. He had heard rumors that Hideki had well-placed partners in successfully swindling a number of rich Tokyo businessmen out of more than thirty billion yen. His partners apparently had threatened to kill Hideki if he didn't keep his silence. Yamato was personally directing the task force assigned to protect Hideki and get him on the witness stand alive.

For the first time in months Tak felt energized. Someone must have reminded Knuckles Yamato that Hideki Kohno and he were boyhood pals and so Knuckles wanted him on his task force.

"An American known as . . ." Yamato glanced at a slip of paper . . . "James Tucker—what strange names these people have—claims that someone stole his wallet this afternoon on the subway. Ridiculous, of course. Tucker is a businessman visiting Tokyo with his wife. He is also a personal acquaintance of the American ambassador, so we must treat him carefully. Tucker is staying at the Okura. Get over there and take care of the matter."

Yamato passed the slip of paper to Tak. A flat-featured man with no hint of humor in his manner, Yamato's lips now parted slightly in what may have been, for him, a rare smile. "Your kind of case, is it not, Saji-san?"

Tak was stunned. *This* was the reason for the summons? A damn tourist had lost his wallet?

As he took the slip of paper, Tak's eyes strayed to Yamato's hand, to the badly misshapened knuckles. It was whispered that Superintendent Supervisor Yamato had made a nice extra income in his days as a beat policeman in Ikebukero from extorting money from prostitutes. When the girls were slow to pay, or when they tried to shortchange him, Yamato was said to have beaten them with his fists. And hence the damaged knuckles and the nickname.

Yamato caught Tak examining his hand and quickly lowered it. His mouth set. "Get to work, Saji-san. Take care of your precious *gaijins.*"

He turned his back on Tak and focused his attention on the more important task of protecting Hideki Kohno's life. Tak crumpled the slip of paper in his fist and left the office without another word.

Senior Inspector Ueno was loitering in the hallway, full of curiosity. "There you are, Saji-san. Repeat your assignment to me, just so I know you have it straight."

Tak suppressed an urge to smash Ueno's bland face. "Red Army terrorists have infiltrated the Mitsukoshi department store on the Ginza. They're planning to destroy the Gucci display and Ralph Lauren collection. I've been sent to arrest them."

Senior Inspector Ueno called out as Tak went by him: "All by yourself?"

Tak drew a car from the motor pool and drove through midday traffic to the Okura Hotel, which was just down the street from the American embassy.

The fact that James Tucker and his wife were staying at the Okura was enough to alert Tak to their importance. No hotel in Tokyo housed as many important foreign dignitaries and businessmen.

He parked in the underground garage and went directly to the Okura's assistant manager, who gave him the bare bones of the story and the number of Tucker's suite. The assistant manager was nervous that Tucker's loudly voiced complaints about crime in Tokyo might in some way reflect badly on the hotel.

Tak went to suite 412 and knocked on the door.

"It's open!" a woman's voice called. "Come in."

A woman of about fifty, auburn-haired and stylishly dressed, was sitting in a chair painting her nails. She smiled vaguely at Tak and returned to her nails.

At the far end of the suite James Tucker, also about fifty

years of age, large in build, heavy in the gut, with a florid face and a nose reddened with spidery capillaries, was talking on the phone.

"Uh huh . . . uh huh . . . no . . . uh huh . . . two thousand shares . . . tomorrow at the opening price."

Tak took out his notebook and pretended to be going through it so that Tucker would not think he was listening to the conversation, which of course he was.

"I don't give a damn . . . just a lousy broker, that's all . . . not even a very good one. You can tell him I said that, Teddy. Yeah, screw him. That ethical behavior stuff is bull. We didn't get any information from him we couldn't have gotten from someone else. I shopped around for a broker who'd place the order for a smaller commission. Nothing wrong with that."

For the first time Tucker glanced at Tak. Tucker had small eyes for such a big man. "Listen, I'll call you back at 10:00 A.M. New York time. I've got a problem to deal with here. Okay? See you, Teddy."

Tucker put down the phone. "Who are you?"

"Detective Inspector Takeo Saji, Tokyo Metropolitan Police Department." He accorded Tucker a respectful bow, then showed his police identity card. "I'm sorry to hear you have had a problem. Please tell me about it and I will try to help."

"Try to help? Did you hear that, Janice? He'll *try to help.* Isn't that a kick in the ass?"

Janice shrugged, kept painting.

"At least you speak English. I had my wallet stolen on your subway this afternoon." He went to a side table, splashed some Scotch into a glass and added ice.

Tak's mouth moistened. He loved good Scotch even more than he loved good *sake.*

"We were shopping in the Ginza. My company had hired us a car and driver for the day but Janice here thought it would be *fun* to take the subway back to the hotel. *Fun.* To take a *subway.* You ever heard of anything like that?"

Janice sighed. "Everyone told us the subways in Tokyo are clean and safe. But when we were coming up the steps, Jim noticed that his wallet was missing."

"There must have been *a thousand people* on our train." Tucker's face went red at the idea of so many people presuming to use the subway with him. "I *know* that I had my wallet with me when I got on the subway because I'd just forked out twenty thousand yen for a tie at the Mitsukoshi department store. I mean, you want a two hundred dollar necktie, Tokyo's the place to shop."

Tak was writing in his notebook just to avoid looking at Tucker's face. He had never seen such a red face. He hoped Tucker's color didn't mean he was on the verge of a heart attack. Ueno would be certain to claim Tak had caused it.

"Is it possible you simply lost your wallet?"

Tucker reacted as if Tak had spit in his face. "Is that the deal? You're gonna try to tell me there are no pickpockets in Tokyo? Eleven million people, every one a goddamn saint?"

"Very few saints in Tokyo," Tak said. "Very few subway thieves either."

"You did take your coat off, Jim." Janice Tucker looked at Tak. "He said it was stuffy in the subway."

"Whose side are you *on*?"

"If you were coming back from the Ginza you must have been on the Hibiya line. I'll call the subway station at the end of the line and see if your wallet has been turned in."

Tucker made a scoffing sound. "I was carrying maybe a hundred thousand yen in cash plus all those credit cards. You think anyone's gonna *turn in* that much cash?"

Tak was already on the phone to the lost articles office at Naka Meguro. The manager of the office came on and Tak spoke quickly to him in Japanese, pleased to note Tucker's irritation at being unable to follow the conversation. He kept his expression neutral even though the news was good.

When Tak put down the phone, Tucker said: "No sign of my wallet, right?"

"They have your wallet. It was turned in about an hour ago."

"That's a relief," Janice Tucker said mildly. "You see, Jim, the subways here really are safe."

Tucker shook his head. "I'll bet the wallet was cleaned out."

"The station manager told me the wallet contains ninety-eight thousand yen and several thousand U.S. dollars in traveler's checks." Though he remained impassive, Tak took pleasure in adding: "Your credit cards are there, too. There was a room slip from the Okura in the wallet, so the station manager sent a messenger to bring it to you. He should be here soon. You did not really need a policeman for this."

"Well, I'll be dipped in shit."

"Jim!" Janice Tucker shook her head. "You'll have to excuse my husband, he's not used to dealing with such honest people." She examined her nails critically. "There! All done! How do they look?"

"Very lovely," Tak said. "That shade of red is similar to the color of our Japanese azaleas. I hope you will be here to see them."

"I'm afraid we're leaving in a few days."

Tucker had recovered from the shock of learning that his money had not been stolen and seemed to want to make up for his rudeness. "Detective . . . uh . . ."

"Saji."

"Yes. Detective Saji, would you like a drink?" He waved at a cart sagging with bottles of liquor. "Help yourself."

Tak reminded himself that he was here representing the Tokyo Metropolitan Police Force. "No, thank you. Not while I'm on duty."

"Where did you learn your English?" Janice Tucker asked. "It's very good."

"I went to UCLA."

Tucker's eyebrows went up. "Oh, yeah? I'm an Ohio State man myself. UCLA plays pretty good football, but you were never in Big Ten class."

"I'm afraid that's true," Tak said.

"You're a big guy for a Jap. I mean for a Japanese. You look like you might have played football yourself."

"In high school, yes. Not at UCLA."

"How'd you happen to go to school in the U.S.?"

Tak was mercifully delivered from answering that question by a knock on the door. The messenger from Naka Meguro had arrived with a manila envelope containing Tucker's wallet. Tak signed a receipt and wrote his rank and personnel number beneath it, then dismissed the messenger.

"That's it," Tucker confirmed. "I'll be damned and gone to hell if it isn't."

"You'd better check the contents."

Tucker thumbed through the cash, counted the traveler's checks and looked at each credit card. "All here." He looked embarrassed.

"This would *never* happen in New York City," Janice Tucker said. "Drop your wallet on Lexington Avenue, it'll be stolen before it hits the ground."

Tucker slipped the wallet into his back pocket and patted it self-consciously. "Guess I'd better be a little more careful."

"Up to you." Tak went to the door. "Goodbye, I'm glad everything worked out."

"Hey, is there someone who should get a reward?" Tucker lumbered forward, dragging the wallet out heavily, as if it now held too much money.

"That's not necessary."

"I mean, you might want to spread a few bucks around

. . . the guy at the station . . . whoever turned in the wallet. You'd know better than me."

"Not necessary." This time Tak put some steel into his voice, which brought Tucker up short.

"Whatever you say. At least take my card. Maybe you'll be in New York sometime, we can take you to dinner."

"We'd love to do that," Janice Tucker said.

The *gaijin* in Tak wanted to refuse the card, but his Japanese instinct toward courtesy prevailed. He accepted the business card from Tucker and left the suite.

Outside, standing in the hallway, he turned the card over and over while he cast around for a way to express his dislike of Tucker short of face-to-face discourtesy. A smile came when he found one.

Tak carefully tore Tucker's business card in half and then into quarters. He slipped the pieces back under the door one by one, then went to assure the assistant manager that the problem of the "stolen" wallet had been resolved.

As he left the Okura, Tak realized he was still smiling and that, for a change, he felt halfway satisfied with himself.

Chapter 3

THE PORSCHE WAS ONLY three weeks old and so the engine still sounded tight and the steering felt stiff. Cricket Kimura decided to let it out a little even though he was winding his way through some narrow back streets.

He crossed Aoyama-dori near the cemetery and let out the Porsche down a neighborhood shopping street. There was no sidewalk, just a white line along one side to set off the pedestrian walk. Kimura was amused to see the neighborhood ladies with their bundles of laundry and bags of groceries jump in fright when he blew by them.

His route to Turo Kajima's sword shop in Shinjuku took him close to Nishi Azabu, so he detoured a couple of blocks in order to deliver a message to one of his clients. A warm-up for the main event with Kajima.

Kimura stopped in front of the client's shop, ignoring other cars that came to impatient halts behind him, and peered through the plate-glass window. Tashio Sentaka owned the store and sold golfing clothes and equipment. Kimura just stared through the window, revving the Porsche's engine loudly until Sentaka noticed him. Kimura pointed a finger at Sentaka, then drove off.

A month earlier Sentaka had borrowed five million yen from Kimura to buy new stocks of golf clubs and bags and designer sports clothes for the spring season. Payment was due tomorrow. Kimura wanted Sentaka to know that he expected it on time. No excuses. No postponements. Kimura wanted his five million yen plus twenty percent monthly interest. In cash. In the palm of his hand. Tomorrow. Because Japanese were so crazy for golf, Sentaka did a nice business. Sentaka would pay.

Kimura pushed the Porsche hard, enjoying the tight turns down crooked streets and the sidelong glimpses of cats and children scurrying out of his way.

It was smart to stir up some fuss on the streets. Everyone in this part of Tokyo knew Cricket Kimura but were not yet familiar with his new car. He wanted his car to be recognized, people to fear him and stand aside for him.

He had two quick stops to make before the sword dealer. The first was at a dusty shop on one of the humblest side streets in the city. The establishment was run by a bent, elderly man known only as Torigako. Kimura entered the shop in a more gentle manner than usual and even favored the proprietor with a deep bow.

"Torigako-san, I've come for my new pet."

The elderly proprietor smiled. "Kimura-san, when I received your message I immediately set aside my very best specimen for you."

The shelves of the shop were lined with tiny cricket cages made by hand by the proprietor. As far as Kimura knew, this was the last shop in Tokyo where cricket cages were made in the old way, by hand, and where one could also buy a cricket to take away in one's cage.

The gentle chirping of the crickets made Kimura smile. He liked crickets much more than people. The little creatures were harmless and made lively music. He had loved them as a boy, believed then, as many did, that crickets were good luck, and still believed.

"A big one!" Kimura peeked through the wooden slats of the cage and made a face at the cricket as if it were a baby. "And your cage is handsome, as usual."

"Thank you, Kimura-san."

"I like the cages with the red-and-blue slats. Make some more of those."

"I shall do so."

Kimura put a ten thousand yen note on the counter. "Never mind the change."

Kimura consistently overpaid, but this was too much. "You are even more generous than usual."

Kimura shook the cage a bit to see if the cricket could be nudged into a song. "I have an important job to do. I need a *very* lucky cricket today. An *extraordinary* cricket."

The proprietor was saddened by the compliment, though he did not dare show his feelings. Kimura was Yakuza, and always bought a cricket for luck before "an important job." Sometimes Torigako would read in the newspaper of a murder or other major crime the day after Kimura bought a cricket from him. He did not like to think of his gentle crickets bringing good luck to such enterprises, but, of course, there was little he could do about it.

Kimura put the cage under his arm. "I'll see you soon, Torigako-san. Keep a good supply of our little friends in stock."

"I shall do that."

Kimura placed the caged cricket on the floor of his Porsche and headed for his next destination, Azabu Juban. In the Juban he parked next to a run-down building and went up a flight of outside iron steps to a second-floor loft. A glance at his Rolex told him he would have to make this fast, his important business for the day was in Shinjuku.

He strode into the loft, heels clacking on the plank floor.

"Hello, Matsuka-san. Hello, girls. You all look beautiful. What's the matter, why the sad faces?"

The girls didn't look sad, they looked and were terrified. Most of what they knew about Cricket Kimura was rumor. Some were seeing him for the first time, and they didn't like what their eyes told them. Kimura wasn't tall, but inside the beautifully tailored Armani suit his body was thick with pads of muscle, and the way he moved implied a threat. His expression was purposefully impassive, but his eyes were malevolent.

Nobuo Matsuka did not look very happy either. He bowed deeply, the palms of his hands on the front of his thighs. "I am most distressed, Kimura-san, that you feel it necessary to speak to my girls."

"Your gross is off thirty percent. I want to know why."

"Discourtesy." Matsuka gave the girls a contemptuous look. "They don't treat their customers as well as they should. I tell them what to do, Kimura-san, you know that. I've trained each of them just as you've instructed. They're supposed to be refined and charming. Seduce their customers, not just stick a hand down their pants. But instead they giggle and carry on like schoolgirls and too often the customers go to another house. I am disgusted with them and embarrassed that they are not bringing in more yen for you."

Kimura was looking at the girls and their surroundings, taking his own measure of the situation. The girls were pretty, all twelve of them. None was older than twenty, a couple only fifteen or sixteen. Along one wall stood racks of dresses Kimura had paid for. Very stylish, some expensive.

The girls stood in three groups. Two Japanese together. Five Filipinos. Five Koreans. He noted that their futons were laid out together in the same pattern. At the end of a night's work they would want to sleep next to their own kind. Kimura approved of that.

"All right, I see the problem and the solution is obvious.

You ladies must become more serious about your work." He crooked a finger at one of the Filipino girls. "You . . . come here."

The girl was the thinnest of the group, with a round, angelic face, big eyes as brown as tilled earth. She trembled slightly as she stepped forward, everyone watching her.

Kimura took hold of her arm with his left hand and slapped her with the palm of his right hand. The rest of the girls drew back. Kimura slapped her again, and again, until blood flowed from her nose. But not too much. He didn't want to soil his suit. He then knocked her to the floor and began kicking her. He knew the routine well, had been taught by others. Three minutes and he was done. He had heard bones crunch, seen a tooth fly. He hadn't lost his touch.

"Matsuka-san, put this girl in hospital. When she gets out ship her back to Manila." He turned on the others, now cowering in silence against the bare concrete wall of the loft. "The rest of you had better bring in more money. You aren't geishas, you know. You're whores and you owe me a living."

Useless speech, half of them didn't know more than a few words of Japanese, but for form's sake it had to be said.

"Matsuka-san, come with me."

Kimura went down the outside steps and into the nearest alley with big Matsuka at his side.

"Beautifully done, Kimura-san. I would have handled it but I knew you wanted to deal with them yourself—"

"You're wrong," Kimura said. "It's no longer my responsibility to manage whores." He jabbed a finger into Matsuka's chest. "That's your job. I only showed my authority so that you wouldn't lose face in front of them. The problem is not *them*, Matsuka-san. It's *you.* You've only got two Japanese girls in your string. *Two.* You know better. Yes, our customers will tolerate Koreans and Filipinos but they won't pay as much for their pleasure. They want *Japanese* girls, Matsuka-san. You know that. Japanese girls bring the highest price, that's why I've told you to make sure at least fifty percent of your string are Japanese."

"Kimura-san, it's so hard these days to recruit our own girls. They used to come in from the countryside by the hundreds . . . the thousands . . . but there's too much prosperity out there . . . companies opening offices in every prefecture. They get jobs these days and turn up their noses at our kind of work—"

"That's not the problem. There'll always be girls who can be turned into whores. The problem is you. You spend too much time drinking and dancing in the Roppongi discos. Get yourself out into the country, find new girls. *Japanese* girls. If you don't I'll have to give your string to someone else. I would hate to do that, but I have people to answer to myself."

Anger contorted Matsuka's face. Ignoring the fact that big Matsuka towered over him, Kimura drove a fist into the man's stomach, grabbed his shirtfront, pulled him up, hit him once more. Matsuka gasped for air. "I'm a patient man, Matsuka, you know that, but I have my limits."

Matsuka collapsed against a wall. When he could speak and stand straight again he bowed even more deeply than when Kimura had walked into the loft.

"I apologize, Kimura-san. You are the best boss in the Yamaguchi-gumi. I let you down. Please forgive me."

"*Shatei*," Kimura said. "Little brother, you're young. You need more experience, that's all. Do you think I didn't make the same mistakes when I was your age? Some nights I fucked my own whores so much that they became too tired to take care of the customers. But I learned better, just as you will. I have great confidence in you. You're strong. You're tough. You're loyal. But you do owe me an apology. A *real* apology. Do you understand?"

"Yes, *Oyabun*." Matsuka nodded gravely. "It will be done."

Kimura looked again at his Rolex. "Time enough for apologies tomorrow tonight." He left the alley and walked toward the Porsche. Over his shoulder he said, "Give that girl some money when you send her back to Manila. The Filipinos speak badly enough of us Japanese as it is. We don't want them to say we're cheap, too."

Chapter 4

"THIS IS WHERE I store my most important treasures."

Turo Kajima opened a double-door safe concealed behind a screen at the back of his showroom. The large safe held only two swords, each resting on its own wooden stand. He removed one sword along with its stand, swung the door of the safe closed and placed the stand and sword on a felt-covered worktable.

Kay admired the sweeping lines of the scabbard and meticulous detail on the handgrip. "Beautiful workmanship."

"Yes, this is a sword most worthy of an Emperor," Kajima said with quiet pride. "Let me tell you something of its history. Emperor Meiji came to power in 1867. He was a very young man but already wise and determined. One of his first decisions was to move the capital from Kyoto to Edo, which he renamed Tokyo. This sword was presented to him during the ceremony commemorating the new name for our nation's capital. The Emperor was convinced that Japan needed to adopt some western ways to avoid being invaded and overrun by Russia or another power. Modern military strength was a priority. The government's slogan became *fukoku-kyohei,* which means *rich country, strong arms.*"

Kajima had not yet taken the sword from its scabbard. As he spoke he gazed at the weapon as if it were his young Swedish mistress.

"But the Emperor had enemies who wanted *nothing* to do with the west. They found many reasons to oppose him. Although the Emperor followed the Shinto religion, he was tolerant of other beliefs. When he allowed Christianity to be legalized in 1873, many people were outraged. Emperor Meiji also abolished the feudal system, creating prefectures in place of fiefdoms. And he disbanded the samurai, who by that time had become brigands and hired swords. He gave the samurai pensions to keep them from organizing a revolution. In their place he created a genuine army and opened military academies to train officers.

"So many changes coming so fast stirred unrest. The most serious challenge to his rule was the Satsuma revolt in 1877. The revolt was put down by the new army, with the help of several hundred samurai who were called back for one last glorious battle, and that's where the legend of this weapon was born."

Kajima drew the blade from its scabbard, the steel glittering under the fluorescent lights.

"To discourage others who might have traitorous thoughts, Emperor Meiji ordered the beheading of the leaders of the Satsuma revolt. He gave this weapon to the samurai to use for the beheadings. No one can say exactly how many were put to death. Legend has it that twenty-five heads rolled under this sword. But don't think that Meiji was a cruel man. His reign was enlightened. He gave us our constitution, universal education, land reform. When necessary he could be strong but he regretted having to behead the traitors. Soon after the incident he gave the sword to a member of his court. That is how this sword came to be in private hands rather than in the museum at the Meiji shrine."

Kay took a pair of gloves from her purse and slipped them

on. She made it a practice never to touch a metal antique with her bare hands. Moisture from the skin could cause rust as surely as a bucket of seawater.

Kajima approved. "I was told you would be very professional." He too drew out a pair of gloves from a drawer in the worktable and passed the sword to her.

There were no photographs of the sword that Kay had been able to find. She had discovered several written descriptions and made detailed notes that she laid out along with a magnifying glass and polishing cloth. Then, point by point, she began to compare the sword with the facts from her research.

"As you can see," Kajima said, "this is a *daito,* a long sword. The blade is curved rather than straight. We call a curved blade *shinogi zukuri.*"

Kay used the magnifying glass to examine the point. She had learned that Japanese swordsmiths of the eighteenth century, the Shinto period of swordmaking, used several different styles in making the sharp point of a blade. This was a curved *kissaki* point, as it should have been. The sword also had a curved edge, a *fukura-tsuku.* She then moved to the blade itself.

Each part, large or small, of a samurai sword had a name. *Shinogi-takashi* was the name for the raised ridge line that ran the length of the blade. Two narrow grooves along the blade were called *futasugi-hi.* She also found the delicate engraving of a chrysanthemum, the symbol of the Japanese imperial court, on the hand guard of the grip, the *tsuba.* She used the polishing cloth to help bring out a faded detail. Kajima frowned over that until he was satisfied she was not going to harm the weapon.

"*Buke-zukuri,*" he said, indicating the leather wrapping around the handgrip. "It is rare to find the original leather on a sword that is more than two hundred years old."

"Yes, it's been wonderfully preserved." Kay turned the weapon over and studied the blade again under the magnifying glass. "I'm sure you're responsible for that. How long have you owned this sword?"

"Thirty-eight years."

Kay was troubled again by Kajima's willingness to part with something that had become a part of his life. She again wanted to ask why he was selling it, but not at the risk of losing the piece for her client. Anyway, it was better to withhold judgment until she was completely satisfied with the sword's provenance.

"I need to examine the tang."

"Allow me." Kajima picked up the sword and pointed to a wooden pin in the handle. "The hardwood pin that fastens the handgrip to the sword is probably not original. Over the decades it must have been changed often."

She watched as Kajima used a small hand tool to push the hardwood pin through the handgrip. With the pin removed, the sword came apart in two pieces—the grip and the long steel blade itself.

The tang, the part of the blade that fitted inside the handgrip, held the real history of the sword.

"You will find all the information you need on the tang," Kajima said. "Our Japanese swordsmiths were meticulous."

The characters etched into the steel of the tang were identical to those she had copied from her source books, but she had no idea what they meant. "This is obviously the year the sword was made—1750. So it couldn't have been made for Emperor Meiji. He wasn't even born yet."

"Correct. I suspect the sword was originally made for an earlier shogun. I know it was presented to Emperor Meiji on the day the new capital was commemorated, but there is no record of its original owner. Would you like me to translate the Kanji for you?"

"Yes, please."

He pointed to the Kanji characters engraved near the top of the tang. "This says: *Made in Mino province . . . one lucky day in February, 1750 . . . by Sagan-no-kami . . . of tempered wootz steel from India.* You'll also notice the shape of the end of the tang. A ship-bottom tang, as collectors say. Sagan-no-kami was the best swordsmith of the eighteenth century. He always used this distinctive ship-bottom style in his tangs."

Kay straightened up. "Thank you, Kajima-san. I'm satisfied. If you have the certificate of authenticity we can conclude our deal right now. I have the check with me."

"Yes, let's do that before I become as melancholy as an old *ojiisan.*"

Finally Kay had to ask. "Why are you selling? Why haven't you even asked who my client is? And if you have to sell, why not to some rich Japanese collector?"

"Oh, my contacts in the U.S. have given me the name of your client. Walter Emerson of Philadelphia, trucking business, wealthy collector of antique swords and flintlocks. I know him, he has tried to buy this sword before, through other dealers. I always turned him away."

"Then why are you selling *now?* Why do you want this sword taken out of Japan?"

Kajima inserted the tang into the hilt, reconnected the two pieces with the sturdy wooden pin and slid the sword into its scabbard. "My reasons are not your concern, my dear. And you may consider yourself lucky on that score. Please advise Mr. Emerson to avoid taking the sword apart too often. Tell him to give it a light coating of oil once a month. Keep it under climate control. Polish the blade yearly but *never* polish the tang, you risk damaging the historical markings. And tell him not to sharpen the blade, he will only ruin it. The blade is razor sharp already and will stay that way for the next century if oiled regularly."

The actual transaction took only five minutes as Kajima signed the certificate of authenticity. Kay had brought a bill of sale that was already filled out. He signed that too and Kay handed him a cashier's check for two million three hundred thousand U.S. dollars, the price they had agreed upon by letter. As soon as Kajima signed the bill of sale he stamped the back of the check with a personal seal and locked it in his safe.

"I have several aluminum carrying cases built expressly for swords. We'll pack it into one for you and then go out for a drink." His eyes had regained some of their light. "Perhaps we can also have a quiet dinner together, and a little wine. In your hotel suite?"

"Why, Kajima-san, I suspect you're trying to seduce me. What would your young mistress say if you didn't come home until morning?"

He gave Kay the sly fox look she was beginning to know. "I am a fortunate old man. My little Swedish girl understands that I have a roving eye and a remarkable sexual appetite."

"I'd love to have dinner with you but I'd feel more comfortable in a public place."

Before Kajima could press his case for a private dinner the door opened and a thickly built Japanese strode aggressively into the shop. He seemed annoyed to find that Kajima was not alone. He assessed Kay quickly before bowing to Kajima.

Kajima did not return the bow, which struck Kay as odd.

The two men exchanged brief and, Kay thought, sharp words in Japanese. Kajima, clearly uncomfortable, said, "Miss Williams, would you mind waiting upstairs for a few minutes? I have some business with this . . . this person . . . and then we will pack up the sword and be on our way."

"Of course." Kay went up the steps to the office. The apparent hostility of Kajima toward his visitor seemed out of character.

There was a window in Kajima's office that overlooked the showroom. The slat blinds were closed. Kay opened them slightly, just enough so that she could look down on Kajima and his visitor. Now they appeared to be arguing, and she noticed that Kajima had made a point of stepping between his visitor and the sword she had just bought, which still lay on the worktable where she had examined it.

Her throat went dry. Without question, she suddenly knew that they were talking about the sword for which she had just paid two million three hundred thousand dollars.

Cricket Kimura had timed his visit for exactly 3:15 P.M. His patron had told him that Turo Kajima was always in his shop between two and four. That was usually a slow time for him, so the shop would probably be empty. Even if it were not, Kajima seldom had more than one customer at a time. Whoever was there could be dealt with easily enough.

Finding a *gaijin* in the shop was something of a shock to Kimura. A pretty one, too, if you liked *gaijin* women, which Kimura did not. He knew, however, that Kajima did. In his briefing, Kimura had been told that Kajima had a Swedish mistress. Perhaps that was who this woman was.

No matter. Kimura went straight to his business. "I'm Cricket Kimura. Perhaps you've heard of me. My patron sent me for a sword once owned by Emperor Meiji. He has already spoken to you regarding this matter. He told me to assure you that you will be well paid. Set your own price and it will be delivered to you in cash tomorrow morning. That way you won't have to pay a *ku* tax on your profit. A good deal for everyone."

Kajima said something to the *gaijin* woman in English. Evidently he asked her to leave, because she immediately went upstairs to his office. That suited Kimura. He had looked at a floor plan of Kimura's shop and knew there were no other doors on the second floor.

When she had gone Kajima said, "It's not possible. The sword has already been sold to another buyer."

"I don't believe you. Why would you sell the sword to someone else?"

"To keep it out of the hands of people like you and your patron. I have a good idea how you would use it. I refuse to let a samurai sword be desecrated in that way."

Kimura began to accept the idea that the antique dealer was telling the truth, but sensed it wasn't the *entire* truth. If he had sold the weapon, why was he so nervous? Why was he fidgeting around, moving himself here and there?

It struck Kimura that the old shopkeeper was making a point of placing himself in front of a worktable where a sword had been laid out on a piece of felt. He could see only the handgrip and hilt but it looked very much like the description of the sword he was after.

"Ah! Now I understand. The weapon on that table is the one I've been sent for—"

"No," Kajima said too quickly. "The sword you want is in my safe . . ."

Kimura had expected the sword to be locked away. If Kajima refused to sell, as he had expected, his plan was to close the shop and torture the old man into giving him the combination. This was so much easier. He pushed Kajima aside and moved to the table. He must not make a mistake. His patron had described the sword in detail. He drew the sword from its scabbard and studied the shape of the blade, the design of the handguard, the ornamentation on the scabbard, the distinctive style of the blade's tip. All the telltale details were correct.

"A poor lie, Kajima-san. This is what I've come for."

"You cannot have it . . ."

The shopkeeper was on him then. Kimura was so surprised that he actually stepped back a pace or two as the old man's fists pummeled him. Pathetic blows, but enough to make Kimura angry.

"Stupid old man . . ."

He gripped the sword with both hands and raised it high. Kajima cringed from the threatening arc of the blade. Kimura let it hang in the air for a moment so that Kajima would have time to taste his own death, then struck. The blade made only a whisper of sound as it sliced through Kajima's neck. Kimura marveled at its sharpness.

Kajima's head was severed. His body toppled first, falling in stages. The force of the blow caused Kajima's head to hang in the air for a second, the eyes staring at Kimura in shock and surprise. Then it fell to the floor, sending Kajima's glasses skittering across the floor.

I've done it, Kimura thought. I've killed a man with an *emperor's* sword.

His reverie was broken by a woman's scream.

Kay had watched the argument develop between Kajima and his visitor with growing alarm. It was clear to her that Kajima didn't want the man to see the sword on the table.

As their argument became more heated Kay thought she heard the word Meiji. She definitely heard both men use the word *katana* . . . sword. She did not like the visitor's looks. His voice was crude and guttural. But what really caught her eye was his left hand. As he gestured with it, she noticed that the top halves of the little finger and middle finger were missing.

It could have been that the two men were arguing about some other weapon but she didn't think so . . . Kajima was trying so desperately to hide the sword she'd just purchased.

Evidently the visitor noted Kajima's body language too, because he suddenly pushed Kajima aside and picked up the sword.

Which did it for Kay. He had his hands on *her* sword. Someone had better straighten him out.

Before she could rush downstairs and flash her bill of sale, the sword was pulled from its scabbard and raised. The blade cut through the air with dazzling speed. At first she thought it had missed Kajima. Then she saw his body fall. Incredibly, his head . . . Kajima's *head* . . . hung suspended, then it, too, fell to the floor. She thought she was throwing up, but what emerged from her mouth was a scream.

Startled, Kajima's killer looked up at the slatted window. Their eyes met. The man *smiled*. Actually *smiled*. He said something, more to himself than to her, then he started for the stairs.

He was coming for *her*. For precious seconds she was immobile. Then instinct took over and she moved. No thought to it. Just instinct and movement.

There was a latch on the door that she turned to its lock position. She seized Kajima's desk, pushed it in front of the door, threw the chair on top, realized she would need the chair and yanked it down again.

There was no other door but there was a window behind her that looked down on a narrow alleylike space between buildings. The space was no more than two feet wide but it appeared to be the only other way out of Kajima's office.

The killer tried to open the door and was stopped by the lock, though not for long. His shoulder hit the door, wood splintered, the lock sprung. Kay heard a grunt as he pushed hard to open the door and dislodge the desk.

By now she was up on the chair and halfway out the window. Not a long drop into the alley space, thank God. She kicked off her high heels, balanced herself on the sill and took a deep breath.

As the killer smashed his way into Kajima's office, Kay dropped through the narrow space. The walls were so close together that she was buffeted between them as she fell. She hit the concrete hard, tried to roll with it, felt a stab of pain in her left ankle and took a blow to an elbow. She got to her feet by clawing at the close-in walls and quickly looked up at the window.

Kajima's killer stared down at her. He held the sword in one hand and the scabbard in the other. Kay did not wait to see what he would do next. She ran, limping, careening off the walls, as fast and as far as she could.

Chapter 5

THE BEEPER ON TAK'S BELT went off while he was unlocking his car in the Okura Hotel's parking garage, having resolved the wallet problem of Kick-in-the-Ass James Tucker. He used his cellular phone to call the Special Crimes Unit and was put through to Tadashi Ueno.

"Saji-san, get over to the police box across from Shinjuku station. Some hysterical American woman just stumbled in there. Lost her shoes, apparently. She doesn't speak Japanese, of course. The police-box officer knows a few words of English. He says she's babbling about a *murder*. With a *sword*. Crazy talk. Since she's American, the chances are she's on drugs. Get over there and take charge of the situation."

"Don't you have someone else to send? I've just done my part for Japanese-American relations."

"No, you're the department expert on *gaijins*. By the way, your joke about the Red Army infiltrating the Mitsukoshi department store was not funny. National security is a serious matter, try to remember that."

Ueno hung up and Tak headed for Shinjuku, convinced he was about to meet a female version of James Tucker—a loud,

41

belligerent American incapable of humor. First a "lost" wallet. Now "lost" shoes. What a lost day.

For a change traffic was light and Tak made it to Shinjuku relatively quickly. He pulled up in front of the *koban* and went inside. Two uniformed police officers stood over the American woman, who was hunched down in the police box's only chair. She was trying to drink a cup of tea one of the officers had given her, but her hands were shaking too badly.

She's lovely . . . was Tak's first thought.

And terrified . . . was his second.

"I'm Detective Inspector Tak Saji. Are you all right? You look like you've been through a war."

Her head jerked in surprise at Tak's faultless English. "I just saw a man horribly *killed.*"

Tak expected additional words to come spilling out but she was still too upset for coherent talk. She shuddered and her eyes, her big blue eyes, blinked rapidly.

She wasn't a California girl, he decided quickly. He knew all about California girls, had almost married one in LA a thousand years ago. She was wearing a tailored suit done in the muted colors favored by stylish, successful New York women. Not that she was one of those thin-lipped career types either. This was a beautiful, well-endowed woman of about thirty who would look womanly whatever she wore.

"What's your name?" Tak asked quietly.

"Kay . . . Kay Williams." Answering the simple question seemed to take a lot out of her, because she immediately started to cry.

"May I see your passport?"

She shook her head. "In my purse . . . left it behind."

Tak thought the claustrophobic atmosphere of the small police box was making it difficult for her to answer questions. He asked the two uniformed officers to wait outside. "Is that better?"

She nodded. "I could hardly breathe. Detective . . ."

"Saji."

"Detective Saji, I just saw a man *beheaded* by a sword. . . ."

"What man? Where did this happen?"

"Turo Kajima, a dealer in antique swords. In his shop just a few blocks from here. I got away, climbed out a window and fell into an alley. The killer was . . . oh God . . . he might still be there, you've got to hurry . . ."

The woman's palpable fear gave her remarkable story the ring of truth.

"Just a moment." He went outside and asked the senior uniformed officer if he knew of an antique shop in the neighborhood owned by a man named Kajima. The officer did, of course, know Kajima and his shop. That was part of his job, to know everyone in the neighborhood by being *Omawari-san*—"Mr. Walk Around."

Tak went back into the police box and gently lifted the cup of tea from Kay Williams's shaky hand. "Come on, we'll go to Kajima's shop." When she drew back he added, "Don't worry, one of these officers will come with us. You'll be well protected."

With that promise stiffening her nerve, Kay let herself be put into the back of the police car.

Tak followed the beat officer's directions and within two minutes was pulling up in front of the small shop on a back street less than three blocks from the police box. The front door was ajar.

He told the beat policeman to stay with the young woman, then went to the front door and pushed it all the way open with the toe of his shoe. From his vantage point on the sidewalk he could see the decapitated body of a man lying inside. Blood had flowed along the floor and splattered on the walls and display cases, which held antique swords.

Tak drew his pistol and entered. It had been four years

since he had fired his Walther in the line of duty and perhaps two years since he had last qualified with it on the range in the basement of Tokyo Metropolitan Police headquarters. He wished he had cleaned it more often. The damned thing would probably explode in his face if he tried to use it.

Inside, the shop was completely quiet except for the hum of a climate control unit. The downstairs was small enough to take in with a single glance. No killer here.

Tak moved forward until he saw the head of Turo Kajima lying under a display case. His stomach clutched up. He had seen many corpses, but this was the first time he had come across one with a detached head. The head lay on its side, the veins and muscles and severed spine exposed like some sort of elaborate biology-class specimen.

He looked away from the grisly sight and noted the door at the top of the stairs. It had been smashed in. He went up the steps quietly as possible, his pistol cocked and ready, and slid into the room low and fast.

No one in the office. The desk had been pushed over on its back and a chair was standing next to the room's single window. He went to the window and looked down on a narrow breezeway, the space into which Kay Williams must have jumped to escape the killer. Her purse was on the floor along with a pair of high-heeled shoes. He gathered up the purse and shoes and carried them downstairs.

He was about to go outside and call headquarters from his car when a memory clicked in his mind. A week or so ago he had been in a bar somewhere, Shibuya maybe, drunk and feeling vaguely suicidal. The urge toward suicide had been growing in him lately. He had gone into the men's room and unloaded his pistol to make sure he wouldn't hurt himself with it, accidentally or otherwise.

I reloaded the pistol the next morning, he told himself. Didn't I?

He ejected the clip from the butt of his Walther. It was

empty. The cartridges were probably still in the pocket of the suit he had been wearing that night, the suit that lay crumpled on the floor of his closet.

Tak, you are a total fool. If the killer had hung around, there'd be *two* heads lying on this floor. What's happened to you? Have you become as incompetent as Senior Supervisor Ueno, or are you just looking for an unusual way to kill yourself?

He holstered the useless weapon and went out to his car. "She's right," he said to the beat officer. "There's a murdered man in there, separated from his head. Take charge of the entrance. Don't let *anyone* into that shop, especially curious fellow officers. From this moment the medical officer, the technical supervisor and the crime-scene supervisor are the *only* people who can grant entrance to that building."

"Hai!" The beat officer moved from the car and took up his post.

Tak called in a code seven—signifying a crime of severe violence—and gave the dispatcher the location.

All this was done in rapid Japanese. Kay had listened closely and thought she understood what was being said from Tak's attitude.

He turned and put his hand on her arm in a steadying way. "Everything you said checked out. There's a dead man in there. Kajima, I assume. You were right, his head has been severed. And I saw the window you narrowly escaped through, you were very lucky there. Here's your purse and shoes."

"Thank you," Kay said in a small voice.

Tak had kept his hand on Kay's arm. It was a very nice arm, he reflected, firm and strong under the soft fabric of her suit. "The killer sensibly cleared out before we got here. I'm sorry but I have to ask you this while it's still fresh in your mind." Tak took out his notebook and pen. "What did he look like?"

"He'll always be *fresh in my mind.*" Kay forced herself to

think about the killer. "Let's see. He was Japanese, thirty-five, forty years old, not big, maybe five-eight or -nine but *powerful*-looking." She paused. "He was dressed in a very good suit, maybe Italian. There was some sort of pin on his lapel, a gold pin . . . Oh, and he was missing two joints from his left hand. Yes, the tops of his little finger and middle finger were both missing."

"Yakuza."

"What?"

"Yakuza. Our Japanese version of the Mob. We have several big crime syndicates here in Japan. Taken together they're referred to as *Yakuza."*

"How do you know he was one of those?"

"When he does something wrong, makes a mistake or disappoints his boss in some way, a *Yakuza* atones by cutting off part of a finger. For a Japanese gangster it's a badge of honor to be short a few finger joints. I wonder what connection Kajima had with the *Yakuza,* and which gang had him killed?"

Kay shook her head. "I can't see Turo Kajima being mixed up with gangsters. He was a cultured man. And he loved his country far too much, I'm sure, to have anything to do with such types."

"You'd be surprised at how many distinguished Japanese have an association with the *Yakuza."*

"Not Turo Kajima. You're talking as if he was some sort of gangster himself. He's a *victim,* Detective Saji."

"Yes, he's certainly that. Do you have any idea why this gangster killed Kajima?"

"Oh, my God." The shock of Turo Kajima's beheading and her own close call had temporarily wiped everything else from her mind. Now she saw the killer again, standing in the window looking down at her, the samurai sword in one hand and scabbard in the other. "Yes, I do know why he was here. That murdering son of a bitch came to steal my sword!"

* * *

Within twenty minutes at least a hundred policemen descended on the neighborhood around Kajima Katana.

The street was quickly blocked to traffic by several gray police vans, out of which poured uniformed police in combat fatigues in a shade of gray that matched the vans. In the States they might have been called SWAT teams. They were armed with belted service revolvers rather than automatic weapons. Each man carried as personal protection a long shield made of some sort of lightweight, bulletproof plastic. They wore helmets with clear plastic face masks. To Kay they appeared to be preparing for a riot rather than searching for a killer.

Inside, photos were being taken of Kajima's body and evidence gathered by technical teams. A medical officer had pronounced Turo Kajima officially dead. Not that there could be any doubt, she thought grimly.

So far the only solid piece of evidence to emerge, aside from Kay's eyewitness statement, was one clear footprint of a man's shoe in the puddled blood near Kajima's body.

Detectives and uniformed police were going up and down the street talking to shop owners, residents and anyone else who might have seen the killer come or go. Kay remained in the back seat of Det. Insp. Tak Saji's police car trying to curb her natural impatience.

Occasionally Detective Saji would confer with one of the other policemen, and Kay noticed something strange about their dealings with Saji. The policemen were elaborately polite with one another but treated Tak Saji in a brusque, almost rude fashion.

There were, she thought, some intriguing differences between Saji and the other policemen, and Kay wondered if those differences were the reasons for their attitudes. To begin with, he spoke English without a trace of an accent. Tak

Saji was also much taller than any of the others, six feet or possibly an inch more in height, and rather handsome. He had a lean face with a squared-off jaw, sad eyes, wide shoulders, an absurdly narrow waist, almost no hips at all and a smooth, athletic way of moving. She also detected the fact that Tak Saji was a heavy drinker. Her own father had been a drinker, a hell of a drinker, and she knew the signs too well. At least he carries it well, she thought. Better than Pop did.

She decided the worst thing about Tak Saji was his suit. It didn't need to be pressed, it needed to be *burned.* The other cops' suits were as neat as the ones on department-store mannequins.

Tak came out of Kajima's shop now and eased into the front seat. "They're going to open Kajima's safe in the morning. If they don't find the combination anywhere in his office they'll bring in a torch bar and cut through the lock."

"What about the check I gave to Kajima?"

"It seems that whatever is in that safe is now part of Turo Kajima's estate. I telephoned our legal office in Ohtemachi. They were definite about that. They can't return the check you gave to Kajima."

"But I paid Kajima two million three hundred thousand dollars for a sword *I don't have.* That killer has it!"

"Legally the killer stole the sword from you, not from Kajima. Wait a minute, did you notice whether Kajima endorsed the check? That might make a difference."

Kay tried to remember. "No, I think he stamped the back of it."

"Too bad. In Japan a personal stamp . . . a *han* . . . is as legal as a signature. When Kajima put his *han* on the back, that check became his."

"And I can't even stop payment, that was a cashier's check." Kay felt a massive headache coming on. "Well, that settles it. I can't go back home until I've got the sword back."

"Why not?"

"The check came from my client. Obviously I didn't have time to insure the sword against theft so I either have to give the money back to my client out of my own pocket or deliver the sword. And my pocket sure as hell isn't that deep."

"Bummer."

Kay found herself smiling. "Bummer? You didn't learn that kind of English in Tokyo."

"No, I went to school in the States." Tak quickly changed the subject. "Maybe we'll get lucky and find the killer right away. If he's Yakuza I doubt that he'll leave the country with your sword. More likely he'll try to sell it. You say the sword once belonged to Emperor Meiji?"

"Yes, it was used to behead the leaders of Satsuma revolt."

Tak nodded. "I remember reading about the revolt and the sword in my history class."

"I thought you went to school in the States."

"Just high school and college. Actually I never finished college. I dropped out of UCLA to come back to Japan."

"Why didn't you finish?"

"The family that took me to the U.S. came back here. I'd just been dumped by the girl I thought I was going to marry, so the timing seemed right to come back with them." Another swift change of topic. He was already talking too much. "Can I get you some tea or coffee?"

"No, I'm fine, thanks."

"Your color is better. When I first saw you I thought you'd lost a lot of blood, you were so pale."

"Well, I was absolutely terrified. You did all the right things to get me back on track."

A little man in a tight suit came hurrying up to the car. He snapped out some Japanese words at Tak with a minimum of courtesy, frowned over Tak's reply, seemed suddenly agitated, gave Kay a frightened look and walked away. He stopped in front of one of the uniformed officers guarding the door and shouted something in his face before rushing back into Kajima's shop.

"Who is that weird little man?"

"My boss, Senior Supervisor Tadashi Ueno. He's been appointed crime-scene supervisor for this case. At UCLA we would have called him a nerd. Here we bow deeply and call him Ueno-san."

"What's his problem?"

"He's scared because Knuckles Yamato, his superior, is on his way here." Tak looked bemused. "Which is strange. Knuckles hardly ever goes to a crime scene. Stranger still because he's very busy right now protecting Hideki Kohno."

"Kohno. I read that name in your English-language newspaper, the Japan *Times*, this morning. He's a gangster too, isn't he? Getting ready to testify about some big scandal?"

"Hideki's no gangster, just a fast-talking con man who let the Yakuza use him to front a swindle."

"You seem very familiar with Hideki Kohno."

"It was Hideki's family that took me to the States when I was a kid. Uh-oh, here comes Knuckles Yamato. Watch Ueno's performance. You know who Uriah Heep was?"

"Sure, he was the obsequious little kiss-ass in a novel by Charles Dickens."

"Uriah Heep was Mr. Courageous compared with Tadashi Ueno. Excuse me, I'd better find out what Knuckles is up to."

Tak left the car and joined his two superiors in a sidewalk conference. Kay did not like the looks of Knuckles Yamato. His face was flat and emotionless and he reacted to everything said to him with a cold expression and curt answers. His questions, whatever they were, came accompanied by chopping gestures no doubt intended to intimidate his underlings.

The gestures certainly worked with Tadashi Ueno. The little man couldn't stop bowing. His head went up and down as if bobbing for apples. Even from twenty yards away Kay could see that Ueno was sweating like a stevedore.

Tak, on the other hand, had accorded Yamato one brief bow and now seemed to be disagreeing with him about something. Their disagreement sent Ueno into a veritable frenzy of bowing. After a time Yamato, with Ueno trotting at his heels, crossed the street and went into a coffee shop.

Tak came back to the car. "Knuckles would like to talk to you."

"Good!" Kay got out of the car.

"Brace yourself. He doesn't want you to stay in Japan. He wants me to put you on tonight's plane to New York."

"What?"

"He says you're in danger because you saw the killer's face."

"But that means I'm the only one who can *identify* him."

"Yamato seems to be looking at the politics of the case. He's afraid of having a murdered American woman to explain to the U.S. embassy."

They joined Yamato and Ueno at a table near the coffee shop's front window. Neither of them rose to greet Kay. Yamato simply pointed to a vacant chair.

"My English is not good," Yamato said.

"You speak it very well." Kay was trying to keep her temper and deal with Yamato.

"I'm sorry you have had such a . . . painful time? . . . are those the right words? . . . in Japan. I have asked Saji-san to take you to your hotel so that you can . . . can pack. And then take you to the airport and escort you to your plane. I will have a reservation made for you." He gave her a clumsy smile and Kay thought she heard creaking noises from facial muscles seldom used. "The police department will pay for your ticket. As . . . ah . . . com . . . pen . . . sation for your terrible experience."

"That's very generous, thank you for the offer, but I'm not leaving Japan just yet."

The seldom-used smile cracked a bit. "I must insist. The killer saw your face. You saw his. He may try to eliminate you as a witness."

"If I leave Japan you won't *have* a witness."

"You may return for the trial after we have caught the killer."

"How the hell are you going to catch him if I'm not here to identify him? But that's beside the point. I'm staying here until I have my two million three hundred thousand dollars *or* my samurai sword."

"You will leave Japan," Yamato said flatly. "Tonight. I will take the matter to your embassy if I must."

"You do that. Do you know the U.S. ambassador to Japan? I do. I was his daughter's roommate at Bryn Mawr. That's a college in the U.S. Her name is Elizabeth but I call her Peaches. The ambassador calls me Kaybird and I call him Uncle Wiggily because he's cute as a rabbit. What I'm telling you . . . *Knuckles* . . . is that I'm practically a daughter to the U.S. ambassador to Japan. I don't like to presume on my friendship with him but I sure as hell will if I have to."

"Miss Williams, you had better—"

"Do you know what he'll tell you if you try to ship me out of your country? He'll tell you to fuck off. Has that phrase reached Japan? Only he'll do it in much more diplomatic language because he's a really polite man, which is how you get to be an ambassador."

So much for keeping her dignity, Kay thought. Probably an overrated quality anyway.

During her outburst Yamato had drawn in his breath with a hiss, which made him sound like a snake that wanted to strike. He didn't otherwise react but neither did he try to hide his opinion of her. Kay could read his eyes very well. In them she saw neither hatred nor anger, just an entrenched contempt.

He tried on his false smile again. "I'm very sorry if I did not make myself clear. As I said, my English is . . . I suppose I should say . . . not adequate. My only concern is for your safety. So let me make a . . . um . . . proposal?"

"Proposal," Kay repeated. "Yes?"

"You appear to have confidence in Detective Saji. I will put Saji-san in charge of this case. And I will also put him in charge of your safety. Is that . . . um . . . satisfaction to you?"

Kay elected to be gracious in victory, sort of like Katharine Hepburn after she won the big court case from Spencer Tracy in her favorite movie, *Adam's Rib*. "Thank you, Yamato-san. That sounds like a very good plan."

Yamato gave Ueno the order putting Tak in charge of the case. Then he rose, gave Kay a nod and walked out of the coffee shop. Yamato's sudden departure confused Ueno. He looked at Kay. At Tak. He had no idea what Kay had said to the superintendent supervisor but the tone had sounded harsh. Sensing that Yamato was displeased with both the American woman and Detective Inspector Saji, he got up and followed Yamato.

"Do you really know the American ambassador that well?" Tak asked.

"I don't know the man at all, don't even know his name," Kay admitted.

"You mean the ambassador doesn't have a daughter named Elizabeth, also known as Peaches?"

"He might. Who knows? Hell, I didn't even go to Bryn Mawr. I was accepted but my pop blew my tuition money on a three-week binge and a girl in Boston. So I went to U. Mass instead."

"That was a nice bluff."

"You don't ever want to play poker with me," Kay said, and smiled. "I'm *good.*"

"I'll bet."

"I'm sorry I called Yamato by his nickname. He didn't seem to like it and he'll know you were the one who gave it to me."

"Doesn't matter. Yamato couldn't dislike me any more than he already does."

"Then why did he put you in charge of the case? And appoint you as my protector?"

"He gave me the case so I could fail. So I could disgrace myself. And maybe get you killed in the bargain."

"Well, I hope you don't let either of those things happen. Why does Yamato have it in for you? Why do the other policemen treat you with such . . . I'm getting like Yamato, I don't know what the right word is . . . with such condescension?"

Tak gave her a bleak smile. "Because I'm the two things the Japanese hate most. I'm *burakumin.* And I'm *kikokushijo.* You wouldn't want to be me."

Kay had no idea what he was talking about. Worse, she could feel him pulling back from her. She wanted to ask what *burakumin* and *kikokushijo* meant but this didn't seem to be the time. He'd become too withdrawn. Not now, Kay thought. I'll wait and let him tell me when he's good and ready.

Chapter 6

CRICKET KIMURA KEPT SEVEN different places in various neighborhoods of Tokyo, two of them expensive and professionally decorated apartments and the other five simple rooms furnished with a few pieces of rough old furniture.

He never slept in the same place two nights in a row and he never told anyone at which place he would be sleeping. He kept in touch with his half-dozen lieutenants over the cellular phone he carried with him at all times.

Kimura's caution stemmed from an incident that took place fifteen years earlier, when he was just a youngster brand-new to the Yakuza.

The *oyabun* for whom Kimura worked at that time was Kato Kobayashi, a former sumo wrestler who had made his way up the organization by virtue of his ability to crush skulls. Kobayashi loved to drink and eat; each day he drank at least two cases of beer and ate seven meals. He weighed 420 pounds. Kobayashi owned a Mercedes with a special driving seat built to fit his ample proportions. His specialties were pimping and extortion. It was rumored that one of his prostitutes had smothered to death in his flesh while he was having sex with her. As big, strong and feared as he was,

55

Kobayashi's obvious fatal flaw was that he was a slave to his appetite and had gotten into the habit of going into particular restaurants at predictable times.

For example, every Tuesday night at about eight he dropped into a small inn in Kando for his sixth meal of the day, *shabu shabu* washed down with a dozen beers. One night a rival from the Sumiyoshi-rengo walked into the place while Kobayashi was on his last course of *shabu shabu* and fired four shots point-blank into Kobayashi's chest. The noise startled him, but the bullets failed to penetrate very far into his huge bulk; they damaged no vital organs and in fact, he barely felt them. Kobayashi was rising from the table in anger when his assailant fired the last two bullets into his brain.

Kimura had learned from that. He had no wish to meet Kobayashi's fate and so a few hours after he had beheaded Turo Kajima he turned up unexpectedly in Meguro at a Turkish bath in which he owned a small interest.

The operator of the *toruko* nervously escorted Kimura to his room and asked if he wanted one of the girls from the baths to be sent up.

"Later," Kimura had answered tersely. "I'll let you know. Just leave me. See to your customers."

Kimura had arrived carrying his newly acquired cricket in its brightly painted cage and a long parcel wrapped in brown paper. He put the cricket on the bedside table and unwrapped the parcel. The brown paper fell away to reveal the samurai sword.

Kimura drew the blade. It was still sticky and black from Turo Kajima's blood, the sight of which raised again the vision of Kajima's head being separated from his body.

How easy it had been. This sword was, indeed, a marvel. No wonder the shoguns of old were so feared. Look what they had to work with. Guns were nothing compared to this weapon.

Kimura found a towel and carefully cleaned the blood from

the blade. When it was dry and shining he raised it above his head. On the table stood a vase of flowers. Violets, Kimura thought, though he had trouble telling one flower from another.

He swung the sword deftly and the blossoms were separated from their stalks in a wink, falling gracefully on the table and floor.

A true marvel.

He returned the sword to its sheath, rewrapped it in the brown paper and placed it under the bed where it would be near to hand while he rested. Then he undressed and lay down with the lights off and his eyes closed.

A reverie came over him in the darkness, or perhaps it was a vision. He saw himself at the head of a column of men in samurai dress, riding a great tall horse. The horse was white. Crowds on either side of the road cheered and waved as he passed. Eyes lingered on the sword sashed to his waist. Fear and admiration were in the eyes of the people who lined the road.

Kimura lingered over the vision. He found he could rerun the scene over and over in his mind, like a videotape of a favorite movie. Only this was better than a mere movie. This was what his life would have been if he had lived two hundred years earlier.

Even now, in these modern days and on the streets of Tokyo, he had made a large part of the vision come true. People *did* look on him with fear and admiration. He *did* now own a sword of great name and honor. And now he *was* a samurai in deed and name.

This time he called up the vision of Turo Kajima's head disembodied and floating in the air. How the dead eyes had stared. How surprised Kajima had looked.

Cricket Kimura considered the prospect of killing again with the sword. There would be several people to kill, he had been assured of that. He did not yet have the list of names;

that would be given him later tonight. How many names would be on the list? Six or seven, Kimura guessed. It would take that many murders to achieve the goal Kimura's patron had set.

Yes, at least three more heads would fall, a prospect to look forward to.

The darkness had inspired the cricket to begin a song. Kimura listened with simple pleasure. Imagine a little cricket able to make such a strong sweet sound. Nature was so interesting, Kimura wished he understood its mysteries. Why did crickets sing? Why did lions roar? Why couldn't a big giraffe make any noise at all? He lay for a while listening to his cricket, and when the cricket's song faded he turned on the light and went into the hall.

"All right, send up a girl," he called down to the proprietor. "A fresh thing. Not some old tramp who's been had a million times."

"Hai! As you say, Kimura-san."

He went back to the bed and lay down again, now ready for some sex. He knew what he wanted the girl to do. She had better be a pretty one or he'd break a few of the proprietor's tired old bones.

A minute later the girl entered the room. Her footsteps were hesitant and she stood with her back to the wall after closing the door.

"Come closer, don't be afraid."

She approached Kimura warily.

"What's your name?"

"Candy."

"Candy! That's not a Japanese name."

"It is my working name. The customers like it."

"What's your real name?"

"Miko."

"That's better." Kimura spread his legs. "Do you like what you see, Miko?"

She looked at his body with interest, perhaps feigned, perhaps real. "I've never been with a man who had such tattoos."

"Then you've never been with an *oyabun* of the Yakuza. Even if you had been you would not have seen tattoos like these."

Kimura was extremely proud of his tattoos. Actually, his body was covered from front to back with one enormous tattoo of a red dragon. The dragon's head covered his chest and stomach. Running out along his arms and legs were its green-scaled legs. Its wicked, winding tail curled out along his back. "It took three years to cover my body with the dragon."

"Was it painful?"

"Of course, but what does that matter? Come here, Miko. Kneel beside me."

The softness of his voice had relaxed the girl. She did as she was told, kneeling by the bed and automatically caressing his arm. She was about twenty years old, slim. Her jet black hair was cut short, creating a frame for her face. Enormous brown eyes. Very small nose. Tiny mouth, too. Kimura liked what he saw.

"How long have you been working here?"

"Six months, ever since I came to Tokyo from Kyushu."

"Do you have parents there?"

She shook her head quickly, the subject one she didn't like to discuss. "They don't consider me their daughter anymore."

"That must be painful for you. I never knew my parents. They abandoned me and I grew up in an orphanage."

"Maybe you were lucky," Miko said.

"No, I wasn't. Family is important. That's why I became Yakuza, to have a family."

Miko's caresses became more spontaneous. "I was told to be careful with you, that you have killed people."

"Yes, but you don't have to worry." He gave a rattling laugh. "I've already done my killing for today."

She laughed with him, unaware that he was not joking. "I do like your tattoos." With a graceful movement she slipped off her loose dress and slid her naked body on top of his. "They make you very sexy, Kimura-san."

"Did you notice the tongue?"

"What?"

"The dragon's tongue!" He was annoyed that she had missed it.

Miko looked at the dragon again, saw that the jaw extended all the way down to Kimura's loins. In fact, the open mouth and teeth of the dragon surrounded his loins so that Kimura's cock was right in the center of the mouth.

The girl drew in her breath as she grasped the fact that the dragon's tongue was tattooed onto Kimura's cock.

"The tongue . . ."

"Yes. Having the tongue put there was the most painful part of the job. Took the tattoo artist twenty days, he could only do a bit at a time. Each night I drank *sake* and wept. But in the end it was worth it."

Miko put her hand on Kimura's cock and watched it grow. "Ah, the tongue gets bigger!"

Kimura put his head back on the pillow and closed his eyes. "Put the dragon's tongue in your mouth." He felt her mouth close over it. "Yes . . . that's the way."

She sucked at him.

"Yes . . . take the tongue . . . the dragon's tongue . . ." He felt himself become the dragon, a huge and powerful beast who could not be vanquished or denied or killed. Being the dragon was as good as being a samurai. He felt mythic. Reborn.

The girl worked at him with her considerable skill, understanding his needs and doing her best to fulfill them. His balls were cupped in one of her hands. With her other, she massaged the insides of his thighs.

Kimura groaned. After a time he spoke, his words slurred but commanding. "Yes . . . the dragon is almost ready, almost ready!"

The girl increased the rhythm.

"That's it, here comes the fire!" Kimura felt the dragon's fire belch from his loins, twisted so the girl's face was rubbing against him. The fire kept coming. The girl gulped, swallowed noisily. The dragon writhed on the bed until all the fire had been consumed. And slowly Kimura ceased to be the dragon and became himself again.

The girl slid off him onto the narrow bed and lay with her arm around him, waiting to see what he wanted next. The proprietor had warned her not to hurry him, to spend all night with him if that was what he wanted.

Kimura did not bother to compliment Miko on her expertise. Never treat a whore too well, that was one of his fixed business principles.

"You can go now."

She crawled gently over him and stood next to the bed while slipping back into her dress. "Do you want me to return later?"

"No, I have appointments to keep. Just get out."

When she was gone Kimura dressed himself. Looked at his watch. Two appointments to keep and then he would begin his mission. Will I be the dragon for the rest of the night, or the samurai?

The samurai, he decided. Steel instead of fire.

Chapter 7

Tak could almost admire the way Knuckles Yamato had maneuvered him into taking on two tough assignments at the same time—solving a lurid murder case *and* protecting the only witness to the crime from the Yakuza.

He was especially leary of trying to protect a woman as headstrong as Kay Williams. When he told her that he was on his way to search the victim's house she demanded to come along. Tak had tried to convince her to stay in her room at the Imperial with a guard on the door while he did his job, but she said: "There's no way you're leaving me behind. I'll find Kajima's house on my own if I have to."

So he was driving to Turo Kajima's home with Kay Williams sitting next to him. If his colleagues found out he'd be laughed off the police force.

"What are you muttering about?" Kay asked.

"Nothing."

"I can tell you're pissed . . . that means angry."

"I *know* what pissed means. I'm *not* pissed."

"Yes, you are."

"No, I'm just worried about you, Miss Williams. Although I don't think you're in any immediate danger from the

Yakuza, I can't be certain. I don't even know what's behind Kajima's murder. I'd bet it's about more than the sword itself. And for all I know the killer may be ransacking Kajima's house right now. We might walk in on him."

"I told you to call me Kay. You don't have to worry about me. I've been taking care of myself ever since my pop drank himself to death and my mom went off to live with a philosopher. At least he calls himself a philosopher. Actually, my mother's boyfriend earns his money betting on horses. But he likes to read Plato and Montaigne between races, so I guess he can call himself a philosopher if he wants."

This woman's conversation was becoming harder and harder to follow. "Miss Williams . . . Kay . . . I shouldn't be taking you with me while I search the victim's house and question his mistress. That goes against every regulation of the Tokyo Metropolitan Police—"

"I've got a hunch you're the kind of cop who breaks lots of regulations, when *you* feel it's necessary. When *I* think it's necessary . . . *me* . . . a *gaijin* . . . a *woman* to boot . . . you get *pissed*. There, I said it again."

She was right and Tak hated that she was right. In defense he said: "I don't break a lot of regulations."

"No? I'll bet it's against regulations to drink on duty. And to wear a suit that looks like it's been slept in for a month. And I noticed that your gun's got rust spots. I'll bet that's *really* against the regs."

Tak had no good answers.

After a minute Kay said, "I apologize, that was mean of me. You've been wonderful and I'm being a bitch." She sighed. "I guess I'm scared that losing the sword is going to cost me my business. When I'm scared I get bitchy. Can't help it, it's the way I am."

Driving in a car with this woman was like taking a roller-coaster ride standing up. "You're right about some of that," Tak admitted. "I did have a couple of drinks earlier today.

And my Walther is a little dirty. But I don't sleep in this suit, I just haven't had time to get it cleaned and pressed."

"It's actually a very nice suit." Kay wanted to make peace. "Potentially."

Tak noted the "potentially" and decided to spruce up. Buy a new tie. Get his shoes shined. And *definitely* take this suit to the cleaners. It had been a while since he'd worried about his grooming. Couldn't hurt to make a few changes.

Turo Kajima had lived near Zojoji temple, practically in the shadow of Tokyo Tower. His home was a narrow, two-story building on a quiet street off Hibiya-dori. The neighborhood looked quiet and expensive and pleasantly old-fashioned.

Tak found a parking place around the corner and with Kay at his side went to the front door. The steps leading to the door were littered with broken crockery. Kay looked at Tak and shrugged.

Tak rang the bell. When there was no answer he persisted. If the house was empty he could still get in with the set of keys he'd taken from Kajima's body.

The keys proved unnecessary. The door was yanked open by a tall girl with ash-blonde hair, blue eyes and the full-chested figure for which Swedish women were famed. She was dressed in a red tank top and jeans and was barefoot and crying.

"Please go *away*. Just go away and leave me alone."

The girl's accent was slight. Kay decided she'd learned her English at a very good private school, probably in Switzerland.

"I'm Detective Saji, Tokyo Metropolitan Police." He quickly showed her his ID. "This is Kay Williams . . . It looks like you've already heard that Turo Kajima has been killed—"

"Yes!" She began wailing louder. "Some *reporter* was just here. He wanted my *comments*. I threw *dishes* at him. When he left he was bleeding and I'm *glad.*" She spun around and ran into the house.

They followed and closed the door behind them.

"I'll stay with her," Kay said. "You go ahead and look around if you need to."

Looking around Kajima's house was exactly what Tak wanted to do and he was grateful to Kay for accepting the job of calming the girl. He was desperately awkward when it came to dealing with crying women. He had had no experience at it. His mother had never cried, at least not that he had ever seen.

Tak first took a walking tour of the house. The place had only a few rooms. The largest was a long living room, where the Swedish girl sat on a couch crying, with Kay's arm around her. Then a dining room. Kitchen. Two bedrooms. A study. Each room was decorated with exquisite Japanese antiques and art. The furniture was low and simple with traditional lines. Kajima had lived well but the only mild extravagance was an enormous water bed in the master bedroom.

It was the study that attracted Tak's close attention. He used Kajima's keys to unlock the desk and settled back for a quick inventory of the late antique dealer's papers. He found well-organized files that held bills for home repairs, letters to and from friends, a folder full of stock shares in various Japanese companies, old photographs, travel brochures.

The file that interested Tak was a series of letters to and from Tak's old friend Hideki Kohno. Apparently Turo Kajima had lost money investing in Hideki's company—Seisa-ko Securities. Kajima had written three outraged letters to Hideki and kept copies.

Hideki had responded with correspondence that promised Kajima he would "look into the matter of the missing funds and settle all questions, arguments and unfavorable results to your full and complete satisfaction."

That was Hideki talking, all right, Tak thought. Verbose.

Evasive. Fast to make promises he didn't intend to keep. No, that wasn't fair . . . Hideki always *intended* to do the right thing, he just never got around to it.

Interesting coincidence, Tak mused, that Turo Kajima was one of those who had lost money in the Seisa-ko Securities fraud. A lot of money, too. Almost a hundred million yen, according to the correspondence.

Tak also found an address book in the desk. He thumbed through it, recognized the names of a few prominent Japanese business leaders and stuck the book in his pocket.

The girl's sobs had tapered off to the point where Tak thought it would be all right to sit down and ask her some questions. He went to the living room and found Kay and the girl talking to each other. Kay was no longer sitting next to her on the couch. She had moved to a nearby easy chair. Both women were holding glasses of white wine.

"Detective Saji," Kay said, "this is Ingrid Thorsen. She's been a student at Sophia University here in Tokyo for two years."

"Hello, Ingrid." Tak sat down across from her. "I know you were very close to Kajima-san and I'm sorry for your loss."

"Thank you." Ingrid was pale but more composed. Her paleness made her hair look even more blonde. "He was such a gentle man, I can't *believe* he's been . . . murdered." She shook her head. "Just *can't* believe it."

"May I ask you a few questions?"

"I suppose." She drank some of her wine. "Oh, do you want anything to drink?"

"No, thanks, not while I'm on duty."

Tak needed a drink but he wouldn't take one while Kay Williams was around. Her remark about his drinking had hurt. He liked to think that no one noticed his little faults. "Did Kajima-san have any serious enemies?"

"None that I knew of."

"How long have you known him?"

"About a year. And I've lived with Turo for . . . oh . . . eight months now."

"Did he have any business or money problems?"

"I don't know exactly what Turo had, but he was very well-off."

"Had he seemed moody or worried about anything else lately?"

Ingrid thought that one over. "He lost a lot of money in a bad investment this year. Losing the money didn't bother him so much as the way it was lost. He said he had been cheated, along with a lot of other people."

"Seisa-ko Securities," Tak prompted.

"That's right." The color had begun to return to her cheeks and her rigid posture began to soften. "Turo was looking forward to seeing that man, that Hideki Kohno, go to prison."

"Was he going to be one of the witnesses against Kohno in the trial for fraud that begins this month?"

"No . . . but I think Turo was part of a group that was bringing a civil suit against him."

"What about a weapon once owned by Emperor Meiji?" Kay asked. "Did he ever talk about it? Mention that he was going to sell it?"

"Yes, though he didn't say why. I assumed it was just a business deal, but you say he was killed by someone who wanted the sword."

"We can't be certain about that," Tak said. "The killer may have just found the sword to be a handy weapon."

"I don't understand 'handy,' " Ingrid said.

"Nearby . . . there when it was needed."

"Oh." She turned to Kay. "And you were right there when it happened? When Turo was killed?"

"Yes. There was nothing I could do, it happened so fast."

"The killer tried to get at Miss Williams with the sword, too," Tak said quickly. "She was very lucky to escape." He paused. "The killer was about thirty-five years old and well dressed. A Japanese. The tops of two fingers of his left hand were missing. Despite his appearance he had the voice and manners of a thug. He sounds like Yakuza. You've been in Japan long enough to know who the Yakuza are. Does that description fit any of Turo Kajima's friends or associates?"

"Of course not." Ingrid's eyes began to mist over again. "He wouldn't have anything to do with that kind of person. The *way* Turo died was so awful. He *loved* his swords. To be killed by one of them . . ."

"Why don't you come and stay with me at the Imperial tonight," Kay offered.

"Thank you, no." Ingrid shook her head and her blonde hair swished. "I need to be in Turo's house tonight. I hope you find that madman soon. I wish you'd put *him* to death by sword." She sat back heavily. "I loved Turo so. He was much older than me and my parents hated that. Other people wondered why I took up with him, too. But he never seemed to me to be seventy-eight years old, or even thirty-eight. He was so sexy. I've never known a man who could turn sex into such an elegant, rich experience."

"What are you going to do now?" Kay asked.

Ingrid drank off the rest of her wine. "I don't know. Move into a dormitory at the university perhaps. Or maybe go back to Stockholm, after the baby is born."

Kay's jaw literally fell. "The baby?"

"Yes." Ingrid looked from Kay to Tak. "That's the worst thing of all. I just found out that I'm pregnant. On Saturday night I was going to make a big event out of telling Turo. A private party with catered food and candles. Poor Turo." Ingrid began to cry. "He died without ever knowing he was going to be a father again."

"Again?" Kay felt even more bewildered. "Somehow I had the impression Turo Kajima never married."

"That's true, he never did marry. But he did have children . . . lots of them . . . children all over the world. The oldest is sixty-one." Her eyes flashed with pride. "Turo Kajima had twenty-six children and he was still making babies at seventy-eight. Believe me, Turo Kajima was a very unusual man."

Kay thought that might be the understatement of the century.

Chapter 8

CRICKET KIMURA DRESSED for his evening appointment in a new wool suit from Paul Stuart, dark blue with muted stripes, a light blue Brooks Brothers shirt, a paisley tie from Mitsukoshi and handmade English shoes. Anyone who failed to notice his hard features or the bulging muscles under the suit might have taken him for a stockbroker or banker.

He felt uncharacteristically nervous about this meeting. The afternoon assignment had gone well, except for the unexpected presence of the *gaijin* woman who had seen his face. However, Kimura doubted that his patron would chastise him for that. The girl could be dealt with, if necessary, *gaijin* or not.

Nor was it the killings to come that were making Kimura nervous. What did worry him . . . just slightly . . . was their aftermath. Would his patron reward his courage by elevating him in the Yamaguchi-gumi, as he had implied? Or would he become a liability?

Kimura knew what happened to liabilities. They were dropped into Tokyo Bay with tire rims chained to their ankles or found dead of gunshot wounds in the trunks of their cars.

He must carry out this assignment in such a way that he would become a power in his own right. Not easy. But it could be done.

He parked near his patron's home in Omotesando and removed the sword, still wrapped in brown paper, from the trunk of the Porsche. The package was so bulky that it looked nothing like a sword. He walked around the corner to the side door and rang the bell. The door was opened by Yoshi Hasegawa himself, looking at ease in a maroon turtleneck sweater by Ralph Lauren and dark brown slacks. "Kimura-san. It's good to see you. Please come in."

Kimura followed Hasegawa down a hallway and into a paneled study lined with both Japanese and English books.

"You must allow me to pour you a drink," Hasegawa said. "We will toast today's success. Scotch?"

"*Hai*, thank you."

Drinks were poured into Hoya crystal and one glass was handed to Kimura.

Yoshi Hasegawa raised his glass. "To our venture, and to the sword. *Kanpai!*"

Kimura took a deep drink of the fine Scotch and allowed himself a rare moment of pure relaxation.

"Sit down, please," Hasegawa said.

They sat opposite each other in red leather chairs. As he looked at his host, Kimura saw all that he wanted to be in life. Yoshi Hasegawa had begun his career as a pimp and extortionist, the same path Kimura had taken. Hasegawa had been a strong-arm man, a tough boy from the Yokohama docks who knew how to use a knife and a lead pipe. But that had been four decades ago. Hasegawa, now in his middle fifties, had long since become the elder statesman of Japan's network of Yakuza gangs. He was a man of influence in many avenues of Japanese life. Photos of him were seen in the newspapers, usually in the company of important political figures and businessmen. Kimura had even seen Hasegawa in a television news program playing golf with a former president of the United States and Japan's foreign minister.

Over the years Hasegawa had worked assiduously at wearing away all his rough edges. Now, sitting across from Kimura, Hasegawa was the picture of an urbane Japanese gentleman, from the casual elegance of his clothing to the smooth, agreeable lines of his face. His hair was gray only at the temples, which suited him. Seeing him in the Ginza, in the back of his chauffeured Rolls-Royce with a cellular phone at his ear, no one could suspect that Yoshi Hasegawa had begun life selling the sexual favors of cheap dock girls for a hundred yen.

"I've been monitoring the television news shows and the police channels. Everyone knows that the sword used to kill Kajima-san was also used by Emperor Meiji to behead traitors. It's a big story. Tell me, did the old man give you much trouble?"

"No, that part was easy. Though he seemed to know why I wanted the sword."

Hasegawa nodded. "Kajima was a wise old fellow. I approached him about acquiring the sword. At the time I thought his silence might be bought. I offered to cover most of his losses on the Seisa-ko deal as well as pay a premium price for the sword. A very generous offer, I thought. But Kajima was stubborn. He wanted to bring Kohno to justice. And he was intelligent enough to guess why I wanted the sword."

"A fatal mistake," Kimura said.

"Yes."

"You heard there was a *gaijin* woman in Kajima's shop?"

"That was also on the news."

"She jumped out a window before I could deal with her."

"No matter. An interesting development, though. The *gaijin* had just bought the sword from Kajima-san."

"He claimed he had sold it. I didn't believe him."

"It is true. She purchased it for a collector in the States. Kajima-san wanted to send the sword out of the country to stop me from using it. You got to him just in time, Kimura-san."

They finished their Scotch and Hasegawa asked to see the sword. Kimura removed the paper wrapping and handed the weapon to Hasegawa.

"How very beautiful." Hasegawa drew the sword and admired it. "I once used a sword to kill a man who was trying to take over a gambling house I owned. I ran him through twice. Interesting experience. But that sword was nothing like this, it was an ordinary blade. This weapon is different, history and magic all in one."

Kimura noted how well Hasegawa handled the weapon.

"It's been twelve years . . . no, fifteen . . . since I had to kill anyone." Hasegawa sheathed the sword and handed it back to Kimura. "Those were exciting days, Kimura-san. Though we hardly realized it at the time, we were building an empire. Of course, the Yakuza were considered nothing more than street criminals then. That was before we got into banking and stock deals and solidified our relationship with the government. Now we're one of the largest industries in Japan, did you know that? If we were listed on the Nikkei index we'd be number ten or eleven in the nation. Right after the communications and auto companies." He gave a short laugh. "Maybe we will be listed on the Nikkei someday."

"Business is always good," Kimura said, "if you pay attention to your business."

"I've always liked your attitude. You understand that a Yakuza can never let up in business, never take a whole day off. If you let your guard down even for an instant . . ." Hasegawa's voice trailed off and he completed the point by bringing down his hand with a chopping motion.

Kimura basked silently in his patron's approval, content to wait for him to outline the next steps in his plan as they

lingered over their Scotch and talked about the new first
baseman for the Seibu Lions. Hasegawa was a rabid baseball
fan. He had a box seat for all the Lions home games and liked
to send expensive presents to players who had outstanding
games. To a player who had hit three home runs in a single
game he once presented a solid gold Rolex for every member
of the player's family.

After a time Hasegawa rose and went to the desk in his
study. He took a tiny gift-wrapped box from a desk drawer
and presented it to Kimura. "I have a small gift for you,
Kimura-san. I hope you will accept it."

Kimura quickly stood and bowed. "I'm honored to receive
any gift you would bestow upon me, Hasegawa-san."

"It's a modest thing, a trifle in comparison with all you are
doing for me."

"I'm honored." Kimura bowed again before unwrapping
the gift with care. The box was quite small. A ring box,
Kimura decided. But when he lifted the lid he found a gold
key engraved with the distinctive Rolls-Royce logo.

"I took the liberty of choosing a white Rolls. You'll look
rather splendid in it. Drive through Ginza on a Saturday
night and you'll have every girl in Tokyo throwing herself at
you."

Kimura was staggered. This was more than a luxury toy. It
was Hasegawa's way of announcing his elevation into the
highest ranks of Yamaguchi-gumi. Only an *oyabun* who re-
ported directly to Hasegawa was allowed to drive a Rolls.

"I don't know what to say."

"Words are unnecessary. You've earned your position,
Kimura-san. No one could question that. We'll have another
drink to it."

While Hasegawa poured Scotch, Kimura could only stare at
the gold key and imagine the figure he would cut driving
down Roppongi-dori in a white Rolls-Royce.

"The car is being prepared by my personal coachmaker."

Hasegawa added ice cubes to the Scotch. "Your initials are being engraved on the doors and I've taken the liberty of having a personal crest designed for you. The car will be ready to drive when our project is completed."

The slightest of chills went up Kimura's spine. The killings had to be accomplished first. And done right. If not, the white Rolls-Royce would vanish—along with Cricket Kimura. "I understand."

"I knew you would." Hasegawa passed him the glass with a smile. "Now, let us talk some real business. Sit down at my desk."

Kimura seated himself and watched Hasegawa take a stack of manila folders from the bottom drawer.

"There are twenty-two files here, Kimura-san. Each contains personal data on one of the investors who lost a large sum in Seisa-ko Securities. Address. Business affiliation. Hobbies. Daily routine. Photograph. Everything you need."

Kimura flipped open one of the files and looked at the photo of a middle-aged man with bags under his eyes.

"You must kill six of these people within the next two weeks. Any six, it doesn't matter which. I want their heads cut off with the Meiji sword. I want people to see you and see the sword. I don't want them to see your face, of course. Wear a hood, Kimura-san. Look like an executioner. That's what you'll be."

Kimura wanted to understand the entire purpose of this project. "You want me to kill six people in such a way that the surviving sixteen will be too afraid to continue with the lawsuit."

"Exactly. This sword was used to behead traitors. This is already starting to come out in the newspapers, I've seen to that. The message is clear—traitors will die by the sword. You may not have to kill six. Three or four might be enough. But you should plan for six."

"These people must be very dangerous. I thought Hideki Kohno was the only one who could really hurt you—"

"Kohno! He's a flea, what the *gaijin* call a front man for our operations. He will say nothing important at his trial. He will plead guilty and go to jail. He knows I could end his life with one phone call. These others are much more trouble because they don't even realize how dangerous they are. The problem, you see, is that a civil lawsuit would bring intense public scrutiny to much more than just the swindle itself. We cannot afford that."

Kimura nodded. He knew that money from Seisa-ko Securities had been funneled not only to Yoshi Hasegawa but to a number of politicians including members of the Diet. That was why a reign of terror had to be imposed on the Seisa-ko investors who had brought a civil lawsuit against the corporation.

"When you become a member of my *sanro-kai* you'll learn much more about our operations," Hasegawa promised. "And I think you will be impressed by the extent of Yakuza influence."

Kimura was still studying the files. "Kohno-san must know a lot more than the investors who lost money to him. I don't understand why we don't kill him. That way you can be *sure* he'll never talk."

"There is one good reason for keeping Kohno alive, at least temporarily."

A doorbell rang. The side door again, the same door Kimura had used.

"And you are about to meet that reason."

Kimura continued to study the files while Hasegawa answered the bell. There were servants in the house but they had been instructed to let the master of the house answer his own door tonight.

"Kimura-san, I'd like you to meet one of our most valuable allies."

Kimura looked up from the files and received a shock.

"I know Kimura-san," said the visitor. "At least by reputation."

"My reputation is only a small shadow compared with yours," Kimura answered graciously. Not certain what else to do or say, he stood and bowed respectfully to Police Superintendent Supervisor Knuckles Yamato.

Yamato returned the bow. Ha! The sight of one of Tokyo's senior police officials bowing to a Yakuza *oyabun* would have bewildered the ordinary Japanese citizen.

"Sit down." Hasegawa took a chair between them and dispensed with his role as host. "Yamato-san can't spend too much time with us, it's dangerous for him to be here."

"Your house isn't being watched," Yamato assured him. "Not tonight, at least. I made sure of that. Still, I'd like to be in and out of here in ten minutes."

"Of course. Kimura-san, you should know that Yamato-san is aware that you killed Turo Kajima. I told him that myself. Don't be alarmed." Hasegawa put up a calming hand. "Yamato-san is in this with us. He has a great deal to lose personally if the Seisa-ko scandal grows any wider."

"I see." Kimura still hated the idea of this policeman having evidence against him.

"No, you don't yet see," Hasegawa said. "But you will. Yamato-san also knows that you are going to kill several of the investors who are suing over the large sums they lost in the Seisa-ko fraud. Now control your temper. Yamato-san will protect you. That's his job. You kill those people and he will make sure the investigation comes nowhere near to you."

Some of the tightness in Kimura's chest began to ease. "How will you do that?"

"I've already begun." Yamato's flat face took on a self-satisfied glow. "I assigned Detective Inspector Takeo Saji to the Turo Kajima murder case."

"Tak Saji? That big fellow who killed those two assassins who tried to get at the Emperor's nephew? He's nothing but trouble. I don't see how assigning him to the case helps me."

"Saji-san is a hard man, I agree," Yamato said. "But he has also become a burned-out drunk who hasn't a friend inside the department. In addition to putting him on the murder case I've made him responsible for that *gaijin* woman who saw you at the scene. And I personally removed your photo and fingerprints from the department's computer files."

Kimura was pleased by that news. "Will you make him responsible for investigating all the sword deaths?"

"That, of course, is my plan." Yamato was smug. "He can't succeed. The case is too big and he's just one policeman with no one to help him. Oh, I'll assign a few people to him, but nobody will do anything. Not for Tak Saji."

"Why not? Nobody cares if a man drinks too much. What else is wrong with him?"

"He's *burakumin*," Yamato said. *"And* he's also *kikoku-shijo."*

Which changed everything. "All right," Kimura said, "now I see. I can almost feel sorry for Tak Saji. How did a man like that get onto the police force to begin with?"

"He had a patron, Hideki Kohno's father, in fact. When the father died Saji-san lost what small influence he had. He would have been kicked off the force long ago if he hadn't once saved the life of the Emperor's nephew."

"The Kohno connection again." Kimura was troubled. "I still don't see why I don't just kill this Hideki Kohno."

Hasegawa interceded smoothly. "The problem there is quite simple. The superintendent general of the Tokyo Metropolitan Police put Yamato-san in charge of Kohno's safety. If we let you kill Kohno, our good friend Yamato-san would be disgraced. He would have to resign his position or be demoted. Either way we would lose a most valuable ally in the department."

Everything in Japan is politics, Kimura thought.

"After Kohno is convicted and goes to prison," Yamato went on, "we can arrange for him to have a very bad accident. Then his death will be no reflection on me." He looked at his watch. "I should go now." He stood and gave Kimura an almost friendly look. "Trust me, Kimura-san. I will keep you safe."

Hasegawa escorted the policeman to the door. When he returned he said, "I can see you are still worried about Yamato-san. Why? You have police on your own payroll."

"Yes, but I don't deal with them personally. I don't like policemen, especially the ones who play both sides."

"I don't like him either, my friend. But Yamato is well bought and paid for, I can assure you of that."

Kimura was touched that Hasegawa had used the term *my friend.* That was the first time he had ever called him anything but Kimura-san.

"Why are you smiling?" Hasegawa asked.

"I was thinking about Yamato-san's remark when he left. *Trust me.* What a stupid thing for a policeman to say."

Chapter 9

It WAS MIDNIGHT in Tokyo, 10:00 A.M. in Philadelphia.

While Tak watched over her from the lobby bar at the Imperial Hotel, Kay Williams called her client from a bar phone using her credit card. Speaking to Walter Emerson was the last thing in the world she felt up to but it had to be done.

Getting through to Walter Emerson was a chore. She dialed direct to his corporate headquarters in Philadelphia and was greeted by a third-line gatekeeper secretary. By pleading urgency Kay's call was bucked up to an executive secretary who didn't have the authority to put Kay's call through to her boss so she routed it to an administrative assistant.

Fortunately the AA understood how passionately Emerson felt about his collection of antique swords and flintlocks, and when Kay made him understand that her call was important, the AA put her through to the Man himself.

"Walter Emerson here."

"Hello, Walter, this is Kay."

"Kay! Did you get it? Did Kajima finally come through? Christ, I thought the old bastard would *never* sell that sword."

"He sold the sword," Kay said. "The deal went through."

"Wonderful! I can hardly wait to hold it in my hands. You have no idea, Kay, how many years I've wanted to own that sword. The mystery of it . . . the history . . . wait . . . is it in good condition?"

"Yes, excellent condition . . . But there's a problem."

"Problem?" The enthusiasm chilled. "I don't want to hear about any problem. The sale went through? He accepted my check? As my agent you accepted the sword?"

"Yes."

"Then I don't see how a *problem* could exist."

"Let me tell you what happened." And she did her best to summarize the incredible sequence of events that occurred after Turo Kajima accepted Emerson's check and locked it in his safe. She managed to describe how brutally Kajima had died without becoming sick to her stomach, and she explained why the Japanese police would not let her retrieve his check for $2.3 million. "Legally, the check now belongs to Kajima's estate."

"And the *sword* belongs to me," Emerson said. "Not that it seems to do me much good at this moment. This guy . . . actually cut off Kajima's head? With only one blow? The sword must be in terrific condition."

Kay was disgusted by Emerson's pleasure over the sharpness of his sword. Kajima's murder seemed to have little effect.

"Has anyone figured out who the killer was?"

"The officer handling the case thinks he's one of the Yakuza."

"He's what?"

"The Japanese mob."

"Oh. Christ, what a mess. What are you going to do? Stay there until the police recover the sword?"

"Yes. Or until I believe there's no chance it will be recovered in the near future."

Silence while Emerson digested her remark. "I don't intend to lose two point three million on this deal, Miss Williams."

It was no longer *Kay*. "I understand your position. I'd feel the same way."

"My first priority is to take delivery of the sword. And it must still be in collector condition."

"Of course."

"I'll give you two weeks to deliver it to me. Two weeks from *today*."

"Yes . . ."

"If I don't have the sword by then I'll have to file a lawsuit against your company. I'm sorry, this isn't personal."

"I understand that." Kay's stomach seemed to be twisting itself into a large knot.

"What I really want is the damned sword."

"And I intend to get it back for you."

"Keep me informed." Emerson hung up.

When Kay left the phone her legs felt wobbly and she wondered if her anxiety showed. That question was quickly answered. As soon as she sat down at Tak Saji's table he said, "You look worse than you did this afternoon."

"Thanks."

"I'm sorry, I just meant you're very pale again."

"Yes, I get that way when I see people murdered or when my livelihood is threatened."

"Your client was angry?"

"Determined. He wants to hold the sword he just bought in his hot little hands. I can't blame him for that, he already shelled out more than two million for it. If he doesn't get the sword within two weeks he'll sue me. He's got about fifty lawyers on his payroll, real sharks. They'd make a snack out of my little company."

"Can you cover a loss that big?"

Kay shook her head. "My biggest asset is my shop in Connecticut. It's in an old restored farmhouse on Route 35 in

Ridgefield with about ten acres behind it. I bought the property at a tax sale, fixed it up and the value's gone way up. But my equity's only about six hundred thousand. I've got maybe another four hundred thousand in stocks and bonds and a hundred and fifty thousand worth of antiques in stock in the shop. I thought I was doing pretty well, a millionairess at thirty-four. On *paper* at least. Now it all might well go down the drain."

"You don't look thirty-four," Tak said. "I thought you were twenty-eight or twenty-nine."

"Thanks. This time I mean it."

Tak cleared his throat. "Would you like a drink?"

"Okay . . . why not . . . make it a double something. I need to sleep tonight." She noticed that Tak was drinking Perrier. "Look, I was a bitch to go on about your drinking. I shouldn't have done that. I'm sorry. Have a real drink with me."

"You were right." Tak took a swallow of Perrier and pretended to like it. "I've been drinking pretty hard for four or five years now. Sometimes I can't even remember where I was the night before." He leaned forward. "Most of the time I don't even *care* where I was. I can't drink like that when I've got a real case to work on."

"What do you mean *real case*?"

"Usually they give me all their *gaijin* jobs because I speak English well. You know, bodyguard for a visiting American or Australian dignitary. Handle the arrest of a foreigner who gets in trouble. Earlier today I helped a businessman from New York find a lost wallet. I'm a gofer, Miss Williams."

"Kay."

"Right . . ."

A waitress came up and Tak ordered a double martini for Kay.

Meanwhile she tried to divert herself from all the problems at hand by looking around the Imperial lobby at the graceful columns and the impressive mosaic covering the far wall. "This is such a beautiful hotel."

"Frank Lloyd Wright designed the original Imperial Hotel. It was the only major building in Tokyo that survived the great *Kanto* earthquake of 1923 without any major damage. They dismantled the original building about twenty years ago. This one was built in its place using a lot of Wright's fixtures and designs. Frank Lloyd Wright is revered in Japan because he did quality work. Japanese do admire quality."

"My father was an architect," Kay said, "though not in Wright's league. He might have been, except he was too fond of the grape. Drank himself to death while he was still a young man."

Tak wondered if she was giving him a not-too-subtle message about his own future, or lack thereof.

"Pop was a great guy, though." Kay's drink was served. She picked up her glass and looked into the pale liquid as if delving into the past. "He could always make me laugh, even in the worst of times. He had a gift for making the most common occurrence sound funny."

"No small gift," Tak said.

"Phil, my ex-husband, could be funny, too." Kay drank some of her martini and the slight smile left her face. "But Phil could *not* be described as a great guy. He was more like your basic scum-sucking rat."

"How long were you married?"

"Ten or fifteen centuries. Actually, Phil and I were only together a year before I discovered it wasn't just *my* body he craved, it was the body of *any* girl between the ages of fifteen and twenty-five. No, make that thirteen and twenty-five." She felt a little dizzy, either from the liquor or the memory of her marriage. "What about you? Any wife, ex or otherwise?"

"No wife. No girlfriend, either. Not for a long time now."

Kay decided it was time to find out what was behind Tak Saji's problem with liquor and women. "What was that stuff you were telling me earlier? About why I wouldn't want to be you?"

Tak knew she had been waiting to spring that question on him, and that sooner or later he'd have to tell her. Kay Williams wouldn't give up on it. She was the type who never gave up on anything, except a husband who turned out to be "a scum-sucking rat."

"I said that I was *kikokushijo* and *burakumin*. *Kikokushijo* is a word for a person who goes away to a foreign country and comes back so different that the Japanese won't accept him. That's what happened to me. I spent seven years in LA, and when I came back I was too different to be accepted. Not that I would have been accepted anyway because I'm also *burakumin*."

"And what's *that*?"

"Everyone knows that India has an untouchable class. Most people don't realize that Japan does too. They're called *burakumin* and I happen to be one."

Kay looked skeptical. "An untouchable class? In a modern country like Japan?"

"Centuries ago the *burakumin* did all the dirtiest work, like bury corpses. Our ancestors were forced to live in ghettos that weren't even shown on maps. Well, the *burakumin* are still around. And still discriminated against. Most of us can't get decent jobs. My father did better than most, he was a gardener."

"That sounds impossible, in this day and age. I mean, you look like any other Japanese. How could people tell you're a . . . what is it . . . *burakumin*?"

"In Japan everyone is listed at birth in an official family register. When you apply for a job an employer looks up your family register as part of a background check. Or if you want to marry a girl, her parents will look you up. When they discover you're *burakumin*, forget it. No job and no marriage."

"That's medieval!"

"No, that's just Japan."

"If *burakumin* are so discriminated against, how did you get to be a detective inspector?"

"Hideki Kohno's father got me onto the police force. He pulled a lot of strings because he thought he owed me. And then I got promoted, something no one expected to happen. Especially me."

"You must have done something right. Something that overruled the fact that you're *burakumin*."

"Yes, I did." Tak wished he was drinking something more interesting than Perrier. "I killed two men in the line of duty, and they turned out to be exactly the right men to kill."

Listening to Tak's problems was taking Kay's mind off her own. "Please tell me more." She saw him flinch. "No look, this isn't just idle curiosity." A lie. She was insatiably curious, always had been. "You've been assigned to protect me, right? If I'm going to put my life in your hands I need to know more about you, that's all."

Tak, giving in, sat back and told her all of it, from the beginning:

"My father worked for Suro Kohno, Hideki's father, as a gardener here in Tokyo. Kohno had a big house and garden and a high position with the Bank of New Tokyo. Then one day Kohno was transferred to Los Angeles as vice president for the bank's operations on the West Coast of the U.S.

"He decided to take with him a cook, a maid, a driver and a gardener—my father. My mother refused to go to the U.S. She wouldn't leave Tokyo even to visit relatives in other prefectures, she was very old-fashioned that way. So my father went without her. There was no question of refusing to go. As a *burakumin* he couldn't afford to anger his boss. My mother sent me along to look after my father, who worked six or seven days a week and never thought to take a meal unless it was prepared for him.

"I was fourteen years old when we flew to LA. I spoke no English. I'd never been out of Tokyo. And I was terrified.

"Kohno and his family rented a house in Pasadena, just northeast of LA. I should say he rented a mansion, a big estate with extensive grounds on Orange Grove Boulevard. That's why he needed a gardener. Kohno brought his family with him, of course, his wife and his son Hideki.

"At first my father and I didn't live on the big estate. Kohno had rented a little bungalow in the black neighborhood of Altadena for my father and me. Tough neighborhood, lots of gang stuff going on but that didn't bother me. I'd grown up a *burakumin* in a very hard part of Tokyo. I knew how to use my fists and a knife too if I needed it.

"What did bother me was being put back to fourth grade because I didn't know English. There I was, fourteen years old and sitting in a class of nine-year-olds! I felt disgraced.

"Hideki didn't know any English either, so his father hired tutors to help him. Funny thing, though. I seemed to have an aptitude for languages. I studied hard and was speaking English pretty well in about six months, while Hideki could hardly say more than good morning or the weather is hot today.

"When Hideki's father heard how well I was doing, he decided to move my father and me into a room above the garage on his estate. That way I'd be around all the time to help Hideki with his English.

"And that's how Hideki Kohno and I got to be friends.

"At first, of course, Hideki didn't want to be my friend. I was *burakumin*. Untouchable. But Suro Kohno was a very practical man, very modern. He didn't believe in that old stuff and told Hideki to stop complaining and start getting along with me.

"Do you ever watch squirrels running around? They go

from one thing to another. Always moving. Not getting much done but always busy. That's Hideki for you. A lot of energy going nowhere.

"His English got a lot better from spending time with me, and I learned some things from him, too. He taught me how to look at the next kid's paper during a test to get answers I didn't have. I also learned from Hideki what sex was about. By the time he was fifteen Hideki was going with girls and carrying rubbers in his wallet. He also taught me how to creep under the stand at a football game and look up the girls' dresses. Yes, Hideki knew a lot, but not nearly as much as he thought he knew.

"Hideki also had a big mouth on him. One day he said to a big black kid, LeRoy Tate was the kid's name, 'We don't allow blacks to come to Japan. They steal and make other trouble. No one in Japan likes blacks, except for Little Black Sambo. We read about him all the time.'

"I wasn't there when Hideki said that, you understand. I just heard about it later. LeRoy Tate kind of smiled and said, 'That's too bad, 'cause we niggers just *love* you Japs. You got all the money, right? All the loot? And you like to share it, I hear.'

"LeRoy grabbed Hideki, turned him upside down and shook him by the ankles until everything in his pockets fell out. LeRoy's friends scooped up Hideki's money and whatever else they wanted. Then LeRoy turned Hideki rightside up and beat the living shit out of him. Put him in the hospital for almost a week.

"While Hideki was recovering, his father called me into his study. We sat down together and Suro Kohno got right to the point. You're a senior in high school, Tak. Doing well, too, I asked your teachers about your grades. They say you're quiet and shy, something I already knew, but quick. You're quick on the football field, too. A very hard player. I like that."

" 'Thank you, sir,' " was all I could say, wondering what Suro Kohno was getting at.

" 'Hideki isn't a good student.' " Kohno fidgeted and grumbled. 'He doesn't like to work hard and he's always in trouble. Now he's in the hospital because of his loud talk and I'm afraid that might happen again.'

"All I could do was listen.

" 'Have you thought about going to college?' " Kohno asked.

"That was a big surprise. No, I hadn't thought about it. College cost money and Kohno didn't pay my father enough to send me to college.

" 'I'm sending Hideki to UCLA to study finance,' Kohno said. " 'Pretty good school. I couldn't get him into Stanford or USC, his grades aren't high enough. But UCLA will give him a good education. I'd be willing to pay your tuition and room and board, even give you some expense money, if you'll agree to go to UCLA and be Hideki's roommate.'

" 'Why?' I asked.

" 'To help him with his studies and keep him out of trouble. Hideki does enough bad things living right here under my roof. When he gets away to college I'm afraid he'll go wild. I want you to keep him in line. Oh, you can't run his life for him, I know that. Just try to keep him out of the *worst* kinds of trouble, like this thing with the black boy. I don't want Hideki to be beaten up again or to run his car into a wall while he's drunk. Yes, I know how much he drinks.'

" 'And for that you'll send me to college?'

" 'It's a good arrangement for both of us. I've already spoken to your father and he's agreed. What do you say?'

"I said yes, of course.

"That's how I went to UCLA on a personal scholarship from Suro Kohno. And I loved it there. I was majoring in education, I wanted to be a teacher, help other kids get a start. I worked so hard they called me a grind, you know what that is.

"Hideki did not do well. I helped him as much as I could. Tutored him, nagged him into studying, helped him write his papers, prepped him for exams, took his car keys when he had too much to drink, which was pretty often.

"We'd been semi-friends all through high school, probably because I was no threat to Hideki then. In high school he had his own car, his own circle of friends. So I wasn't around all the time. We might hang out together once in a while but in those days I was just on the fringe of his life, correcting his English.

"But now I was his roommate. And sometimes I was telling him what to do. One night when I was trying to help him study for a test he got fed up with me.

" 'You're nothing but a goddam jailer! I *hate* having you for a roommate. What was my father thinking of? You probably tell the old fart everything I do.'

" 'No, I never tell him anything,' I said, and that was the truth. I had told Suro Kohno I'd help Hideki all I could but I wouldn't spy on him.

" 'I don't see why I have to live with a *burakumin*,' he said.
" 'This would never happen in Tokyo.'

" 'You wouldn't be going out with blondes and redheads in Tokyo either,' I reminded him.

"That calmed Hideki down. He did have a lot of *gaijin* girlfriends, and when they were mentioned every other thought went right out of his head, even his anger against me.

" 'Hey, I've got a big date tomorrow, Tak. You should see her. Beautiful! And built like a brick shithouse.' "

"That was one of Hideki's favorite expressions. Built like a brick shithouse. He used it to describe any girl who was at all attractive. I like American slang but I've never been able to figure out that one. What's so attractive about a brick shithouse?

"Anyway, Hideki forgot he was sore at me and started making plans for his date.

" 'For some reason this babe doesn't want to go out with me alone. Says I've got a *bad reputation.*" Hideki laughed at that, he loved having a bad reputation. 'Hey, you come along with us, Tak. Then when I give you the signal, get lost somewhere, okay?''

" 'No, thanks.'

" 'Hey, come on. We're just going to the Westwood Cinema, catch a flick. After the movie you split and I'll take care of Sandra.'

"That was the first time I heard her name—Sandra.

" 'You do me that favor and I'll hit the books real hard tonight. How about it? She won't go out with me if I show up alone. Please, Tak. I'm really nuts about this girl.'

"I could see he was serious, he really did want to go out with this girl, this Sandra. So I promised I'd go along and even that I'd get lost after the movie.

"The next night we went to pick up Sandra and that's when my problems started. I took one look at Sandra and totally lost my head. I mean, I was *in love.* No control. No common sense. A total head case.

"What a girl she was. Long blonde hair almost down to her waist. A face with green eyes, strong chin, and very sweet nose. Soft voice, body all whippy, blue eyes with highlights of green, funny, irreverent, a little wild. A genuine California girl.

"It turned out that Sandra went for me, too. Instead of Hideki losing me, Sandra and I managed to lose Hideki in the crowd coming out of the movie. We headed down Sunset Boulevard to the beach in her car and sat up the rest of the night talking and touching each other.

"Sandra knew very little about Japan, wanted to learn it all in one night. Didn't care that my father was a gardener, hers was only a desk clerk at the Ambassador Hotel. Didn't care that I was Japanese, told me I looked like a young samurai. We watched the sun rise over the cliffs at Santa Monica and made love for the first time right there on the beach.

"When I got back to the dorm it was noontime. Hideki was madder than I'd ever seen him. All I can say is that for the first time ever I was swept up in my own thoughts, my own life. I didn't know what a swamp being like that could be, the mistakes you can make.

"Over the next couple of weeks I spent every spare minute with Sandra. I pratically forgot Hideki existed. My grades started to slip. I was still in the top ten percent of my class but I was no longer at the very top. That would have bothered me before, but with Sandra at my side I didn't worry about anything.

"We got engaged. I met her father, she met mine. She thought my father was cute. I thought hers was a moron, couldn't believe he'd fathered a girl as wonderful as Sandra. My father was alarmed that I was going to marry a *gaijin* but he didn't know what to do about it. He took out his frustration on the estate's rosebushes, pruning them back almost to nothing.

"What was Hideki doing all this time? Whatever he wanted. I'd stopped being his keeper. If Suro Kohno wanted to cut off my money I couldn't blame him. I'd learned that in the U.S. you can work your way through school and that would have been fine with me.

"As it turned out, I never did get my degree. One morning I walked into my room after class to find two cops going through my things. A guy from campus security was with them. They had a warrant to search my part of the room. A lot of stuff had been stolen from rooms in the dorm over the past few weeks and an anonymous phone call had sent the police to me.

"They found some of the missing stuff hidden at the back of my closet, a stereo and a portable TV and some other stolen merchandise in my desk, two watches and a whole slew of other people's credit cards.

"I was taken to the Westwood police station and booked for grand larceny, twelve counts.

"I called my father and he talked to Suro Kohno, who came to see me. He listened, seemed to believe that I was innocent and said he'd do what he could to help me. Meanwhile I'd have to stay in jail. He was a bank vice president, couldn't afford to bail me out until he was certain I was innocent. Might look bad to his bank if I turned out to be guilty.

"So I sweated out five days in the county jail. What killed me was that Sandra never showed up. I couldn't figure that one out. Where the hell was she?

"Hideki had talked to her. He'd told her I'd been in that kind of trouble before, shoplifting and stealing auto parts, and that he'd had to cover up for me several times. He also told her I was *burakumin*, a Japanese untouchable, and he made that sound as bad as AIDS. Told her *burakumin* have hereditary defects and venereal diseases passed from one generation to another. By the time Hideki was finished with my character and lineage, Sandra was finished with me.

"How could I refute him? I was *burakumin*, and stolen goods had been found in my closet and desk.

"Sandra couldn't see that Hideki was out to destroy me. Hideki can be very convincing, just ask the people who invested in Seisa-ko.

"Suro Kohno finally bailed me out of jail and got the charges against me dropped. Though he never mentioned Hideki's name, he obviously knew that his son was behind my problems.

"I tried to explain everything to Sandra but it was too late. She cried and said things like 'I don't really know you,' and 'What if our children had one of those hereditary defects?'

Then the semester ended and she took off on a surfing trip to Hawaii. Hideki took a holiday, too, knowing I'd kill him if I saw him.

"When Suro Kohno announced that the bank was calling him back to Tokyo to become its new president I was ready to come back with him. To hell with UCLA, I didn't even want to be on the same campus with Hideki. And my father was delighted; seven years in the U.S. was more than enough for him.

"Kohno then got me onto the Tokyo police force and I took the job just to be doing something. I spent the first two years in a *koban*, a police box, way out toward Narita airport. Then they put me on the permanent detail that guards the many cousins and nephews of the emperor who live outside the palace grounds.

"It was a dead-end job, sitting in a police van all day outside some nonentity's home. Officers assigned to that duty usually realize they have no future in the department and resign. That's what the department hoped I'd do. They had no place for a *burakumin*, they were just paying off a debt to Suro Kohno.

"If it hadn't been for The Sons Against the Emperor Society I probably would have quit. The Sons, as they're known, is an offshoot of the Red Guard. A bunch of terrorists determined to bring down the emperor. They can't get at him, of course, though occasionally they lob a pipe bomb at a *koban* near the imperial palace or do some other kind of petty damage.

"One afternoon I was sitting in my van in front of a house that belonged to a nephew of the emperor. It was a hot muggy day so I was half-dozing and hungover besides. I hardly paid attention to the car that cruised by the house a couple of times. Maybe more than two times, I don't know for sure.

"Anyway, I finally did notice the car. There were three men inside. It was an old Honda and the license plate was smeared with mud so that you couldn't read the numerals.

That's what caught my eye. It hadn't rained in three weeks, so where did all that mud come from?

"I pulled out my pistol just as two of the men jumped from the car, leaving the driver behind the wheel. One headed for the house, the other came for me and was unslinging a stubby little Uzi. Before he could fire a burst through the windshield I put my pistol out the window and fired one shot at him. My round caught him in the chest and he went down. I jumped out of the car and ran after the second gunman. The guy behind the wheel took a couple of shots at me and missed. I ignored him because I heard the other gunman fire his Uzi. He was shooting away the lock on the front door.

"I caught up with him just as he entered the house. Someone was screaming, a woman, and a baby had started to cry. I didn't give the gunman any warning, you don't have to do that in Japan. Before he could get far enough inside to do any damage I shot him twice in the back. From the way he fell I knew he was either dead or too badly hurt to be of any more danger to anyone. By the time I got back onto the street, the third man had driven away in the Honda.

"It turned out that the gunmen were members of The Sons Against the Emperor Society. Their pockets were stuffed with declarations against the imperial family so people would know what their cause was in case they died in their attack, which they did.

"What good would it have done them to kill a rather obscure nephew of the emperor? I don't know. Crazies don't think straight. Anyway, for a brief time I was a hero. None of the newspapers even mentioned that I was *burakumin*. Because the emperor was grateful that I'd saved some of the lesser members of his family from harm I was promoted to detective inspector. I was beginning to think my life had turned around.

"But others in the department resented my promotion and soon I was back where I started, a *burakumin* with no friends

and no future. I have a better job, more pay, an office in
Metropolitan Police Headquarters. I'll probably never be
fired, at least not while the current emperor lives, no matter
how much I drink. But neither have I ever been given any
really good cases—until now. And the only reason I've been
given this case is because Knuckles Yamato wants to see me
fail.

"So you see, Miss Williams, I mean Kay, you do not have
the star of the Tokyo police department guarding your very
pretty rear end and looking for your sword. Instead you have
the department outcast. But let me tell you this. When I'm
sober, and thinking clearly, and have something worth working on, I'm a pretty good cop. In fact I'm a *damned good* cop.
When somebody commits a crime that really annoys me, I go
after that person whether I'm assigned to the case or not. I've
brought in quite a few perps, as the U.S. police call them,
much to the annoyance of my superiors, who wish I would
just stay at my desk and blend into the woodwork.

"So don't worry, I'll do a good job for you. I promise."

Kay had been listening carefully to Tak until he reached the
point where he talked about his sexual relations with his
California girl. Then her mind started to drift. She lost the
thread of his story to an image of Tak in bed with that girl
from UCLA. And when he promised her that he'd protect her
"very pretty rear end," a rush went through her.

I've been without a man for too long, she thought. But is
this a guy I really want to go to bed with? A drunk and an
outcast from his own society? A man who shoots people in
the back without even a warning? A man who quite obviously doesn't have a friend in the world?

God help me, I think I do.

"You should file a lawsuit," Kay said. "That's the best way
to fight discrimination."

"This isn't the U.S. We settle most of our differences by negotiation instead of litigation. People say that's one of the nice things about our country."

"Well, you've got to do something. That *burakumin* stuff is bullshit."

Tak had to laugh. You couldn't explain to her that Japan didn't work like the rest of the world. "Maybe you're right, maybe that should be our battle cry: BURAKUMIN IS BULLSHIT." He finished his Perrier. "Come on, I'll walk you to your room. I'll pick you up at 9:00 A.M. We'll go to headquarters and you can look through the Yakuza photo files."

"You think I'm in any real danger from Kajima's killer?"

"A Yakuza doesn't like to get rough with *gaijins*, that kind of behavior attracts too much attention. But when we get closer to him, he may decide that he has to get rid of you. Then we'll have to take special precautions. Tonight you can sleep soundly."

"I feel like I haven't slept in ten days."

Tak went upstairs with her. When she opened her door he said, "Just let me check the room." He looked around the room and then made sure there were no ledges or other easy ways to get inside. "I've talked to hotel security. They have someone down the hall watching this door from the linen closet. No one will get in here tonight."

"Thank you."

"See you in the morning."

Tak seemed to linger, and for a moment Kay thought he might try to kiss her, or at least put a hand on her arm. But instead he said, "I'm sorry you've gotten such a bad impression of Japan." And then he was gone.

The first thing Tak did when he got home was to find the bullets for his Walther, then he sat down and cleaned the weapon and reloaded with a full eight-shot clip.

Next he shined his shoes, threw out every tie that had food spots and set up an ironing board to press the suit he'd left crumpled on the floor.

He had intended to empty into the sink the almost full quart of Nikka Scotch that was in his cupboard but couldn't bring himself to do that. He tried to tell himself that would be a waste of money, he'd rather give the Scotch away. The truth was he needed the comfort of having a bottle of Scotch sitting in his cupboard.

Before he could pull his futon out of the closet and lay down to sleep his phone rang.

"Moshi-moshi."

"Tak? Is that you?"

A voice from the past. "Hideki?"

"Yes . . . yes . . . it's me. Look, I'm speaking English in case someone overhears me. I don't want anyone here to know what we're talking about."

"Where are you?"

"They've got me in an apartment in Meguro. Two police guards. But that's not enough, Tak." Hideki Kohno's voice began to break up. "I'm not safe here. They're gonna *kill* me. Sooner or later I'm gonna *die.*"

"Who's trying to kill you?"

"Yakuza. You know those guys, they'll get me even if they have to wait until after my trial. You saw what they did to Kajima-san. That's gonna happen to *me.*"

"Turo Kajima? Hideki, do you know who killed Kajima-san?"

"I don't know *who* did the job. I only know Kajima's murder is connected to Seisa-ko, and I heard on TV tonight that you're running the case. Goddamn, Tak, I don't want to die. It was just . . ." Now he was simultaneously sobbing and whining. ". . . just easy money. How was I to know it would blow up into something so big?"

Tak had an urge to hang up. Hideki Kohno had never given

him anything but trouble, this time would be no different. "Where are they holding you?"

"Lion Mansion in Meguro."

"Where are your guards right now?"

"Asleep . . . the one who's supposed to be awake is dozing in the next room . . . I'm *scared*, Tak."

"Are there guards outside, too?"

"One, I can see him from my window. He's patrolling around the apartment house."

"Then it sounds like you're safe for tonight. Are you really going to testify against the Yakuza?"

"Hell no! Hasegawa-san would have me killed right there in the courtroom."

"Was Yoshi Hasegawa behind Seisa-ko?"

"He was part of it, Tak. But *I'm* the only one going to jail." Hideki's voice dropped to a whisper. "The guard woke up, I can hear him moving around."

"Hideki, calm down. Do they ever let you out of the apartment?"

"They let me take an exercise walk at night," he whispered. "Two of them come along with me."

"Do you stop anywhere?"

"There's a public toilet in the park down the street. Sometimes I go in there, take a leak."

"Lion Mansion in Meguro. I'll find it. What time do you take your walk?"

"About nine."

"Go in the restroom tomorrow night. I'll be there. Don't worry, I won't let them kill you."

"Thanks, Tak. I knew I could count on you. Hey, I'm sorry for all the trouble I caused . . . I mean . . . back in California . . . that was . . . I gotta go!"

The connection was broken. Tak put down the phone with a strong sense of *déjà vu*. Ten years. That's how long it had been since he had talked to Hideki Kohno. Not since California.

I ought to let Yoshi Hasegawa kill him, Tak thought. That'd be a simple way to even the score.

Chapter 10

TORIGAKO HAD ONLY JUST OPENED his shop and put on a pot of tea when Cricket Kimura roared to a stop outside in his new Porsche. So early, and Kimura was dressed in a black sweatshirt, black pants, black shoes. Torigako had never seen him in anything except a tailored suit.

Kimura came in with his usual brute authority. "Good morning, Torigako-san. I am here for another of your pets."

"Oh, my." The old man was momentarily upset. "The cricket I sold you yesterday was not satisfactory?"

"No, no, nothing like that. He's a fine little fellow, sang to me beautifully last night. And very lucky for me, too. No, I simply need another playmate." With a touch of belligerence. "Anything wrong with that?"

"Of course not. I am delighted to have such a satisfied customer. Let me see . . ." Torigako was flustered; usually Kimura gave him some notice that he was coming, allowing him time to pick out a good specimen.

"I don't have all day," Kimura said.

"Here you are." Torigako reached out blindly and picked up a handsome yellow cage in which a smallish cricket had nestled itself into a clump of grass.

"Not very big," Kimura said.

"Ah, but wait until you hear his call. Beautiful!" A desperate lie; in truth this cricket sounded like any other.

"But is he lucky?"

"All my crickets are lucky, and blessed."

"Shinto blessed or Buddhist blessed?"

Aiii! Kimura had never asked that question before. Torigako had no idea that Kimura was religious. A religious Yakuza? What a thought. "Shinto," he said out of desperation.

Kimura shrugged. "Doesn't matter, I suppose. So long as he's really lucky."

"I would not sell you an unlucky cricket." Torigako truly did believe that all his pets were lucky for their owners.

"I know that. You have been a good friend to me, Torigako-san." He laid a ten thousand yen note on the counter, as he had the day before.

"I am embarrassed by your generosity. That is simply too much to pay for one cricket and one cage. I cannot allow you to overpay me two days in a row."

"I'm not overpaying. Good luck is worth a lot to me." He picked up the cage and smiled at the creature inside. "Let's go for a ride, little friend. See you again, Torigako-san. Very soon. Be sure you have a good selection, I'll have need of several lucky crickets this month."

Torigako wheezed a sigh of relief when Kimura left his shop. A valuable customer, but a difficult one. He poured a cup of tea, sat down at his worktable and began to paint the slats of three cages he had made the day before. When all three cages had been painted, Torigako picked up his newspaper and began to read the lead story in the Asahi *Shimbun* about the murder of a dealer of antique swords in Shinjuku. The killer had cut off the head of the antique dealer, a man named Turo Kajima. And the killer had stolen a famous sword once owned by Emperor Meiji and used to behead the leaders of a revolt. The killer was described as a man of about thirty-five, well-dressed. Nothing more was known about him except the possibility that he was Yakuza.

That last made Torigako bite the tip of his tongue. Could it be? Yesterday Kimura had bought one of his crickets for luck and paid a lot of money for it, too much money. Hours later a man was brutally slain, possibly by a Yakuza gangster.

Torigako put the paper aside and began laying out strips of wood for new cages. This was the day most parents passed out small amounts of money to their children. The boys and girls would be coming in after school to buy cages and crickets and he wanted a nice stock for them . . . But as hard as he tried to put the murder of the sword dealer out of his mind, he could not. Cricket Kimura was a Yakuza, a killer, he knew that in his mind and in his bones. Probably he killed that poor man in Shinjuku. But what should he do about it?

Nothing. Even though others would die, too. Why else would Kimura purchase still another cricket this morning, two days in a row? Because he had someone else to kill, the only logical answer. A lucky cricket to keep him from getting caught, that was how this man thought.

A strip of wood snapped between Torigako's fingers. Stop it. You can do nothing. Kimura would find out and kill you too . . .

He drank another cup of tea and sat for a long time just looking out his window. After a time he would feel better, he told himself. But he did not.

Kimura found a parking place on a side street near the German embassy and made a walking tour of the neighborhood. The Hiroo section of town was full of embassies. The German one looked like a squat desert fort inconguously set down in the middle of a city. The place he was interested in stood near the German embassy, a two-story building in which several doctors and accountants had offices.

Dr. Tetsuo Wako, plastic surgeon, rented a suite on the first floor. Kimura had, of course, heard of Dr. Wako. Dr. Wako advertised heavily in newspapers and in publications like Tokyo Journal. He promised to make you a new person through liposuction and "cosmetic surgery of Beverly Hills quality." People said Dr. Wako had become rich charging a hundred thousand yen for every kilo he sucked out of your body. He was also famous for giving people new noses and chins. Kimura was sure Dr. Wako did do well in his business, he had seen the man driving around Tokyo in a green Jaguar.

Kimura did not seek out Dr. Tetsuo Wako for his professional services. His was one of the names on Kimura's list, and he had decided that the doctor should be his next victim. There was a nice symmetry in using a sword to kill a man who made his living with a scalpel.

Kimura entered the office building carrying a fake package, as if he were a messenger making a delivery. He went to the end of the corridor where Dr. Wako's suite was located but didn't go inside. Instead he opened another door that led to the car park under the building. Someone came toward him and he turned his face away, pretending to examine the label on the package. When the passerby had gone into the building Kimura looked for Dr. Wako's green Jaguar. It was there, which meant that the good doctor was in his office sucking fat out of someone this morning.

Kimura knew that doctors liked to have private exits from their offices, ways to get in and out without being waylaid by unhappy patients—in Wako's case patients whose fat may have come back or whose new noses didn't look as pretty as they'd expected.

He found the private door that led from Dr. Wako's suite into the car park and quickly opened the simple lock with a picking tool. Kimura enjoyed picking locks, somehow the act made him feel that no one in the world was safe from him. A very good feeling.

On the other side of the door was another corridor, very short and leading to two separate doctors' suites. The suite on the left was identified as Dr. Wako's. He listened at the door and heard voices. Also the sound of a girl crying. Probably didn't like her new nose, Kimura decided as he tested the handle and found that the door wasn't locked.

Kimura retraced his steps out of the building and walked quickly around the corner to his Porsche. He took out the sword from the trunk, the sword still wrapped in nondescript brown paper, locked the trunk and walked back to the medical building around the corner.

Minutes later he was again standing in the short corridor behind Dr. Wako's private exit. He slipped a black hood over his head, unwrapped the sword and again listened to the voices. Soon the patient would leave. Then the famous plastic surgeon would learn just how sharp a blade could be.

The girl had been crying for ten minutes while her mother and father sat on either side of her squirming with discomfort. Dr. Wako was getting sick of her. Tiresome girl. Spoiled rotten, like so many Japanese girls these days. Not that he should complain, it was the spoiled ones who spent money on cosmetic surgery.

Still, this one was noisy as well as spoiled. He wished her parents would tell her to shut up. It was their place to do so, not his. How could they discuss the problem at hand when she was wailing so loudly? Nevertheless, Dr. Wako decided to broach the issue again in order to force a decision.

"Let me say once again," he began, "that it is not possible for me to replace your daughter's hymen. There has simply been too much . . . damage to the area involved. To the vaginal wall, that is."

Which made the girl cry louder, even though she now buried her face in her hands.

Damn them, Dr. Wako thought. They screw every boy in sight, then they expect me to give them back their virginity with a wave of my scalpel.

"Moto-san," he said to the father, "I suggest that your wife and daughter wait in my outer office while we complete our discussion."

The father sent the wife and daughter out of the office, then sat back down with a heavy sigh. "Wako-san, this is a terrible problem for my daughter." The father, who was so ugly that Dr. Wako thought he should consider cosmetic surgery for himself, lit a cigarette and settled into his chair as if he might stay all day.

"My daughter is getting married in two months. Very fine boy. He works for Mitsubishi Bank, excellent future. However, he expects his bride to be a virgin. Unfortunately Kimiko made one little mistake last year and so of course she is no longer a virgin. We were told that you could replace the hymen, make it seem that she is still a virgin."

Dr. Wako wanted to laugh. The man's daughter had not made "one little mistake." From his examination he could tell that the girl had been sexually active for years. He wanted to tell the man to face facts, that his precious daughter had been fucked a hundred times. But there would not be any point . . . or any fee . . . in saying such a thing.

"In your daughter's case I cannot replace the hymen, that's definite. You can go to another surgeon, seek another opinion, but I'm afraid you'll get the same answer."

"Doctor, what can I do?" The man was plaintive. "The wedding night is only eight weeks away."

"There is one solution." Dr. Wako caught a glimpse of himself in the mirror and, just for a moment, didn't recognize his own visage. He had begun his adult life with a rather plain, nondescript face. That had seemed a bad advertisement for a plastic surgeon so he had had another doctor "do" his nose and chin and cheekbones. Now he had a straight, handsome nose, a jutting movie-star chin and cheekbones so straight one could eat *sashimi* off them. Yet somehow the total effect made it seem as if his face was made up of spare parts from other people. Bothersome, though as far as he knew no one else had ever seen him in that light.

The father was waiting anxiously for Dr. Wako to continue.

"What I can do would not even be considered surgery. Just a simple procedure that I think would solve your daughter's problem."

What he was about to suggest was unethical, yet what choice did he have? His losses on the Seisa-ko deal had cleaned out his savings and jeopardized his whole financial structure. He needed yen, lots of it, and he needed it fast.

"This would have to be a very confidential matter because what I'm suggesting is not an accepted medical procedure . . ." It genuinely pained Dr. Wako to sink into quackery. Only the thought of how much debt he was carrying could make him go on. "If your daughter came into my office the night before her wedding, I could implant a small, thin sac of blood in her vagina. Stitch it to the vagina wall. On the wedding night, during intercourse, the sac would rupture and she would appear to bleed copiously, thereby convincing the groom that your daughter is indeed a virgin."

The father's face lit up. "A wonderful solution! It wouldn't be, you know, painful to my daughter, would it?"

"No. She would also have to come here the morning after her wedding night to have the stitches and sac removed."

"I can arrange all that. How much would this cost?"

Dr. Wako weighed this question carefully. Moto-san, the father, was president of a construction company. Very well-off. A conventional sort of man. Worried about the reputation of everyone in his family. The image of his daughter as a virgin was therefore important to him as well as to the girl herself. "One million yen."

Moto-san swallowed hard.

"I realize the cost is high. That's because, as I said, this is not an accepted medical procedure. That's not to say it isn't safe. Believe me, it is safe. Your daughter will have very little pain or discomfort. But I must be compensated for going outside the bounds of traditional medical practice." To salve his conscience he added: "I'm willing to do this only because I hate to see a young girl's wedding night ruined by accusations and ridiculous finger-pointing."

They talked further and finally came to an agreement. The procedure would be done on the very morning of the wedding at Moto-san's home. The next morning Dr. Wako would again appear at Moto-san's home. The happy couple would stop by the house on the way to their honeymoon in Hawaii. The girl would go upstairs to her parents' bedroom, where Dr. Wako would take out the stitches and remove the shards of the sac in a few minutes time. And then the girl could be on her way to Hawaii. A virgin properly deflowered on her wedding night.

Dr. Wako accepted an advance fee of five hundred thousand yen and showed Moto-san to the door. He promised mother and daughter that all problems had been solved, leaving it to the father to explain the arrangement in the privacy of their home.

When they had gone he told his nurse to give him a few minutes alone before he saw his next patient, then closed his door and threw himself into the chair behind his desk in a fit of sudden depression. His white coat seemed soiled. The handsomely framed diplomas on the wall looked fake. His entire professional life felt like a joke.

Money. Truly the root of most evil. And yet he could not live without it. Not anymore. He was too accustomed to the Jaguar and big house in Nishi Azabu and the best restaurants and finest wines. If only that damned Hideki Kohno hadn't been such a crook . . . if only Seisa-ko had paid off as it should have . . . if only if only if only.

Dr. Wako heard a creaking sound but was too depressed to give it any attention.

Kimura, waiting behind the door to Dr. Wako's private exit, had listened to the conversation between the doctor and the girl's father. The fact that Japanese brides were still expected to be virgins was amusing, and Dr. Wako's solution was inspired. The doctor could have been Yakuza, he was such a magnificent thief. One million yen for planting a sac of blood in a girl's vagina. Imagine!

Finally the arrangements were completed and the father and family left. He heard Dr. Wako tell his nurse to give him a few minutes alone, heard his office door close.

The private exit door opened with a creak as Kimura stepped into the office. Dr. Wako was sitting at his desk, his face buried in his hands. Kimura didn't understand why the doctor looked so depressed when he had just talked a man out of such a large amount of yen. No matter, he would soon be relieved of his problem.

When Kimura unsheathed the sword, Dr. Wako did look up. The sight of a man in black dress and black hood holding a samurai sword caused him to blink and throw himself backward.

"Who *are* you? How the hell did you get in here?"

Kimura smiled beneath the hood. "I'm your fate, Dr. Wako."

"What? What does that mean? Why are you wearing that hood, are you disfigured? Are you a patient of mine? Why are you waving that damn sword around?"

"Enough questions." Kimura moved forward until he was directly across the desk from the doctor.

Still Dr. Wako did not move. He seemed incapable of movement, or much thought. He continued to blink in confusion. His hands now lay palms down on his desk, as if he might try to push himself up out of his chair.

Kimura leaned forward and swung the sword in a ripping, two-handed motion that not only severed Dr. Wako's head but took off the top of the chair as well. Dr. Wako's head fell onto his desk and the body slid away as though with a life of its own. An amusing thought—

A scream filled the office. Kimura was certain that Dr. Wako had screamed *after* his head was severed. He found *that* intensely interesting. Even more fascinating was the way Dr. Wako's eyes continued to blink as the head lay on the desk.

The nurse, reacting to the scream, came running in. She stared at the hooded figure, the sword, the severed head with the blinking eyes, the blood splashed across the desk and carpet, and promptly fainted to the floor without a sound.

Patients who had been waiting to see the doctor gathered at the door. Another scream and another fainting woman. One man, a big fellow in rough workman's clothes, took a step inside as if to try to stop Kimura from escaping. Then he saw the full bloody scene and backed away, making gagging noises. Others began to shriek and fight their way out of the building.

The hysteria didn't alarm Kimura, it worked to his advantage. When the others had retreated, he sheathed the sword and rewrapped it in the brown paper, removed his hood, took a last satisfied look at his work and slipped quietly out of the building.

Chapter 11

"THIS IS OUR CRIMINAL INFORMATION SYSTEM." Tak pressed a command key on the computer and a cruel face with a strangely pleasant mouth appeared on the screen.

"Every Yakuza gangster we know is in this database, about forty thousand of them. Don't worry, you won't have to look at that many." He hit a few more keys. "I'm limiting the search to gangs in the Tokyo area, about seven thousand faces. Still a lot to look at but you don't have to finish today. You can come back tomorrow if you have to. Study each face carefully and take plenty of breaks."

"Look at those eyes. I wouldn't want to meet that character in a dark alley."

Tak looked at the information that ran down the side of the screen in Kanji. "No, you wouldn't. This one's a drug dealer suspected of four killings."

"I heard you didn't have drugs in Japan."

"We have drugs. Not as much as in the U.S. but more every year. If there's money in it, the Yakuza will be there. Can I get you some coffee?"

"Sure, thanks."

Tak left to get coffee and Kay took off her jacket. As she

draped it over the back of her chair she was aware of the contemptuous looks she and Tak had both received from other members of Tak's squad. You didn't have to speak Japanese to be aware that Tak's colleagues disliked him. No one had spoken to Tak or to her. Even the two detectives assigned to help Tak with this case had stood aloof, their faces frozen while Tak was speaking to them. A lousy atmosphere, Kay thought. No wonder Tak drinks too much and doesn't get his suit pressed.

That wasn't true today, though. He'd picked her up at the Imperial in a clean, pressed suit. His eyes were clear and his hands steady. Even his movements were quicker, more decisive. Walking through the lobby of the Imperial, she had noticed three different women sneaking looks at him. No doubt about it, at his best Tak Saji was a genuine hunk.

Kay pushed the key Tak had instructed her to use and a new face appeared on the computer screen. This fellow was older, perhaps sixty. His face was roughened from some sort of pox, his graying hair closely cropped. Definitely not the man who had murdered Turo Kajima. Kay hit the key and went to the next subject.

The computer presented each face in excellent color, both frontal views and profiles. Kay couldn't read the names and other information presented in Kanji, but she was impressed with the clarity of the photos, almost three-dimensional.

The fourth Yakuza she looked at gave her a shock. This screen showed not only front and profile views of the criminal's face; it also presented a view of the man's naked body, which was covered everywhere with elaborate tattoos.

"Here's your coffee." Tak looked over her shoulder. "Sorry, I forgot to warn you. Some of these gang members are heavily tattooed. When we bring one in we take photos of his tattoos. Then when we find someone with tattoos dead in an alley with his face blown away we can sometimes identify him. Almost as good as fingerprints."

"They're so . . . elaborate."

"Tattoos that cover the whole body can take months to do. Very painful, but Yakuza don't care much about pain." Kay moved to the next subject. "Seven thousand faces? This might take me at least three days."

"If you can identify Kajima-san's killer, it'll be worth the time. I'll leave you alone."

Tak went to his desk on the far side of the room and considered what his next move would be if Kay Williams couldn't identify the killer from the Yakuza computer files. The connection between Turo Kajima and Hideki Kohno was clear. But what exactly was their connection with the Yakuza? Who hired the Yakuza? And why? Most likely a person of power and influence was in danger of being revealed through the lawsuit. Yoshi Hasegawa had been delegated to correct the problem and had come up with the idea of silencing the investors who had lost money by killing Turo Kajima in a particularly gruesome way.

The two detectives assigned to help Tak in his investigation came into the squad room. They were simply the dumbest men in the division. Behind their backs the other members of the squad called them Simple and Dim. Even with those nicknames, Tak knew that the two detectives were better liked and more respected than himself.

"Where are the files I sent you to get?"

Simple planted his feet and shook his head. "The files on Hideki Kohno and the Seisa-ko swindle cannot be taken from superintendent supervisor's office. He told us Kohno-san has nothing to do with the murder of Kajima-san."

"The superintendent supervisor cursed us and sent us away. The question alone made him angry."

Simple and Dim glared at Tak for endangering their brilliant careers.

"Yamato-san is a fool," Tak said, more to himself than to the detectives. "The connection is becoming obvious."

"You're the fool, Saji-san," Simple declared, "to talk about Yamato-san that way. Do you believe he doesn't know you say these things about him?"

"No, I'm sure you tell him everything. Go back to Shinjuku and talk to Turo Kajima's neighbors. Someone must have seen the killer enter the shop . . . or leave."

"The neighbors were questioned yesterday," Dim pointed out.

"Question them *again*. The first interviews never turn up all the information, you know that. I want lists of everyone in the neighborhood and their whereabouts at the time. I want the names of tradesmen who might have been working in the area. I want taxi drivers who were working in Shinjuku questioned. You know the system. Follow it."

Simple and Dim left silently enough, with aggrieved looks cast for the benefit of their friends in the squad room.

Tak got out a city map and found the street in Meguro in which Yamato's men were holding Hideki. It occurred to him that he'd seen Lion Mansion before. A big red-brick condominium, very luxurious. Hideki would certainly insist on first-class accommodations.

Senior Superintendent Ueno came charging into the squad room. "Saji-san! Terrible news! Another killing!"

"What?"

"Another man murdered by the sword! His head severed! A doctor this time, in Hiroo." Ueno was sweating so that his shirt had turned gray. "We don't even have a suspect for the first murder and already we have a second one . . ."

"How do you know this killing was done by the same man?"

"I don't. But how many people are going around Tokyo cutting off heads this week?"

For once Ueno was probably right. A singular day. I should mark it on my calendar of memorable events, Tak thought, along with the last lunar eclipse and the emperor's birthday. "I'm going to the crime scene. Will you come along?"

"Umm, I have an appointment. You handle the crime scene, Saji-san. You have your full authority on this case."

And full opportunity to fuck up, Tak thought, finding pleasure in the rough directness of the English language. Ueno didn't want to come anywhere near this case. "Fine, I'll report as soon as I'm able."

"Of course," Ueno said vaguely. "When you're able." And hurried away.

Kay had watched Ueno's performance with an anxious feeling. Though she couldn't follow the Japanese conversation she suspected it had something to do with her sword.

Tak told her what had happened. "Another man beheaded. A doctor this time. Sounds like the same killer."

"My God. Did he use my sword again?"

"Don't know yet. I'm on my way to the crime scene." Kay reached for her purse and started to get up. Tak put a hand on her shoulder. "You can't come."

"That's ridiculous. If someone is cutting off more heads with my sword I have a right—"

"You don't have any place at this particular crime scene. This time you weren't a witness. I'll share my information with you when I have some. The most useful thing you can do is continue searching the computer files. Our killer is probably in there someplace."

"It's so dull—"

"An investigation is dull, plodding work. Even when it's about a murder."

"Oh, all right." Kay was annoyed with herself. With her reaction when Tak had put his hand on her shoulder. It was firm but gentle; she felt her face coloring. She didn't need that, not now. "I'll stay here. But if it's the same man using my sword, don't expect me to just sit around staring forever at a computer."

"I'll see you later. If you get hungry there's a cafeteria just down the hall."

"Wonderful. I'll bring my own chopsticks."

As he drove toward Hiroo, Tak didn't stop thinking about Kay, about the sarcasm in her last remark. She'd been angry at him for keeping her from the crime scene. She was very beautiful and obviously intelligent. But, also obviously, not happy with herself. Tak was something of an expert on that subject . . .

The crime scene was a mess. Barricades had been set up in front of the doctor's office building needlessly blocking traffic in both directions. There were five times more uniformed officers than could be put to good use. They looked very smart and professional, even as they got in each other's way. What he really needed were more detectives, but Yamato would never let him have enough manpower. He'd just have to make do with Simple and Dim.

He clipped his ID onto his suitcoat pocket and threaded his way through the forest of uniforms and shoulders. Everyone knew this was Tak Saji's case and that it had been given to him so he could make a fool of himself. As soon as his failure was official the case would be handed over to another detective, who would be given enough help to solve it.

Knowing this . . . enjoying it . . . the uniformed officers made ample room for Tak to reach the office where the headless corpse lay.

Tak noted the name on the door—Dr. Tetsuo Wako. His body had not been covered or otherwise disturbed. The head lay on the desk, eyes open and staring as if placed for exhibit in a museum of the grotesque. The torso lay on the floor behind the desk. Tak reached out and closed Dr. Wako's eyes. Would his family have the head reattached for the funeral?

What a thought . . . He called over a young patrol officer who had been first on the scene and began asking questions.

"Did anyone see the killer?"

"Yes, he was seen." The officer looked at his notes. "But the man was wearing a mask. I'm sorry. Not a mask. A hood, a black hood."

"How was he dressed?"

"In dark clothes."

"How did he get in here?"

"He used that private entrance."

Tak went through the door behind the desk and followed the short corridor to the parking garage. The uniformed officer stayed at his heels, ready to take more notes.

Tak had hoped the killer would have been spotted either going into or coming out of the building, but that was looking less likely. This was no wild lunatic. The killer knew his business, worked in a meticulous way, planned ahead.

A pair of ambulances arrived to take away witnesses who had collapsed at the sight of Dr. Wako's corpse. One woman might have had a heart attack, Tak was told. The others were badly shaken but not in need of medical care. Had anyone questioned them? No, the patrol officer had been waiting for the detectives.

Tak shook his head. "There'll only be one detective on this case."

The patrol officer frowned and snapped his notebook shut. "I heard that but I couldn't believe it. You're being treated with disrespect, Detective Saji. I find myself ashamed of the Metropolitan Police."

Tak looked at him. "What's your name?"

"Patrol Officer Sasuo Kagayama."

"Kagayama-san, you give me some hope." He patted the man's arm. "Thank you. I'll talk to those witnesses now."

The medical officer arrived and began examining the body, muttering to himself like a child over a broken toy. "Mutilation. Bad business. No respect for anyone, people who do this sort of thing." Tak thought that a curious understatement.

Two of the five people who had briefly seen the killer stayed, the other three were on their way to the hospital in various stages of hysteria. These two were not in much better shape. The nurse, who must have seen a lot blood in her career, was fanning herself with a magazine and pressing a handkerchief to her mouth. She removed the handkerchief to say in a choked voice: "Dr. Wako was a *brilliant* surgeon. Everyone loved him. He was a genius with a scalpel and so fast at his work. He did more than four hundred noses alone last year. The man who killed him must have been a maniac."

Sitting next to her was a salaryman with a wart the size of a walnut on the side of his own nose. "I paid Dr. Wako one hundred thousand yen to remove this wart without leaving a scar. Paid him in advance. Who's going to do it for me now? How can I get my money back?"

The nurse was indignant. "You talk of money at a time like this? What kind of man are you?"

"A man with a big growth on his nose!"

The nurse turned her back on the salaryman and began to cry.

The salaryman appealed to Tak. "I've had this wart for two years. It took me all that time to work up the nerve to see a plastic surgeon and now look what's happened. What am I going to do?"

"The first thing we have to do is find out who killed Dr. Wako," Tak said patiently. "Please think about what you saw. Did the man in the black hood have any other features you could identify?" When the two witnesses looked at him blankly, Tak provided a little coaxing. "Anything about his clothes? His physique? His hands?"

He hoped one of them would have noticed the missing finger joints, the distinctive mark of the Yakuza. The salaryman seemed not very bright and the nurse too upset to be of much help. He pressed them for answers from different angles until he was satisfied there just wasn't much to learn from them, then took their names and addresses and let them go.

Patrol Officer Kagayama reappeared. "Sir, the victim's head and body have been photographed. The medical officer would like to take away the body. Does he have your permission?"

"Yes." Tak looked at his watch and was surprised to find he'd been questioning the two witnesses for almost an hour. "Tell him I'll personally pick up his report this afternoon."

"Sir, there might be another witness."

"What?" Tak stood up. "Who?"

"An accountant has an office on the third floor. One of the other officers heard that the accountant came downstairs about the time Dr. Wako was killed. I don't know whether he saw the killer. Someone said he saw the body, ran to a bathroom to throw up, then returned to his office."

Tak felt as if a sword had been run through his own body. Other officers had known about a possible witness and had deliberately not told him.

"Kagayama-san, I owe you." He looked at the officer more closely. Kagayama was young, not more than twenty-five, lean and hard, with troubled eyes at odds with his calm demeanor. Those eyes seemed to give off an anger, even if suppressed, that was somehow familiar to Tak. In fact, he realized they reminded him of his own eyes when he was younger. In those days he had always found himself staring at angry eyes in the mirror. Gradually, as the years passed, his eyes had become less angry, had slipped into a kind of permanent melancholy. Yes . . . Tak thought he knew now why Kagayama was being so helpful.

"Kagayama-san, I imagine you know I'm *burakumin*. Is it possible you're—"

"Sir, I'll bring the accountant downstairs if you wish."

"Yes, I'd appreciate that."

Kagayama went upstairs and came back with the accountant, a thin, long-jawed little man whose glasses magnified his eyes to twice their normal size.

"This is Sugowa-san. Sugowa-san, this is Detective Inspector Saji-san. He wants to ask you questions."

"I don't feel very well," Sugowa-san said in an unsteady voice. "I'm sorry, Detective. I want to cooperate but I may throw up again. My stomach is cramped and I think I have a fever." He put his hand to his forehead to test that proposition.

"I won't keep you long. Kagayama-san, would you get a cold towel for Sugowa-san's forehead?"

When Kagayama had helped the accountant feel more comfortable, Tak got on with his questions.

"Did you see the killing?"

"No! By the time I came downstairs Dr. Wako was already dead. I saw . . . I saw . . . that *gruesome* sight though. His head! It was . . ." The accountant began to shake. "On his desk!"

"Did you see the killer at all? When he was escaping perhaps?"

"No! I only saw . . . what I said I saw." The accountant's thin shoulders were still trembling and the eyes behind his glasses were enormous, but he did seem calmer. "I hope this didn't have anything to do with the trouble Dr. Wako was having."

"What kind of trouble?"

"Money problems."

"Were you the doctor's accountant?"

"For six years. Until recently Dr. Wako was very successful. Then he went into debt to invest in that scheme and he's been in great need of money ever since."

"What scheme?" Tak asked, certain what the answer would be.

"Dr. Wako invested more than three hundred million yen in Seisa-ko. Do you know the company I mean? It's been in all the newspapers. He thought he was buying shares in a wonderful country club that was going to be built out near Kamakura, but there was nothing behind the company at all. Seisa-ko didn't even own the land they showed to Dr. Wako."

"Why do you think Dr. Wako's death might be connected with the Seisa-ko swindle?"

"He told me the Yakuza was behind Hideki Kohno, the man who sold him all those worthless shares."

"Do you know whether Dr. Wako was part of a group that was bringing a lawsuit related to Seisa-ko?"

"Yes, he was. I did the accounting sheets he submitted to the court."

"Who exactly is this group of investors suing?"

"Why, they're suing the Seisa-ko Corporation, or what's left of it. Dr. Wako claimed that he and some others could prove that members of the government took money from Hideki Kohno and his people to look the other way while they swindled people out of their life savings."

"Do you know of any proof?"

"Me?" The accountant looked frightened. "No. I only know Dr. Wako lost everything he had in that deal."

Tak questioned Sugowa for a few more minutes, then let him go back to his office. He called Patrol Officer Kagayama over to him. "Kagayama-san, I need your help on a confidential matter."

"I'll help if I can, sir."

"I want you to go upstairs and collect from Sugowa-san all of Dr. Wako's records, especially any papers related to the Seisa-ko swindle. Take charge of all the records in this office, too. And this is very important—don't follow the usual procedure of depositing all those papers in the evidence vault.

I'm afraid they might get *lost* if you shipped them there. Do you take my meaning?"

Kagayama did. "Where should I store all those files? They'll take up a lot of space."

"I don't know yet." Tak was improvising. "I may need to rent a private room somewhere."

"I have a friend who owns a loft in Shinagawa. He'll let us store the files there if I ask him."

"You can trust this person?"

The young patrol officer seemed in discomfort as he went through the process of making a painful decision. Finally he said in almost a whisper, "My friend is one of us, sir."

Kay had gotten tired of staring at the faces of Yakuza gangsters. They were depressingly alike. Cruel mouths. Squarish faces. Eyes seemingly full of suspicion and paranoia. Even the young ones, she decided, had eyes that looked a hundred years old.

She stood up and stretched, aware that the men working at desks in the squad room watched her whenever she turned away from them. She knew the glances were unfriendly rather than admiring.

In the corridor just outside was a container of hot green tea that was evidently free, and she helped herself to a paper cup of the tea and nursed it as she paced the area around Tak's desk.

How many faces had she stared at over the last three hours? Hard to keep track. She probably had spent fifteen seconds on each face. Four per minute. Two hundred and forty in an hour. Roughly six hundred and fifty faces over the last three hours. Good lord. With seven thousand suspects to look at she still had at least twenty hours to go.

She tossed the empty paper cup into a wastebasket and continued pacing, trying to get rid of the backache. Her pacing brought her behind Tak's desk and she noticed that he had left out the papers taken from Turo Kajima's house.

Kay took up the papers. Most were useless to her because they were covered with Japanese characters written in Turo Kajima's decisive hand. Only one document was in English, but it was an important one—a list of the names and addresses of the people who were bringing a lawsuit in the Seisa-ko case, along with their telephone numbers.

Kay glanced swiftly around the room. No one appeared to be paying much attention to her. She went to a Ricoh copier in one corner of the room and copied the list.

I'm *not* going to just sit here staring at the ugly faces of gangsters for the rest of the week, she thought. Some of these people must speak English. If Tak won't let me go along with him, then I'll have to look for the sword on my own.

She was about to put the list in her purse when Tak returned.

"How's it going?" he asked.

"Nothing yet. What did you find out? Was it the same killer?"

"Yes." Tak sat down at his desk and reached for his phone. "No one saw his face, he wore a hood this time. But the murdered man, a plastic surgeon, also lost a lot of money on the Seisa-ko swindle."

"Aha." Kay had always wanted to say that. "All right, what does that mean?"

"It means the Yakuza has sent out a killer to terrorize *all* the people who lost money on Seisa-ko. And two killings won't be enough. It'll take more to scare off the other investors. At least the killer can't be sure two are enough." Tak with some irritation snatched up the list of names Kay had just copied. "He'll try to kill another one of these people. If Yamato-san sees that we can solve this case quickly and get the newspapers and the TV people out of our hair, he *may* give me enough manpower to stake out the investors and stop the next killing. He can take the credit, I don't give a damn." He would anyway, Tak added to himself.

Kay watched and listened as Tak spoke in rapid Japanese to whoever was on the other end of the line. He waited a few moments, then was evidently put through to someone else, then waited again.

Kay could tell when Tak finally got through, probably to Knuckles Yamato, his superior. His voice seemed to shift into a heavily polite tone. Tak may have gone to UCLA but he was still Japanese.

As the conversation progressed, though, Tak's voice became more persistent and less polite until he was almost shouting. The other detectives in the squad room were watching him with some surprise. Evidently they'd never heard anyone talk that way to Knuckles Yamato.

Finally Tak said *hai* and slammed down the phone. He looked at Kay and shook his head. "He won't give me any more help. Can you believe it? He says the Seisa-ko case has *nothing* to do with this one. Says I'm determined to drag Seisa-ko into my case just because Hideki Kohno is an old friend."

"He must know better. Two murder victims, both swindled by your one-time pal Kohno, both killed by a sword, on two consecutive days. That's no coincidence."

"Of course not."

"Then why won't he do something to prevent *more* killings?"

Tak lowered his voice. "In Japan they say the Yakuza has a hundred thousand arms for hitting and a hundred thousand legs for kicking. It's possible that some of those arms and legs may be right here in this headquarters."

Chapter 12

THE GINZA DISTRICT OF TOKYO is honeycombed with small expensive restaurants and bars that offer a variety of delights in addition to food and drink. The Ginza hostesses are the most beautiful in the city. From the moment a man enters an establishment they attend to his every wish. Without hovering or being excessively talkative they see that he's made comfortable, that he has exactly what he wants to eat and drink, that his need to talk about his business problems and successes is satisfied, that the lights are not too low or too high, that he has the general feeling he's a very attractive fellow indeed.

By the end of an evening a man will certainly be in a mood to have sex with his hostess, and that can be arranged too. Dinner, drinks and conversation will have cost some eighty thousand yen or about eight hundred U.S. dollars. Spending the rest of the night with a hostess will cost roughly three times that amount.

Each exclusive establishment in the Ginza has its own distinctive clientele. Some are patronized by bankers from nearby Ohtemachi. Others claim Diet members and prominent politicians as their customers. Some are Yakuza bars.

But most are frequented by corporation executives with expense accounts that no one ever audits.

One of those small bars is owned by a man usually referred to as the Former Minister. He doesn't care much for bars himself and the reasonable amount of money this one makes is of small interest to him. He is never seen out front. He uses a paneled room in the rear as his unofficial office, entering and leaving through a private door.

On this evening the Former Minister, a man with a bulldog face and a disposition to match, was eating sushi as Yoshi Hasegawa entered his private room.

"Sit down," the Former Minister commanded. "Have some sushi and a drink." He waved at a sideboard stocked with bottles. "Good *sake* there."

Hasegawa selected Wild Turkey bourbon and ignored the Former Minister's glance of displeasure. The Former Minister was known to hate with a passion anyone and anything foreign. He especially hated Americans and their products, even products as good as Wild Turkey. His mother, father and two brothers died in the B-29 bombings of Tokyo in 1945 and the Former Minister was incapable of forgiveness.

Yoshi Hasegawa declined the offer of sushi. "Nothing for me. I'm having dinner with my *sanro-kai*."

The Former Minister knew each member of Hasegawa's *sanro-kai*, his senior advisory council, and understood that Hasegawa would want to assure them that the plan was on track.

"So . . ." The Former Minister pushed aside his *bento* and dabbed at his lips with a napkin. "As much as I hate television news I've been watching the newscasts. Your man has done well so far."

"Two dead. Two, perhaps three more to go."

"You think five will be sufficient?"

"Yes, though we're prepared for six."

"I talked today to one of those involved in the lawsuit. He's very nervous." The Former Minister smiled. "Kajima-san's killing didn't really affect him, he didn't see the connection between the lawsuit and the death of that sword dealer. Now he does. So do the others, I expect."

Hasegawa sipped at his Wild Turkey and enjoyed its smoky aftertaste. "The problem is that just one of those investors . . . one man not afraid to pursue the lawsuit . . . could bring us down."

"I realize that," the Former Minister said. "I'm not afraid of Hideki Kohno talking, he understands he would be dead within days. But the lawsuit is another matter. I had to spread money all around the Diet to get that deal started. And in the ministries as well. A dozen important government officials could be seriously embarrassed if it came out they received money from the Seisa-ko company. At least two of them call me every day. I keep assuring them the investor lawsuit will be dropped. I hope I'm right."

"Don't worry, my man will do his job."

"Who are you using?"

The question surprised Hasegawa. The Former Minister had never before shown the slightest interest in who was used for dirty work. His interest revealed the depth of his nervousness about this whole business. "I'm using a man called Cricket Kimura."

"Funny name for a killer."

"He thinks crickets are good luck."

"Sounds like a childish type."

"Childish. Basic. Whatever you want to call it. But he's also very bold and ambitious."

"What does he think he's getting out of this?"

Hasegawa got up and added a squirt of soda to his drink. "Kimura-san thinks he's going to become a member of my *sanro-kai*."

"What's really going to happen to him?"

"One of his underlings, a fellow named Matsuka-san, is just as ambitious. When Kimura-san has done his job, Matsuka-san will get rid of him for me."

"So crickets aren't lucky after all."

"I regret having to get rid of Kimura-san, he's a very good man for street-level work. But our enterprise is just too much in the news. Kimura-san must go as soon as he finishes his job."

The Former Minister nodded in emphatic agreement and drank more *sake.* "Is Superintendent Supervisor Yamato-san cooperating with you?"

"Yes."

The Former Minister smiled again, causing the bulldog creases of his face to rearrange themselves into even deeper folds. "He has, of course, no choice. Five years ago Yamato-san killed a hostess during a party in another room in this very club. He didn't mean to do it. He was drunk and became overly enthusiastic in his sex. The girl struggled, he hit her too hard. I settled the matter quietly and since then I've virtually owned Yamato-san."

Hasegawa knew the story. "I still don't like working with him. He's such a smug bastard."

"But useful."

"If he keeps Kimura-san in the clear until this business is over, I'll be grateful to him. But I'll never trust any policeman."

"Or politician?" the Former Minister said, eyeing him.

Hasegawa raised his glass in salute. "Only you."

"You lie beautifully, Hasegawa-san."

"We both do."

They laughed together.

Hasegawa put down his drink. "I must go. I'll call you tomorrow."

"Keep up the pressure." The Former Minister's face lost any trace of good humor. "I want this matter settled quickly."

"It will be. Good night."

The Former Minister worried Hasegawa. The man was past his prime. It was the Former Minister himself who had engineered the Seisa-ko deal and brought in Hideki Kohno to front the swindle. The Former Minister was a gambler who liked to fly to Rio de Janeiro or Macau every few months to try his luck at roulette. The wheels in those casinos were notoriously dishonest and so he usually lost heavily. He might have had better luck in Las Vegas or Atlantic City but he hated America too much to travel there even for the gambling.

Hasegawa knew that the Former Minister owed the equivalent of five million U.S. dollars to various casinos around the world. And paying off those debts had been the impetus behind the disastrous Seisa-ko swindle. A ruthless but increasingly reckless man . . .

A limousine was waiting for Hasegawa. As he stepped into it his bodyguards, who had been in various shadowed areas of the Ginza backstreet, got into two other cars. One preceded Hasegawa's limousine, the other followed.

The Former Minister was still a powerful man, Hasegawa was thinking. But his influential friends were angry at him for involving them in this mess. Sooner or later they would send a delegation to ask Hasegawa what should be done to curb the Former Minister's recklessness . . .

I'll have to tell them the truth—gamblers who lose their ability to set limits always die poor. But first they drag their friends and family down with them. The delegation won't want to hear that, and they will be very upset with the remedy I will propose. But in the end they will go along with me.

And then the Former Minister will become . . . regrettably . . . the Late Minister.

* * *

Cricket Kimura was meeting with his own *sanro-kai* in much less elegant surroundings, the back room of a humble *yakatori* near the Ebisu JR station. They were a raucous bunch, his trusted advisors. But their business abilities in the fields of prostitution, extortion, smuggling and narcotics more than compensated for their lack of sophistication.

The seven Yakuza that Kimura most trusted were thick-necked men who looked like they had been born in suits too tight for their heavily muscled bodies. They were drunk, of course. But not too drunk to realize that Kimura had gathered them for a special reason.

As they sat cross-legged at the low table, washing down barbecued chicken and rice with great draughts of Kirin beer, they would glance from time to time at either Kimura or Matsuka.

Kimura was jovial this evening, almost brotherly in his attitude toward his crew, passing out compliments like small change and urging everyone to eat more, drink more, enjoy themselves.

By contrast Nobuo Matsuka was unnaturally quiet and ate and drank very little. His eyes seldom left Kimura. Was he about to be promoted to a higher rank? He was closer to Kimura than anyone else in the room.

After everyone had eaten and drunk as much as they could hold, Kimura leaned forward and slapped his hand on the table. "Quiet down, I've got something to say. Matsuka-san and I had a little problem yesterday. A disagreement. Nothing serious, these things happen between friends. However, Matsuka-san lost his temper and treated me with disrespect."

Now everyone understood.

Kimura looked at his friend. "Matsuka-san, do you have anything to say?"

Matsuka's bulk stiffened. He lumbered to his feet, faced Kimura, placed his palms on his thighs and bowed deeply. "I apologize for my behavior. I was wrong and I appreciate this chance to atone."

Kimura flicked his hand, granting permission to Matsuka to proceed.

Matsuka sat back down, crossed his legs and unfolded a sharp pocketknife. He then produced a sparkling white handkerchief and twisted it into a rope. He held one end of the handkerchief in his teeth as he wrapped it tightly around the bottom of the fourth finger of his left hand.

The men in the room watched Matsuka for any sign of weakness or hesitancy.

Matsuka put his left hand palm down on the table and spread his fingers. He was pale as he drew in his breath and stared at his left hand with the certain knowledge that it would never look the same again. Then he gripped the knife in his right hand and drove the blade into the flesh and bone of the fourth finger of the other hand.

It took two purposeful cuts to detach the tip of the finger just below the first joint. Because the tightly tied handkerchief had cut off most of the circulation to the tip of that finger, relatively little blood flowed onto the table. What blood did flow turned quickly from bright red to a blotchy black.

The other men in the room murmured their approval as Matsuka, sitting bolt upright, willed himself to keep the pain from showing in his face.

"Well done." Kimura spoke for all of them. "Someone give Matsuka-san a whiskey."

Now everyone was complimenting Matsuka, who was holding out his hand for all to see. The severed fingertip lay in front of him like a child's forgotten toy. Soon Matsuka had to loosen the handkerchief to restore circulation to the finger, and the blood began to flow. A second handkerchief was applied to the wounded finger by the man next to him while Matsuka swallowed whiskey and finally let the effects of his act show on his face.

Sitting around the table were several Yakuza who, over the years had offered up finger joints of their own as apologies. They were the most effusive in their praise, reaching over to slap Matsuka on the back or punch him on the arm.

A man who had given up a section of a finger only in the last year said, "Want to know how to stop the bleeding? Put the stump over a candle."

"Anyone have a candle?" Matsuka laughed. He stopped laughing when a candle was put in front of him and quickly lighted. There was no way to back down. He unwrapped his hand and moved it slowly toward the flame.

"Do it," Kimura commanded, no hint of kinship in his voice now.

Matsuka well understood that he was being ordered to renew his allegiance to Kimura. He thrust his wounded finger against the flame. This time, as his flesh crackled in the orange fire, he did wince in pain. No one held that against him; overall he had carried out his atonement in proper style.

"Give me the part you cut off," Kimura said.

The severed fingertip was picked up, wrapped in a tissue and handed down the table to Kimura.

"For the collection."

His crew, like other gangs, kept an official office where people could deliver mail or come to ask favors. On a shelf in the office stood a large pickle jar of alcohol that held the severed finger joints of several members of the gang. Over time they had shriveled and shrunk until they looked like worms. They represented duty, honor and fealty to the boss. Matsuka's fingertip would be added to the collection in the morning.

As he drank his whiskey, Matsuko felt himself swell with pride—and with anger. Three years ago he had been little more than a pimp who handled Kimura's strings of girls. Now he was a full member of the gang. Over the past two years his responsibilities had expanded. He ran a string of girls, hijacked trucks, beat up people who were slow to pay their debts to Kimura, delivered kilos of cocaine, ran guns down to Osaka. He had even killed two people on Kimura's orders. And the way Kimura had rewarded him was to beat him up on the street because he had temporarily let the profits from one string of prostitutes fall off.

Though he had been careful not to show it, the beating had been a profound humiliation. Matsuka had gone through with this ritual of apology and atonement but he no longer felt any loyalty to Kimura. Only hatred.

Soon he would be able to act on such feelings.

A week ago one of Yoshi Hasegawa's *sanro-kai* had come to him with a secret offer of advancement. It seemed that Cricket Kimura had done something to offend Hasegawa. Matsuka was not told what Kimura had done, but whatever it was, it must have been very serious because Hasegawa now wanted Kimura eliminated, after he finished his work. As a reward Matsuka would be elevated to Kimura's position. At first Matsuka had been shocked and unwilling. Kimura had been his patron and friend. Could he actually kill the cricket man, even for a promotion to *oyabun*? He had not been sure he could.

Until Kimura had beat him up, humiliated him over a bunch of stupid whores. Then Matsuka made up his mind to go along with Hasegawa's offer—kill Kimura and take his place.

Now he was only waiting for the order.

When Matsuka got up from the table he had to steady himself; his hand was throbbing and he felt light-headed.

"Come along." Kimura took his arm. "We'll go have a drink together, just the two of us. Maybe screw a couple of girls. How does that sound?"

Matsuka forced a smile and put a hand on Kimura's shoulder. "I'm always ready to go drinking and whoring with you, my friend."

The only person Kay Williams knew in Tokyo was Hilton Chambers, an antique dealer she would run into at auctions once or twice a year. Chambers was about fifty, slight of build, always immaculately dressed. He wore a toupee designed so well that not even the young Japanese prostitutes he liked to associate with knew his hair was fake.

Kay had called to ask if he would be free about six o'clock for a drink. Chambers said he was and suggested they meet in the Old Imperial Bar in her hotel.

"Thanks for seeing me on such short notice, Hilton," she was saying now. "I appreciate it."

"Always a pleasure to have a drink with a colleague, especially one as beautiful as you. *Kanpai!*" Chambers touched his glass to Kay's. "Besides, this is my favorite Tokyo bar. Look around you, darling. Most of the furnishings were salvaged from the original Imperial Hotel. Frank Lloyd Wright chairs. Frank Lloyd Wright tables. Frank Lloyd Wright mirrors. If I could get my hands on these pieces I could sell them for two or three million, I'm sure."

"I'm sure you've tried, Hilton."

"Of course I have. Just as you would, darling. Don't try to tell me otherwise. Frankly, I'm surprised you called me after I diddled you out of that Queen Anne chest last year."

"Six months ago I would have cheerfully strangled you for beating me to that piece, Hilton. But in this business one can't hold grudges."

"Agreed. Now tell me, who is that extraordinarily stupid-looking chap at the table by the door? The one who keeps staring at us."

"A cop. I don't know his real name. I only know everyone calls him Simple and they call his partner Dim."

Chambers's laugh was a tinkle. "Yes, Simple would be a good name for him. I read all about you in the Asahi *Shimbun* this morning. How terrible for you *actually* to have seen Turo Kajima killed . . . and in that way. I suppose that explains the need for a bodyguard. You were a witness."

"The detective who's running the case wouldn't let me come out for a drink with you unless Simple came along, too. Frankly, I don't think it's necessary."

"Witnessing a murder must have been *awful*." Hilton Chambers had a mouth that puckered when he spoke, so that he always appeared to be probing for information. Which he was.

"I cried like a baby."

"I can't imagine you crying. You're such a resilient and self-reliant lady."

Kay suspected that Chambers was actually calling her a cold bitch. She considered how much else to tell him, finally decided to be candid. They weren't exactly friends but at least they were friendly competitors. And Chambers was the only person who might have the information she needed.

"I may be self-reliant in the U.S., but in Tokyo I'm a fish out of water. Hilton, I need your help."

"Why should I help you?" Chambers was pretending petulance. "I tried twice to buy the Meiji sword from Kajima-san and he turned me down. Then you came waltzing in and he handed it right over. I had a client who would have paid top dollar."

"Kajima apparently knew the Yakuza were after the sword and didn't want them to have it. Selling it to my client was a way to get it out of the country."

"Yes, I can see Kajima-san doing something like that. The old rogue thought more of his swords than he did of his own life. A foolish attitude, if you ask me." He was silent for a moment. "What exactly do you want from me?"

"Information." Kay took a sheet of paper from her purse and unfolded it. "Let me tell you first what's behind all this. You've heard of the Seisa-ko swindle, everyone in Tokyo seems to know about it."

"Yes, but what does that affair have to do with you? Or with Kajima-san?"

"He lost money in Seisa-ko and was one of those bringing a lawsuit against the corporation. The gangster who killed Turo Kajima is linked to Seisa-ko. The Yakuza want to frighten the Seisa-ko investors into dropping their lawsuit."

"A few heads rolling should do the trick, I should think."

She let that pass. "The killer took the sword *after* I'd handed over my client's certified check to Kajima. Kajima had already endorsed it, put some kind of damned *han* on the back, so apparently the check is legally part of Kajima's estate. I can't retrieve it. Which means I have to recover the sword or my client will sue me and take my business."

"The client won't give you any leeway?"

"My client is Walter Emerson."

"Oh, my God." Chambers rolled his eyes. "I've done business with Walter myself. The man is litigation crazy. They say that as a baby he sued his mother to get more milk from her breasts."

Kay half-smiled and went on. "I have a list of the people who invested in Seisa-ko. I thought you might know which ones speak English."

"What if some of them do? Do you think one of *them* would commit murder?"

"No, but they might know something, somebody to lead me to the sword. I'd like to talk to them." She handed him the sheet of paper. "These are the people in the lawsuit."

Chambers put on a pair of glasses and scanned the list. "Hmm. That con man, Hideki Kohno, knows where the honey pots are. I'm acquainted with half of these people, some personally and others only by name. The ones I recognize are all quite well-off."

"Which speak English?"

"Most of them are Japanese businessmen with very little English. But here you are, the Countess Elena Rostov. I happen to know she isn't Russian and she *certainly* isn't a real countess. Elena is the last of a vanishing breed—the international courtesan. Over the years she's been kept by many wealthy men including Count Moritz Rostov, a fake count himself. On the basis of *his* phony title Elena turned herself into a countess. Still, who can blame her?"

"Who's keeping her these days?"

"No one. Elena is over the hill. Still quite passing attractive but no longer a filly. She made a good thing out of sleeping with members of the international set. Which is why she had the money to invest in Seisa-ko."

"Where can I find her?"

"The countess has an apartment in Aoyama. You can get her phone number from the NTT English information operator. Elena is charming. You'll like her."

Chambers continued to scan the list.

"I see Jimmy Sato's name. I've been to his establishment. Jimmy's loaded. He could afford to lose money to Hideki Kohno. He also speaks English like Jimmy Cagney, which is where he took his name from. He learned English by watching old Cagney movies. Ask Jimmy to do his Cagney impression for you, it's a scream."

"What kind of business is he in?"

"Jimmy runs a love hotel. You know what those are?"

"I can guess."

"His place is called the White Heat Hotel. It's in Shibuya, anyone can point it out to you."

"If he's running a whorehouse he probably has connections with the Yakuza."

"Very likely. Jimmy and countess Rostov are the only ones I can guarantee you'll be able to communicate with." Chambers took the olive out of his martini glass and popped it into his mouth. "Can I give you some advice?"

"I'm listening, Hilton."

"Don't go to see Jimmy or the countess. Let the police handle this business."

"You really think it's dangerous?"

Chambers nodded. "Take a long, slow look around you, Kay. Everyone in Japan appears so polite, so kind, so gentle. And most of them are, especially the women. That's why I moved my business to Tokyo more than ten years ago." He set his martini glass aside so that there were no obstacles between them. "But there's a dark side to this society. You've seen a piece of it. The Yakuza has its hand in everything. Business. Government. The arts. And they're *very* dangerous people. Last year a movie director made a film satirizing the Yakuza. Harmless little movie, kind of fun. Soon after it was released the director was stabbed to death on the street."

"Tak Saji, the detective working this case, has sort of told me the same thing."

"And you're still determined to stick your nose into Yakuza business?"

"It *isn't* just Yakuza business. *My* business goes down the tubes if I don't recover that sword."

"A sword isn't worth dying for, darling. Ask our friend Kajima-san."

"Nobody takes what's mine." Kay saw the way Chambers wrinkled his nose and added, "You think I'm a tough, pushy bitch, don't you?"

"Tough and pushy, yes." Chambers gave her one of his professionally charming smiles. "But not a bitch. Look out, though, you're headed in that direction."

"So I've been told." Kay tucked the sheet of paper into her purse. "Thanks, Hilton, you've been a big help."

"I just hope I haven't given you the ammunition to shoot yourself dead."

Kay made her goodbyes, told Chambers she was meeting Detective Saji for dinner and left the Old Imperial Bar.

Chambers stayed, ordered another martini and downed it quickly. Then another. When he had consumed enough liquor to dull his disgust with himself, he took a small address book from his inside coat pocket and looked up a name. His cellular phone was in a briefcase next to his chair. He brought it out and dialed a number in Yurakucho.

In Japanese he said: "*Moshi-moshi.* I'd like to speak to Hasegawa-san, please. Yoshi Hasegawa. He isn't? All right. Can you get a message to him? Yes, please. Ask him to call Hilton Chambers. Yes, he does have my phone number. Tell him . . . tell him it's about a sword. That's right. An antique sword. I'm a dealer. Hasegawa-san is one of my clients. I'll be waiting for his call. *Arigato.*"

Chambers put the phone back into his briefcase and thought about Kiki, the girl he intended to see later that night. Her tongue was velvet. All day long he had been looking forward to lying back with his eyes closed while Kiki rode him.

Alas, Kiki and the other playmates he enjoyed so much were also very expensive. With the disappearance of Japan's bubble economy he wasn't selling as many expensive antiques as in the past. He just couldn't afford to pass up the opportunity to put his hands on the Meiji sword, even if he had to acquire it at poor Kay's expense.

Chapter 13

THE AFTERNOON HAD TURNED into a shambles for Tak, with newspaper reporters and television crews trying to force their way into police headquarters through every door. Seldom did the Japanese press have a story as juicy as a mad killer stalking the streets of central Tokyo with an antique sword. They were happy as jackals over fresh meat.

The department brass ordered Tak to hold a press conference but to give the media as little information as possible. Then they retreated behind closed doors and let Tak face the reporters by himself.

The conference was held in a cramped room in the basement of police headquarters on the theory that if one made reporters uncomfortable they would cut their questions short.

It did not work that way.

The reporters ignored their surroundings and fired questions at Tak for some forty-five minutes. He told them calmly as possible that it looked like both killings had been done by a Yakuza gangster. He gave them Kay's description of the killer. He described the sword in detail. He answered some questions about the condition of the two murdered men, but refused to provide photos or describe the beheadings in detail. On direct orders from Yamato he did not speculate that the two killings might be connected with the Seisako scandal.

After the press conference he spent the rest of the afternoon doing everything in his limited powers to get the bureaucracy of the Tokyo Metropolitan Police on the trail of the killer. Meanwhile Kay continued her fruitless search through the Yakuza computer files.

At five-thirty Kay announced she had stared at the computer screen long enough, she was going back to the Imperial to have drinks with a Tokyo antique dealer she knew. Tak dispatched Simple to keep watch over her.

By 7:00 P.M. Tak, tired and disgusted, called a halt to his work. He met Kay at a *tonkatsu* restaurant in Meguro, where he had told Simple to bring her after her meeting at the Imperial. Simple grumbled that he was hungry too, so Tak sent him home to his simple wife and three simple children.

Over dinner Kay complained again about her passive role in the investigation. She did not mention the names Hilton Chambers had given her.

"You have to finish going through the Yakuza files," Tak insisted. "The killer is *there.*"

"I *will*," Kay promised. "I'm just saying I want to do something else, too. Something more active. Staring at that computer screen isn't only a drag, it's bad for my eyes, I keep seeing color dots floating in front of me."

Tak was disappointed that Kay had gone through almost half the files without recognizing the killer's face. "All right, you can come with me tonight."

"Good. What are we going to do?"

"We're going to help Hideki Kohno get away from police custody so I can talk to him."

"Sounds okay. Can I have another order of these? They're really good. What do you call them again?"

"Tonkatsu. Pork cutlets." Tak was amazed at how many she had already put away. "Do you always eat this much?"

"Sure."

"Japanese girls are too concerned about their figures."

"I'm concerned about mine, too. That's why I do aerobics three times a week and run every morning. The running gives me an appetite."

"Obviously."

She looked at him. "Are you trying to tell me I'm over-weight?"

"No! I'm just surprised at how many *tonkatsu* you've consumed."

"They're not very big." Kay began to worry that maybe she was making a pig of herself. She pushed aside the plate. "On second thought, I've had enough."

"Please . . ." Tak was afraid he had embarrassed her. "Have some more. The cook will love you."

"No, that's okay." She finished the last of her beer. "Explain to me how getting this Kohno person out of custody is going to help us find the killer and my sword."

"Hideki is scared, and he's weak. He'll talk to me."

"Why does he want to get away from his police guards?"

"I suppose he doesn't want to go to court and testify." Tak's smile covered bitter memories. "Hideki was never good at facing up to his problems. He tends to blame others for the trouble he causes."

"Sounds like Phil, my ex-husband." Kay made a face. "I came home early one night and caught him in bed with a girl who couldn't have been more than sixteen. Looked like a high-school cheerleader. Probably was. Phil said the whole thing was *my* fault for coming home so early. Can you beat it?"

Tak couldn't understand why Phil would want to go bed with anyone else when he had Kay. "Do you ever see him? Talk to him?"

"Oh, once in a while he calls, turns on the charm, tells me how much he misses me. Then he tries to hit me up for a loan. The worm."

She still loves him, Tak thought. At least she still feels something.

"I can see what you're thinking." Kay twisted an emerald ring until it bit into the flesh of her finger. "No, I *don't* still love him or want him. I just get emotional when I think about how dumb I was. At nineteen, when I got married, I thought Phil was a genuine Prince Charming. When he turned out to be a frog it just about killed me. For a year I could hardly function, went around all day in my bathrobe eating Oreo cookies and drinking root beer."

"A frog? I thought he was a worm."

"Phil is capable of being two repulsive creatures at once."

Kay wondered why she was talking so much about her marriage. She had never revealed to anyone how much Phil had hurt her, but the way Tak listened had a therapeutic quality. His attention was undivided, right on her. His eyes drew her.

Though she'd come to trust Tak, she still kept her information about Countess Rostov and Jimmy Sato from him. She wanted some investigative work of her own to do and knew Tak wouldn't approve. She no longer believed she would find the killer's face in the police computer. She would have to pursue other avenues, and two of them would be Countess Rostov and Jimmy Sato.

"Where is this Kohno?" she asked.

"Knuckles has Hideki under police guard in a condominium near here." Tak looked at his watch. "His bodyguards allow him a walk in the evening. We'll pick him up then."

Kay thought he sounded awfully sure of himself. "Take him away from his police guards? Just like that?"

Tak responded with the biggest smile she'd yet seen from him. "Yes . . . just like that."

* * *

After dinner they drove a mile to a quietly affluent neighborhood in Meguro. Tak parked away from the street lights and pointed out the building in which Hideki was being held in protective custody, a five-story condominium called Lion Mansion.

"There's a park down the street. Do you see it?"

Kay could make out a wooden section in the middle of a dense cluster of apartment buildings. "Not a very big park. You couldn't lose a couple of police guards in there."

"That's not what I had in mind. The little concrete building at the front of the park is a public toilet."

"Oh, yes." Kay could also make out the small structure.

"I told Hideki to go in there during his walk and use the facilities."

"Then what?"

Tak described his plan to her.

"And you want me to drive this car? I can handle any kind of car, but you Japanese drive on the left-hand side of the street. I don't have any experience in that."

"You'll only have to go a few blocks. When we're safely away with Hideki I'll get behind the wheel."

Kay could tell that Tak was enjoying the prospect of striking back at his department's bureaucracy by stealing Hideki Kohno out from under its nose. His grin was broad and he was keyed up.

"Okay, I'm ready to go," she declared.

"You're sure you know what to do?"

"Do cows know how to fly?"

"What cows?"

"Joke. Forget it. Yes, I know what to do. You go ahead and get yourself set up."

He left the car and walked quickly down the street to the public toilet located at the entrance to the park. The toilet had the same basic design as all other public restrooms in Tokyo. Tak looked up and saw the familiar latticework of narrow beams and struts supporting the roof.

He jumped and grabbed hold of the lowest beam with both hands, swung his legs up. A second beam ran in the opposite direction about two feet higher than the first. He positioned himself so that he was lying on the higher of the two beams and looking down.

With the light fixtures below, he was in a zone of darkness. No one was likely to notice him unless they looked straight up at the ceiling. Even then they might miss him in the dark space he was occupying.

Nothing to do now but wait and try to ignore the aroma that rose toward him and the heat that built up beneath the roof. He hoped Hideki would be there close to nine o'clock. While he waited he tried to take his mind off his circumstances by thinking about Kay Williams. He liked the way her hair shone in subdued light, the way her skin could be both taut and soft at the same time, the curve of her leg, the quickness of her step.

Just when he was beginning to seriously fantasize about her he heard two, perhaps three people approaching the restroom and his mind snapped back to business. Someone said he needed to use the facility. Another voice said to make it fast. Both spoke in Japanese. Tak couldn't recognize the voices, but a moment later Hideki Kohno entered the toilet.

Hideki had changed very little since their college days. He was still thin and wiry with coal black hair, jumpy brown eyes, an unusually wide mouth that always seemed on the verge of a sneer. His air of restless energy and monied authority were undiminished. He wore a pair of dove gray slacks, a red Ralph Lauren sportshirt and black Gucci loafers with leather heels that clacked against the restroom's tile floor. He looked more like a millionaire on holiday than a prisoner waiting for trial.

His eyes darted around the restroom. Muttering, he looked into the two johns. When he couldn't find Tak he ran a hand fitfully through his hair, then went to one of the urinals and began to relieve himself.

"How are you, Hideki?"

Hideki jumped several inches. A stream of pale yellow sprayed the wall, then turned downward.

"Damn!" Hideki slipped easily into English. "You made me piss all over my pants, Tak."

"Keep your voice down."

"You scared the hell out me. What are you doing up there?" Hideki grabbed a paper towel, splashed it with water and gave the soiled place on his trousers a nervous wipe.

"I'm up here to help you get away from your guards. How many are there tonight? Just the two?"

Hideki glanced at the open doorway. "Yeah, two cops. I don't see how we can get past them."

"Let me worry about that. You go back to the urinal and pretend to be taking a leak. When they call for you, don't answer. When they come in, say nothing. Just stand there as if you're still pissing, or trying to. With luck only one of them will come in."

"What's the—"

"No more talk. They'll be getting impatient now. Turn around, Hideki. And keep your mouth shut for a change."

Hideki opened his mouth, shook his head and turned back to the urinal without saying another word.

Ten seconds later one of the policemen called out to Hideki to hurry it up.

"Steady," Tak whispered when Hideki shifted around.

The policeman called to Hideki again, this time in exasperation. Tak heard feet crunching down the gravel path toward the toilet. One pair of feet, the other policeman apparently still waiting on the sidewalk.

As the bodyguard entered he saw Hideki standing silent and motionless at the urinal. No sounds. No movement. Frowning, the policeman approached Hideki and put a hand out for his shoulder.

Tak immediately swung down and landed directly behind the guard. His right arm snaked around the policeman's throat and he applied his left forearm to the back of his neck. Choke hold. The policeman struggled and tried to call for help but the pressure on his windpipe was too strong to allow either sound or air to pass. In moments his resistance withered and he slumped into Tak's arms.

Carefully Tak lowered him to the tiled floor, checked the pulse and probed at the windpipe to make sure he'd done no real damage.

"What about the other one?"

"My partner's taking care of him."

"Partner? I didn't think you had a partner. I'd heard . . . people told me you'd become kind of a . . . I don't know . . . a loner."

"You mean an outcast."

The squeal of tires killed any reply.

"Let's go." Tak pulled Hideki through the door and held tight to his red Ralph Lauren shirt as he raced for the street.

The second policeman was flat on his back. Kay had driven Tak's car down the sidewalk, engine roaring and lights on high beam, straight at the terrified policeman, who had fallen backward over a low wall in his scramble for safety.

Tak yanked open the rear door and pushed Hideki into the back seat, slammed the door shut and dove over the hood, opened the front passenger door and threw himself inside. *"Go."* When Kay didn't respond he yelled: "I said *drive.*"

"I can't find reverse . . ." Kay was yanking the gearshift lever up and down the column. Finally the transmission popped into reverse and Kay jammed her foot against the

accelerator. They shot backward, throwing Tak to the floor-
boards under the dash and sending Hideki flying.

"You'll kill us!" Hideki yelled.

"No way. I was practically raised on I-95." Kay hit the
brakes and at the same time spun the wheel. The car made a
one-hundred-and-eighty-degree turn on a dime. She jammed
the shift lever back into drive, or what looked to be drive in
Japanese, and hit the accelerator again.

Behind them, the policeman was up and waving a pistol.

Tak turned off the lights so his police license plate could
not be read.

"Don't turn off the lights," Kay called out. "I can't see
where the hell I'm going . . ."

"Ten seconds, that's all we need. Just drive." When they
were far enough away so that the cop behind them couldn't
read the plate, Tak switched the lights back on. "Miss Williams, you're on the wrong side of the street."

Kay yanked the wheel and skidded back into the correct
lane. "I thought you were going to call me Kay."

"Please . . . not now . . ."

"You call me Kay or you can drive this damned thing yourself." She was half-smiling, feeling the adrenalin kicking in.

Hideki's head popped up in the back seat. "Who *is* this
woman? Don't let her drive anymore . . ."

"Hideki, do your guards have a car?"

"It's parked behind the apartment house."

At the speed Kay was driving they were already more than
four blocks from the park. "All right, stop the car. I'll take
the wheel."

"What?"

"*Kay* . . . stop right here."

"That's better." She started to pull over to the right-hand
curb, realized she was driving on the wrong side of the road
again and swerved back just in time to avoid a collision with
an approaching Toyota.

"I don't *believe* this," Hideki said from the back seat. "Tak, I thought you were going to save me, not kill me."

Tak grabbed at the ignition key and switched it off, then took his first deep breath since diving into the car. So did I, he said to himself.

Chapter 14

THE TWO WOMEN with Cricket Kimura and Nobuo Matsuka were from one of Matsuka's strings. Both had been brought into Japan illegally. Tamara, a big-chested blonde woman with long legs, was Dutch. Or claimed to be Dutch. She may have been Bulgarian, her papers were unclear. Tamara knew some Japanese but spoke English most of the time in a rough accent.

Shmoozie, the second girl, had long dark hair and a small bust, but her figure was otherwise perfect. She refused to say where she was from. According to an out-of-date Portuguese passport, Shmoozie's real name was Joanna Erfenstras. But whenever someone called her Joanna or spoke to her in Portuguese she seemed not to understand.

Shmoozie's English was a little better than Tamara's but she spoke no Japanese at all. Did not even try to learn. "Japanese guys don't wan' talk with me anyway, they only wan' fuck," Shmoozie would say. Which was true. "And what if I learn Japanese? Just when I get few words they deport me. It happens to me twice before, other countries."

"Fock and move. Fock and move. Is story of our life," Tamara agreed.

Both girls wore tight dresses with no underwear and high-heeled shoes designed more for showing off their legs than for walking. Both were bigger than the average Japanese girl. Both were sleek and pretty and had worked as whores long enough, and in enough countries, so that they knew how to please men of any nationality. They preferred westerners, but the Japanese paid well and seldom hit them, so they were happy enough in the land of the cherry tree, at least for today.

This was the private party Kimura had offered to Matsuka after his friend cut off the end of one finger. The party was being held in one of Kimura's many apartments, this one in a back alley of Roppongi three floors up from the street.

Tamara and Shmoozie were drinking champagne. They had already had sex with the two Japanese and were relaxing in big easy chairs. They knew they would have to perform again, but for now it was pleasant just to sit and talk away the late hours of the evening.

Kimura and Matsuka were on a couch on the other side of the room speaking in low voices. Business, the girls figured.

"You like the tattoos those guys got?" Shmoozie asked.

"What the fock I care about tattoos?" Tamara did not bother to lower her voice because she knew that neither of the Yakuza spoke English. "They pay, that's all I care. Overvise, fock them."

"But his cock, he got *that* tattooed too. Crazy guy, huh?"

"Mean eyes." Tamara poured herself some more champagne. "I don' like men with mean eyes."

"All men got mean eyes," Shmoozie declared.

"Not the pope." Tamara had been raised a Catholic and occasionally got misty-eyed over her fall from grace. "The pope got real nice eyes."

"He so old." To Shmoozie, the worst fate would be to grow old. She did not worry about that, though, because girls in her profession seldom lived past their thirties, and who would want to grow as old as forty anyway? "He gonna die soon."

"And go to heaven," Tamara said.

Shmoozie didn't believe in heaven. Or hell. Or any other kind of purgatory. She figured that being brought to Japan to have sex with men who didn't even speak her language was hell enough for anybody.

From the other side of the room Kimura waved for Shmoozie to come over.

"Well," she said. "He wan' fuck me again already."

"Other guy too." Tamara smiled back at Matsuka, who wanted attention equal to Kimura's.

Shmoozie licked her lips to make them shine and wiggled to her feet, then suggestively walked across the room and knelt in front of Kimura.

Tamara came over too, slid herself into Matsuka's lap and pulled down the zipper of his pants. She saw Matsuka wince and wondered what she'd done wrong, then noticed that one of the fingers of his left hand was wrapped in gauze with blood showing through. About a quarter of the finger appeared to be missing. She did not try to guess why; Tamara had conditioned herself not to be curious, not even to think. She just put her hand inside his pants and coaxed his cock out into the light where she could work on it.

Because this was a double, Shmoozie knew she had to do something different than Tamara was doing. So she slipped out of her dress and straddled Kimura until she was sitting naked on his crotch. Soon he was in her, smiling at her without really smiling, partaking of her without giving her any sense that he liked her. Shmoozie was accustomed to that. She moved rhythmically against Kimura, her head thrown back in a wild fashion. She was also an actress.

Actually, none of the four could really be said to be having a good time. Tamara and Shmoozie did their jobs, Kimura and Matsuka demonstrated their manhood to each other.

Within three minutes the whole event was over, and Matsuka and Kimura lay back to congratulate themselves on their performances.

Shmoozie dressed and joined Tamara, who had already gone back to her chair on the other side of the room and poured fresh glasses of champagne. The women toasted each other.

"Let's drink to focking for money," Tamara said. "Yen. Dollars. Pesos. I don' care which."

They drank while Matsuka and Kimura talked business. Kimura was saying that the Yakuza was gradually changing, getting its hand into more and more respectable enterprises.

"You take a man like Yoshi Hasegawa, he looks like a corporation president." Kimura ran a thumb over the fine wool of his own trousers. "That's why I spend so much on clothes, Matsuka-san. I'm not going to be in this position much longer. I'm moving up, my friend. And you'll take my place."

You're moving down, Matsuka thought. Down and out. You just don't know it. "I'm pleased for you."

"I know you can keep a secret, Matsuka-san. Just hold your silence for a few days and you'll see me become a member of Hasegawa-san's own *sanro-kai*."

"That's great news!" Matsuka clapped his friend on the back. "Can you tell me one more thing?"

Kimura pulled back. "What do you want to know?"

"How did you bring yourself to Hasegawa-san's special attention?" Matsuka reasoned that whatever Kimura was doing to try to please Hasegawa had the opposite effect. Or else why would Hasegawa want to have the cricket man killed?

"I don't think I can tell you."

Matsuka moved a hand dismissively. He didn't want to make Kimura suspicious by pressing the question. "I understand. The fact that you can keep your mouth shut is one of the things that makes you so valuable to Hasegawa-san."

Kimura glanced at the two girls on the other side of the room. He was burning to share his story with someone. Neither Shmoozie nor Tamara spoke Japanese, which was why they had been brought here tonight when business might be discussed. And both girls were tipsy from the champagne.

"Since you're going to become an *oyabun* very soon, I believe I can trust you to keep my secret. But tell no one else. You understand that?"

"Of course."

Kimura leaned closer to Matsuka. "You've seen the television reports about the two beheadings? The antique dealer and the plastic surgeon?"

"You did those?"

"On Hasegawa-san's order. And let me tell you something else, there are more to come."

"Why? Where's the profit in beheading people?"

"Hasegawa-san already has the profit in his pocket. Now he's protecting that profit. The people I've eliminated were investors in Seisa-ko who were making trouble over their losses. All I have to do is behead a few more and the rest of the investors will fade away."

Matsuka thought it was a brilliant plan, and Kimura was just the man to carry it out. But the public attention was intense. And so when Kimura finished his job he would have to be gotten rid of. Matsuka was surprised that Kimura didn't see that for himself. But Kimura was blinded by his ambition and maybe a little crazy too, people had always said that about him.

Matsuka realized that if Hasegawa knew that Kimura had told him of their arrangement he would be a dead man himself. "You can trust me to keep my mouth shut. And you had better not let Hasegawa-san know that you've told me anything."

"I won't." Kimura smiled and gripped his friend's arm. "Would you like to see the sword? It belonged to the Emperor Meiji, the very sword used to behead the traitors who tried to revolt against him. That's why Hasegawa-san wanted me to use it. The . . . uh . . . symbology, you know?"

Matsuka wasn't sure he wanted anything to do with that sword, but the light in Kimura's eyes dictated his answer. "Yes, I'd like to see it."

Tamara and Shmoozie continued drinking and talking in their fractured English as the two Yakuza left the room.

Kimura led Matsuka into the bedroom and turned on the light. Lying on the bed was a long object wrapped in brown paper. Kimura threw off the paper to reveal the tapered beauty of the samurai sword. He drew the sword from its scabbard. "Have you ever seen anything so beautiful? The samurai were giants!"

"Impressive," Matsuka said.

"That's the best you can say?" Kimura started to hand the weapon to his friend so he could feel its power for himself, then changed his mind. He didn't want any hands except his own holding the sword. It was his, for now and all time.

An idea struck him. "I'll show you just how sharp this sword is."

Kimura went back into the living room with Matsuka following uneasily. The look on Kimura's face when he wielded the sword was scary, and Matsuka was not an easy man to scare. Kimura was definitely mad.

Tamara and Shmoozie looked up as Kimura approached. They had spent years reading the looks on men's faces, knowing when they were going to be happy and reasonable and when they were likely to turn ugly. The sword Kimura was brandishing and the look on his face told them all they needed to know.

Shmoozie screamed. Tamara jumped up and ran for the door, but her high heels and the champagne she had consumed slowed her.

Kimura moved forward, blocking her path and driving her backward.

Shmoozie watched from the couch, as though hypnotized by the delicacy with which Kimura wielded the sword. He struck without warning. The sword flashed with a hissing sound and Tamara's head seemed to bounce off her shoulders as her body crumpled to the floor. Her head landed on top of her and rolled across the carpet, leaving an uneven trail of blood.

Now Shmoozie could not even scream. She was paralyzed, unable to think, to move, to look for a way to save herself. One coherent thought penetrated her mind—she had always said she never wanted to grow old, now she realized she had never meant it. She wanted to grow as old as all the bent and crooked old ladies she saw on the streets of Tokyo. As old as the pope. As old as—

Shmoozie never finished the thought. Kimura stepped in front of her, the sword raised above his head. The champagne glass fell from Shmoozie's hand as she raised her arms to protect herself when the sword fell.

Kimura tried something new this time, a downward blow that cut through both of Shmoozie's arms and went on to split her skull all the way down to the bridge of her nose. Her body just sat there until Kimura yanked the sword free, then it fell sideways onto the couch and slid to the floor.

Kimura turned to Matsuka. "Did I exaggerate? Isn't this the most superb weapon you've ever seen?"

Matsuka's stomach had turned to a block of ice. He was willing to say anything Kimura wanted to hear, just to get out of this room alive. "Magnificent. Kimura-san, that was a dangerous thing to do. When these bodies are found the police will see that they've been killed with a sword. They'll connect these bodies with the other killings and maybe trace the girls back to us."

"The whores were illegals. No way to trace them here in Japan. But if you're worried about it, pack them up and drop them in Tokyo Bay."

Take out the garbage, Matsuka thought. That's all you think I'm good for. "As you say, *Oyabun.*"

"Sew them up in canvas and throw in a few chains. They'll go right to the bottom of the bay. Maybe the canvas rots after a couple of years and their bones float to the surface. By then, who cares? Come to think of it, with all the pollution at the bottom of Tokyo Bay the bones will rot too. Then there will be no evidence at all. Maybe pollution isn't such a bad thing, am I right, Matsuka-san?"

Kimura had already lost interest in the girls. He put the sword on a table and began disassembling the handgrip from the tang to give his beauty a thorough cleaning.

To cover his fear Matsuka went to the kitchen and brought out some big plastic garbage bags to begin the job of cleaning up after his *oyabun.* "I'll take care of everything," he said.

Kimura hardly heard him. He was in the thrall of the samurai sword. Cleaning it. Polishing it. Caring for it. Using it like a samurai in the service of the Yakuza had become the purpose of his life.

Chapter 15

ALTHOUGH HE WAS NOT IN UNIFORM Saguo Kagayama saluted
Tak when he came into the warehouse in Shinagawa.

"No need for that. Kay . . . Hideki . . . this is Patrol Officer Kagayama-san. He was the first officer on the scene at
Dr. Wako's office today. And it seems he's *burakumin*. Like
me."

Kay put out her hand. "I'm sorry, I don't speak much Japanese. I'm happy to meet you."

Kagayama, a bit startled by Kay's aggressive friendliness,
bowed and diffidently shook her hand.

Hideki hung back, clearly unhappy to be dealing with still
another *burakumin,* and even more uncomfortable to be in
the dirty, deserted second floor of a rundown warehouse in
Shinagawa. "What are we doing here, Tak?"

"You'll be staying in this place for a while."

"In a *warehouse*? I didn't leave Lion Mansion to stay in
this place."

Tak pointed to an empty crate in the corner. "Shut up and
sit down over there." Hideki tried to outglare Tak but
quickly broke eye contact and slouched across the splintery
wooden floor to sit where he had been told.

158

Tak led Kay to the center of the warehouse floor, which was littered with bits of string, the occasional old newspaper and scrap pieces from bolts of cloth.

A man stepped forward and bowed to Tak. "My name is Oto-san. I am a bank auditor. This old warehouse has been a family property for a long time." With a shy smile he added: "Years ago I bribed a clerk to falsify the family register in my *ku* office so I could find a good job. I am expert at following paper trails. Kagayama-san asked me to go through the plastic surgeon's papers to see what connection could be made with Seisa-ko Securities."

"Thank you."

A girl in a skimpy see-through blouse, tight jeans and a pair of Tony Lama cowboy boots came out of the shadows. "I'm Kiki, I work the streets for the Inagawa-kai." She winked at Kagayama-san. "This handsome young policeman arrest me couple times, that's how he find out I am *burakumin*. I promise listen. Just tell me what you want know. Most nights I fuck three four guys, some Yakuza. I get information for you, no problem."

"I appreciate your help. This is what I'd like you to do . . ."

"Hey . . ." Hideki Kohno motioned to Kay from his crate. "Come here a minute."

Tak was in deep conversation with Oto-san and Kiki and speaking in such rapid Japanese that Kay couldn't even recognize individual words, so she walked over to Hideki.

"A pair of total losers, huh? *Burakumin*, you know what I'm talkin' about? What a *burakumin* is?"

"Tak told me what it means, and that he's *burakumin* himself."

"He would. The guy's a truth junkie." Hideki gave her a full-toothed smile. "You like my English? UCLA. Me and Tak went there, except he never graduated. Tak never does anything right, y'know?" He remembered that Tak had called

Kay his partner. "Don't get me wrong, Tak's a great guy. Love him like a brother."

"I can see that," Kay said, but Hideki was too self-absorbed to recognize her sarcasm.

"He's crazy if he thinks I'm gonna spill my guts about the Seisa-ko thing. All I want is *out*."

"I think Tak will insist you tell him everything you know."

"He can *insist* all he wants, I'm not talking." When Hideki finished looking smug, he began looking sly. "I've got a great deal for you." He lowered his voice to a semiwhisper. "I have money stashed in different banks out of the country. Never mind where. You help me slip out of this dump, and out of the country, and I'll lay some money on you. What do you say?"

"Forget it, is what I say."

"Hey, I'm talking real money. Let's say . . . thirty thousand dollars U.S. or fifty thousand Australian. Name your own currency, I've got money spread all over the place."

"Sorry, Mr. Kohno."

"Call me Hideki. We're friends, aren't we? I mean, you helped me ditch those cops. By the way, that's a crime, what you did tonight. You and Tak'd be in shit up to your eyeballs if I told Yamato what you did."

"I thought you loved Tak like a brother."

"I do, but I can't talk about Seisa-ko, and I've got to get out of Japan, go somewhere the Yakuza can't find me."

"Your best bet is to tell Tak everything you know. Can't you see that?"

"You don't know the Yakuza. They *run* this country. Tak can't stop them from getting to me, not here in Japan. I'm scared, I admit it. You understand that much?"

Tak came up, rubbing his hands together. "Things are moving. Oto-san is going to look through Dr. Wako's papers.

Kiki's going to ask around about the Yamaguchi-gumi. Oto-san also has a friend in the construction business who's fixing up a room for you here, Hideki."

"Tak, I appreciate your help in getting me away from those cops. I was a sitting duck there. But I can't stay in Tokyo, I gotta get out of the country. And I won't answer your questions, you can forget about that right now—"

Tak slapped Hideki so hard that he flew off the crate.

"Tak!"

"Stay out of this, Kay."

Hideki scrambled up, one hand pressed to a blotchy red cheek. "Hitting me won't do you any good. I don't know that much." His voice became high-pitched, reedy. "Really, Tak. I don't."

Tak grabbed Hideki's shirtfront and threw him against the warehouse wall.

Kay put herself between Tak and Hideki. "He's hurt!"

"Hideki's been letting other people take pain in his place for years."

"You're a policeman, you can't go around beating up people to get information."

"This isn't the U.S."

"That's no excuse."

"I don't have to excuse myself. People are dying because of Hideki's swindle. He'll talk to me or I'll give him to the Yakuza myself."

"Are you sure you aren't doing this because he once turned a girl against you back in the States?"

"If that's what this was all about, he'd be dead by now." Tak took Hideki by the collar and dragged him into a small windowless room in the corner of the warehouse where two construction workers were turning the room into living quarters for Hideki. Tak asked them to leave and closed the door behind them.

Kay was beginning to realize that Tak had facets she didn't understand, hadn't been aware of. To escape the curious looks of the workmen, she walked quickly down the nearest steps and out the side door onto the street. The warehouse was located close to Shinagawa station on a dark alley lined with similar buildings, some modern and others, like this one, old and run-down. She could see the trains of the Yamanote line clearly as they pulled in and out of the station, taking on and discharging hundreds of people even at this late hour. Behind and above the station loomed the lights of the Shinagawa Prince and the Meridien Pacific hotels.

"No taxis."

Kay turned to see the pretty girl from upstairs standing alone, smoking a cigarette.

"Guess I have to walk to station."

"I'd give you a ride," Kay said, gesturing at Tak's car, "but I don't have the key."

The girl threw down her cigarette and stepped on it. "I ride in plenty police cars, don't need another one. You're American girl . . . *hai*?"

"Yes."

"Where from? Hollywood?"

"No, I'm from Connecticut. That's near New York City."

The girl grinned. "Hey, I know all about New York. I fuck plenty guys from there."

"I like your boots," Kay said amiably. "I've been thinking about getting a pair of Tony Lamas myself."

"You got the legs for high heels. Like me." She looked down at the toes of her boots, suddenly shy. "They call me Kiki."

"My name's Kay. You're quite beautiful, Kiki, if I may say so." The girl's body was as lean as a greyhound's, her face prim and clean.

Kiki reflexively bowed in such an old-fashioned way that

for an instant she seemed a vision of ancient Japan. *"Ari-gato,"* she stammered. "Thank you so much. I wish . . . I wish I have your looks. Classy. Something I never be."

"Let me go up and ask Tak for the key to his car."

The girl shook off her softness. "Not necessary. See you sometime, Kay. Tell Detective Saji I bring him information soon." She put the strap of her bag over her shoulder and began walking toward the station with a professional strut. Looking over her shoulder, she said, "You fuck Detective Saji yet, Kay? He look like good fuck to me." With a throaty laugh, she continued on her way.

The remark, and the knowing laugh that accompanied it, made Kay uneasy. Why? But of course she knew, she told herself, as she went upstairs to find the door to the little room reopened and the workmen installing a makeshift chemical toilet and washstand for Hideki.

Hideki was again seated on the crate, snuffling, holding his face in his hands. Tak prodded Hideki's shoulder with a silver flask that Hideki grabbed and drank from.

"You'll stay here for the next few days, in the same little room where we had our talk. No window. Oto-san will bring you food and empty the chemical toilet when necessary."

"A jailer. I should have stayed at Lion Mansion."

"Maybe," Tak said, "but you didn't. You were afraid some-body in the police department would tell Hasegawa-san where to find you."

"I'm still a prisoner, only now it's in a *warehouse.*"

Tak pulled Hideki to his feet and walked him into the door of the room. Which did, in fact, resemble a cell. He had a cot, a light, a radio and a washbasin. Not quite a cell, but not Lion Mansion either.

"I get out of here, you'll never see me again, Tak. I promise you that."

"Good night, Hideki. Sleep well."

* * *

When they were in the car and headed for the Imperial, Kay asked Tak what he had learned from Hideki.

"Every government seems to have a man, or a group of men, who run things from behind the scenes. They arrange the deals. Make the payoffs. You know the kind of people I'm talking about. They're the fixers, and the most powerful behind-the-scenes fixer in Tokyo is a man who's only whispered about. Very few people even know his name. I didn't until tonight. He put together the Seisa-ko swindle. Hideki told me his name, admitted that he personally gave this man, who's a retired government minister, the lion's share of the profits from their sale of shares in a nonexistent country club. The Former Minister . . . that's how people refer to him . . . kept a large slice of the cash for himself, of course. The rest he passed around to his friends in government. A lot of people did very well from Seisa-ko. *Except* those who invested in it. Yoshi Hasegawa, the Yakuza boss who bankrolled Hideki, took his cut too."

"But Hideki won't testify to all this in court?"

"No."

"Then what can you do?"

"I need to tie the Yakuza and the Former Minister to Seisa-ko in some other way."

"What about the investors in Seisa-ko? How are you going to protect them?"

"I've called each one and warned them about what's happening. Most didn't need the warning, they can see that the Yakuza is out to scare them off. Some, those who can get away, are leaving Tokyo. Others are hiring bodyguards. A few, though, refused to believe the killing is aimed at intimidating them. They're arrogant and naive. They're the ones I'm most worried about."

They arrived at the Imperial, and Tak put his hand on Kay's arm. "Please don't go jogging in the park tomorrow."

"You aren't going to make *me* a prisoner too. I won't live like that."

Tak irritably passed a hand over his eyes. "Oh, all right. I'll send Simple to the hotel tomorrow morning. He'll bring you to the station and you can look through the rest of the Yakuza photos."

Kay had no intention of looking at more photos of men with tattoos and missing fingers. "Eight-thirty?"

"Yes."

"Are you mad at me?"

"You can be very stubborn."

"There are those who consider that my best trait." She leaned over and kissed him on the mouth. Nothing planned, just an impulse. "That's to thank you for taking me with you tonight. I'd never driven a getaway car before. See you tomorrow."

She stepped from the car and vanished into the elegant lobby of the Imperial while Tak was still trying to say something . . . do something . . . to let her know she had done more than just kiss him.

She had turned him inside out.

Hilton Chambers was standing naked in his bedroom searching through the pockets of his trousers, red-faced. "I've *got* the money. I've always paid you, haven't I?"

"This time maybe not . . . how I know? Money no grow on bush in Tokyo."

"Look, here's twenty thousand yen. I didn't get to the ATM today. I'll give you the rest next time, okay?"

"Next time? No. We got date tonight and you no get enough money? Maybe account empty. How I know?"

Hilton Chambers's account was empty, but he wasn't

about to let Kiki know that. Or anyone else. "Don't be stupid. I just forgot to go the ATM. For God's sake, Kiki, I'm a regular client. Doesn't that count for anything?"

"It count for forty thousand yen, not twenty thousand." Kiki began to wish she hadn't spent so much of the evening with Tak Saji. This was her only sure trick tonight and he didn't even have her usual fee. Kiki sighed like a heroine. At least he had *some* money. "Okay okay, I take twenty thousand yen, you owe me twenty. You no pay, we *both* in trouble. I work Yakuza guys, you know that. They get their money one way or other."

"That's more like it," and Chambers began to unzip Kiki's tight jeans. "I've been looking forward to this all day. I want—"

"You always want, and now for only twenty thousand yen." Kiki rubbed up against him. "But you right, you good customer. So you still get full-rate fuck."

The phone rang and Chambers turned away for it.

"Hey! I do more for you than anybody on *telephone.*"

"I'm expecting a very important call. Get yourself a drink, this won't take long."

Kiki moved away in bad humor and rezipped her jeans.

"Hello."

"This is Yoshi Hasegawa."

"Ah, thank you for calling. I have some information for you." He looked at Kiki, who was pouring herself a drink from the cart of bottles on the other side of the bedroom. She wasn't paying attention to the conversation, and her English wasn't good anyway, so he stayed with English instead of speaking Japanese.

"I have a girl here so I'll speak English."

"All right. Just be quick, I'm busy tonight myself."

"I had a drink earlier this evening with the woman who bought the sword. You know the sword I'm speaking of?"

"I might," Hasegawa said in a guarded voice.

"The woman, Kay Williams, saw the face of the man who killed Kajima-san, the sword dealer."

"What has that got to do with me?" the Yakuza boss asked.

"Nothing, I'm sure. But I thought you might want to know, in case anyone else asked, that she's making trouble."

"What kind of trouble?"

"Tomorrow she's going to see a couple of the investors in Seisa-ko, two who lost a lot of money."

"That has nothing to do with me." Pause. "Which ones is she going to see?"

"Jimmy Sato and Countess Rostov."

"I appreciate the information, even though I have no use for it. Do you understand me?"

"Of course. Hasegawa-san, may I ask a favor?"

"I am listening."

"If . . . and I say *if* . . . that sword ever came into your hands, I'd be privileged to sell it for you. Very quietly, of course. No one would know you were involved. I know a private collector in the States who'd take that item for a very high price, no questions asked."

"Should such a situation occur, I would keep you in mind. What would a sword like the one we are talking about sell for in the U.S., under those conditions?"

"Two million dollars. Minimum."

"Interesting. Good night, Chambers-san."

Chambers was elated as he put down the phone. Soon . . . very soon . . . he'd no longer be short of money for girls like Kiki.

Kiki.

He turned to find her sitting on the bed, legs crossed, looking into a glass of Scotch.

"I told you the call wouldn't take long."

Kiki had heard enough to know who Hilton Chambers was talking to. And what they were talking about, although she had not heard all the names Chambers mentioned. Two of the names did catch her attention—Kay Williams, the woman who was with Tak Saji at the warehouse, and Countess Rostov, who was famous in Tokyo. She had no intention of letting Chambers know she had been listening to his call. With a mischievous grin, she swallowed the Scotch. "Okay then, let's fuck."

Chapter 16

KIMURA AWOKE from a troubled sleep. The killing of the girls didn't bother him, they were only prostitutes and *gaijins* in the bargain. What disturbed him was that the killings had been done on impulse. He had never killed anyone without thinking it out and without first buying a lucky cricket from Torigako-san.

Perhaps, he thought, the cricket I got from him yesterday carried enough luck for the entire day.

Kimura went into the living room and was relieved to see that Matsuka had done a good job of cleaning up after him. The bodies had been disposed of. Only a faint kidney-colored discoloration remained on the carpet. The cushions from the couch were gone, probably at the bottom of Tokyo Bay with the girls' bodies.

After a breakfast of fish and rice and a hot shower, Kimura felt better. He cleaned the sword and wrapped it again in brown paper, then studied the list Hasegawa had given him. There were numerous choices. Most of the potential victims lived close by in either the Minato or Chiyoda wards of Tokyo, a few in Yokohama, one in Kamakura.

He wanted this job over with so he could assume his place

169

on Hasegawa's *sanro-kai.* He wanted the white Rolls-Royce that Hasegawa had promised him, with its rich aroma of good leather and its hand-tooled engine.

The cellular phone that Kimura carried rang and he pushed the button to receive the call.

"Kimura-san?"

He recognized Hasegawa's voice. "Good morning. You've read the newspapers? Seen the television. I hope you are pleased with the way matters are going."

"Very happy. I would say two more . . . assignments and I think your job will be done."

"Only two more? You are making my work easy."

"That is not what I called about. The woman in the shop. You know who I mean?"

"Yes."

"Apparently she has gone off on her own to look for you. Today she plans to visit two of the people on your list."

"Which ones?"

Hasegawa had no intention of using names over a phone line that might be tapped. "The lady who claims to have regal blood and the gentleman who looks through mirrors. Do you know understand what I am saying?"

"Your meaning is clear." Kimura looked at his list and picked out the names of Countess Rostov and Jimmy Sato.

"Avoid those two people. Choose others from the list. I do not want the *gaijin* getting a second look at you."

"I understand."

"Get this over quickly. The news reports are more excited than I had anticipated."

"Completing your contract is my highest priority." Kimura switched to another subject. "If you don't mind, sir, I wanted to ask about the white Rolls. Does it have a CD player? I have a big collection of CDs."

"My friend, it has *everything.* I looked at it again just yesterday. My coachmaker is completing the detail work this week, adding your personal crest to the doors. You will be very pleased, I assure you."

"Thank you . . . thank you . . . I won't let you down."

"I know that. Good luck today. Remember to avoid those two people."

"I will."

Kimura put down the phone and slapped his hands together. The call from Hasegawa had wiped away the slight itch that had bothered him on awakening. Action was the best remedy for doubt, he had learned that long ago.

He dressed and left the apartment with the brown paper package under his arm.

The headlines in the Asahi *Shimbun* were distressing to Torigako the cricket man. *Another* beheading. He couldn't be sure that Kimura was the killer, but the signs were there. He had seen them before. Ignored them before. How long could he go on keeping his mouth shut and his conscience in his pocket? It was one thing when Kimura was killing other gangsters. He could tell himself it didn't matter whether Yakuza killed each other, and he still believed that. But now Kimura was killing ordinary citizens, a doctor and an antique dealer.

If Cricket Kimura was really the killer.

Torigako desperately wanted to be wrong about this. If he was right, then his silence was partly responsible for the killings. He tried to put the matter out of his mind by feeding his crickets and starting work on some new cages. Not that he needed more stock in the store. So few children were buying crickets and cages these days, and almost no adults came in. Without Kimura's patronage he would hardly be able to put rice in his bowl. Even when he didn't buy a new cricket, Kimura would often stop by and drop a crisp five thousand yen note on his counter "for luck."

Was that a reason to overlook *murder?*

All morning long his mind kept circling back to that question. His gloomy thoughts were interrupted only once, when a mother came into his shop to buy her two-year-old his first cricket and cage. It delighted Torigako to watch the child's eyes light up with pleasure when the cricket and cage were put in his hands. *That* was what his business had always been about—giving pleasure and, more times than not, selling good fortune in the form of lucky crickets.

A little after 11:00 A.M. Torigako heard Kimura's Porsche pull to a brake-squealing stop outside his shop. Immediately the crickets quit chirping, as if they too knew an evil force was approaching. Torigako *believed* they did know. Crickets were more intelligent than other insects and had an instinct for people . . . He continued to paint the cage he had been working on while trying to project an air of equanimity.

Kimura came stomping into the small shop in his customary blustery fashion. "Good morning, Torigako-san."

"How are you, Kimura-san?" Torigako put down his brush and gave a deep bow, despising himself as he did so.

"I'm all right . . . just fine." Kimura seemed distracted. "Except for my sleep. I'm not getting enough sleep, can't seem to—" He realized he was about to unburden himself and pulled back. "I'm very well. Why aren't your crickets singing this morning?"

Torigako grasped at straws. "It must be the humidity, the heavy air."

Kimura said, "I find myself in need of another cricket. Let's see what you have, bring them all out."

It wouldn't be necessary to "bring them all out." Every cricket he owned was within sight. Torigako picked up a cage and the cricket inside rewarded him with a song.

Kimura was enraptured. "Ah . . . well . . . I must have that cricket. I've never *heard* anything so beautiful."

Torigako was forced to admit that no one loved the music

of crickets more than this Yakuza thug. "Here you are. It's a new cage, too. I just made it yesterday."

"Good." This time Kimura put *two* ten thousand yen notes on the counter. "People laugh at me for believing crickets are lucky."

"That is a crime." Torigako almost swallowed his false teeth over his careless choice of words. "What I mean is, people should not scoff at things they don't understand."

"Exactly. A few days from now they'll stop scoffing. They'll see all the wonderful good luck your crickets have brought me and marvel. See you soon, Torigako-san."

Kimura left the shop whistling to his new pet, almost prancing to his Porsche. While Torigako slumped on a stool and closed his eyes, muttering the Shinto prayer of purification.

Chapter 17

Aᴄᴛᴇʀ ᴀ ɢᴏᴏᴅ ɴɪɢʜᴛ's sʟᴇᴇᴘ Kay rose early, showered and dressed in a Norma Kamali suit. She intended to visit Countess Rostov and Jimmy Sato whether Tak approved or not.

The only problem was that Tak had detailed Dim to keep an eye on her. She had caught a glimpse of his stolid face looking out from between the curtains of the vestibule on her floor the night before. Well, if she couldn't give the slip to a man whose nickname was Dim there was no hope for her.

She opened her door a crack and looked down the hall. As expected, Dim had pulled back the vestibule curtains so that he could better see her door. He had then made the mistake of settling down too comfortably on the vestibule couch and was dozing peacefully against its cushions.

Kay wrote a quick note to Tak, left it on the desk, swung her purse over her shoulder by the strap and tiptoed past Dim to the elevators.

It was only six-thirty, too early to call on either Countess Rostov or Jimmy Sato, so she caught a taxi to the American Club in Azabudai.

Using her membership card from the Phoenix Club of New York, which had an affiliation with the Tokyo American Club, Kay enjoyed a leisurely breakfast while she read the

Wall Street Journal. After breakfast the American Club's trainer provided her with a jogging suit and shoes so that she could take her morning run around the perimeter of the indoor basketball court.

At about 8:30 A.M., when Simple would be at the hotel to pick her up for another morning of looking at Yakuza mug shots, Kay was starting on the fourth mile of her run. She felt vaguely sorry for both Simple and Dim. Tak would probably chew them out, but she was too pleased about being on her own to feel regrets for long.

Although no one would say why, people were running in and out of Knuckles Yamato's office with expressions that ran from terror to dazed confusion.

For the moment Yamato was doing a good job of suppressing the story of Hideki Kohno's disappearance. There was nothing in the morning newspapers or on the television news. Hideki's trial was almost two weeks away. Yamato had time to find his missing defendant.

Tak felt he had accomplished several things by helping Hideki get out of Lion Mansion. First, he had the pleasure of making life miserable for Knuckles Yamato. More important, he had Hideki's statement that Yoshi Hasegawa and the Former Minister were the brains and bankroll behind Seisa-ko. He had used a pocket tape recorder to get those facts on the record. Unlike in the U.S., Hideki's recorded statement could be used in court.

Tak was feeling reasonably pleased with himself when Simple and Dim appeared at his desk. Dim looked disheveled and grumpy from a night spent guarding Kay's room, and they both looked angry.

"What's wrong?"

"The *gaijin* ran out on us," Dim said. "Somehow she snuck out of the hotel."

"When I came to pick her up the room was empty," Simple put in. "We looked all over the hotel. One of the doormen said she took a taxi but he didn't hear what address she gave to the driver."

Tak leveled his gaze at Dim. "You fell asleep on that nice soft couch in the vestibule, didn't you?"

"No!" Dim looked injured. "I was awake all night. Look at my eyes, I can hardly keep them open."

"There's no need to lie, the damage is already done."

Dim bunched his fists. Tak came around the desk. "Go ahead. I need the exercise."

Dim wasn't a complete fool. He quickly unclenched his fists. "I don't know how she got out of her room. Maybe she climbed through the window."

"On the ninth floor?"

"She left this." Simple handed Tak a note in an Imperial Hotel envelope. "I found it on the desk in her room. I didn't open the note because it's addressed to you. Besides, I can't read English."

Tak,
Awfully sorry to skip out on you. Don't blame poor Dim, he did his best to stay awake. I just couldn't take another morning of looking at Yakuza faces. The killer isn't in your computer anyway, I think you realize that yourself. A thought . . . could someone have tampered with your computer files? I've gone out to do some investigating of my own. Nothing dangerous, I'll be perfectly safe. See you later.

Kay

Simple and Dim were turning to leave when Tak said to Dim: "Aren't you going to complain that you can't work all day after staying awake all night on guard duty?"

Dim had the grace to look sheepish. "I guess I can work today."

When the pair had left, Tak considered Kay's comment about someone in the police department tampering with the Yakuza files. That wouldn't be easy. All officers with the rank of detective inspector and above had access to the computerized photo files. But those files could be changed, or erased, only by officers who held security passwords.

Tak picked up the phone and dialed the internal number for Abo Kenshi, manager of the police department's computer center. This would be a difficult conversation. Kenshi disliked Tak not only because he was *burakumin* but because Tak at times had made fun of Kenshi's cherished computers.

"Moshi-moshi."

"Kenshi-san?" Tak shifted to a whiny, nasal voice. "This is Tadashi Ueno of the Special Crimes Unit."

"Ueno-san, how are you?"

"Very well, thank you."

"When are you going to pay another visit to my computer center? I have a new virtual-memory-imaging system to show you. State-of-the-art hardware from Hitachi."

"Marvelous. I'll come to see it soon, I promise." Tak was beginning to get a headache from the strain of imitating Ueno's obsequious voice. "Right now I have a brief question I hope you can answer."

"If I can I will be happy to do so."

"How many officers in the department have passwords that allow them to alter or erase a Yakuza photo file?"

"If I may ask, why do you need to know?"

Tak cast about for a credible reason. "You see, Yamato-san has given me the task of reorganizing our Yakuza intelligence files." He realized he hadn't complained to Kenshi. That was out of character for Tadashi Ueno, who always had a dozen complaints ready for whoever would listen. In Ueno's most irritating whine Tak added, "As if I don't have enough to do with an enormous caseload *and* the added responsibility of keeping track of that fool Tak Saji."

"A shame," Kenshi said. "That idiot should have been dismissed from the department years ago."

"Years ago. You don't know the trouble he gives me. Now about that list . . ."

"Yes, all right. Let me see. I just have to call up the master password file on my system . . . yes . . . here it is. All names have been color-coded according to their levels." Kenshi tried to sound modest about that and failed. "I tell you, Ueno-san, these new XA 55 monitors have superb color screens. All right, I'll read you the names of those who have authority to enter, alter or erase Yakuza photo files."

Tak scrambled for a pen and paper. "Go ahead."

Kenshi began reading names, which Tak swiftly wrote down. At the end Tak said in a voice closer to his own, "Thank you so much, Kenshi-san, and good health to you and your XA 55s."

He sat for several minutes absorbing the names. He knew each of the senior police officials on the list, and the majority of the low-level clerks who did the actual day-to-day work of keeping the Yakuza photo files updated. Most of the twenty-two people he judged to be hard-working, honorable police officers.

After careful thought he circled the name of the only person on the list he had suspected of having a Yakuza connection: Superintendent Supervisor Tetsuo Yamato.

Chapter 18

COUNTESS ELENA ROSTOV LIVED in Aoyama Towers, a luxury condominium complex near the United Nations University.

A concierge announced Kay by phone and directed her to take the elevator to the penthouse floor. When she stepped off the elevator four Japanese security men in identical black suits with holstered pistols on their belts were waiting. The one who spoke English asked politely for Kay's purse, which was searched with a thoroughness that would have warmed the heart of an FBI agent. He also ran a hand-held electronic metal detector over her body.

When they were satisfied she posed no danger, Kay was ushered into the apartment.

"Come in," a liquid voice said. "Coffee, or would you prefer something stronger?"

For a moment Kay took root, overcome by the panoramic view of Tokyo and the splendid furnishings of the penthouse.

"Coffee would be great."

"The coffee in Japan is wonderful, isn't it?"

The Countess Elena Rostov was resting on a red chaise longue of sleek Italian design. The entire apartment was decorated in minimalist modern. The paintings on the walls were large and powerful works by Frank Zappa and Edward Hopper. Kay recognized a Joan Miró sculpture in one corner.

The countess was in harmony with the surroundings in a red-and-white jumpsuit chic enough to go anywhere in, from the opera to a garage sale.

As Kay approached, the countess said: "Norma Kamali suit . . . Gucci shoes . . . Paloma Picasso pin . . . Hanae Mori handbag. Not bad."

Kay disliked being rated. "My underwear's from Sears."

The countess tossed her wheat-blonde hair and laughed. "Good for you. You're absolutely right, honey. Don't take shit from anyone. Sit down."

Kay sat in a chair that resembled a mammoth nipple with the tip removed. It was surprisingly comfortable. She accepted a cup of coffee from a maid who moved through the apartment as silently as a spectre.

"I'm Kay Williams. I deal in antiques and two days ago I bought—"

"I read about you in the newspapers."

At first glance the countess appeared to be about thirty-five. Over the rim of her cup Kay could see that she was actually closer to forty-five, maybe fifty, but the kind of woman who made her looks a life's work. She was slim enough to make an anorexic envious and probably only an inch less than six feet tall. The word svelte had been invented for her. "Then maybe you know why I'm here."

"You're here for the same reason I've got those rent-a-cops outside my apartment. Some asshole with a big fucking sword has gone bananas."

Kay put down her coffee cup. "What kind of countess are you? You look like you might actually be royalty, but you talk more like a waitress in an I-95 truck stop."

"You just came pretty damned close, honey. I was a waitress once. But I resent the truck-stop crack. I worked the Playboy Club in Chicago. The *original* Playboy Club, when it had class. I wasn't even out of my teens. Tough kid from the North Side, where all the Polacks and Russkies live. Ellie Rostov. I changed it to Elena later. Started calling myself Countess Elena Rostov just for laughs. You could have knocked me down with a wet bar rag when some people actually *believed* I was a countess."

"When was that?"

"Twenty-five years ago, when I first came to Japan." The countess sipped her drink. "I came here with three other hookers, a package deal. The Yakuza brought us over to ball Japanese businessmen. Those guys love tall western girls with blonde hair. I billed myself as fallen royalty, ex-wife of a count, and the Japanese bought it."

"And you stayed?"

"Lots of money here, Kay. You're put together real nice. Makes me a little jealous when I see a girl like you . . . young, pretty enough to turn heads, dressed to the nines, got the world by the balls."

Kay surveyed the lavish penthouse. "I'd say you're the one who's got the world where you want it."

"I discovered Countess Elena Rostov could charge more for a blow job than Ellie Rostov ever dreamed of." She put down her drink and suddenly became serious. "I'd like to help you, honey. You just don't understand what you're messing around in. I've done a lot of business with the Yakuza. They're a real nasty crew. When a Tokyo cop called and told me a Yakuza goon might try to kill me I called in *plenty* of security."

"The killer's using a sword I bought for a client. It's worth more than two million dollars and I have *got* to get it back."

"That's some expensive cheese slicer. But I really don't see how I can help you, Kay."

"I'm looking for a link between Turo Kajima, the sword dealer, and the people who killed him. Anything that might lead me to the sword. You knew Kajima, I assume."

"Oh, sure. I even did him a few times. Randy old devil. You know how many kids he had?"

"Yes, I heard." Kay found herself smiling over the memory of Turo Kajima's audacious sexual overtures. "His latest mistress, a young Swedish girl, is pregnant."

"What an ass hound." The countess smiled over fond memories of him. "Turo was the one who brought some of the Seisa-ko investors together to sue what's left of Seisa-ko. Turo said there was evidence that government officials took their share of the money that idiots like me invested. I personally lost thirty million yen on the deal."

"Why would you invest in a country club?"

"Are you kidding? *Everybody* in Japan plays golf. Haven't you noticed all the stores selling golf equipment? The mini-driving ranges on the rooftops? The nutty part is there are no golf courses in Tokyo. You have to go way the hell outside the city to find one. In Japan a membership in a good country club can cost two, three million dollars. How was I to know that weasel Hideki Kohno, or the people he fronted for, were going to take the money without building a goddamn country club?"

Countess Rostov lifted a silver bell and rang for the maid. "Another Perrier please, and more coffee for Miss Williams."

"Could you get me an entree to someone in the Yakuza? Someone who might help me find the man who took my sword?"

The countess tapped the tips of her fingers on a knee. "You want some advice?"

"I'm listening."

"Forget the sword. Forget the two million dollars. You can always get more money, it's tougher to get another life after you're dead. Get out of Tokyo right now. Me? I'm off to Paris tomorrow morning. And I'll *stay* there, nice and safe, until this business is cleared up."

But Kay couldn't bring herself to take the advice, good as it might be. She had no intention of losing her business. "If I don't get the sword back I'll be broke and as good as dead. Do you know a man named Yoshi Hasegawa?"

The countess put her glass down with a clatter. "Where did you get his name?"

"All I know about him is that he's a Yakuza boss."

"Yoshi heads the Yamaguchi-gumi in Tokyo. They're an Osaka-based gang but they have a lot of operations in Tokyo, too. Sure, I know him. In fact, he was one of the guys who brought me over to Tokyo. I worked in his string until I went out on my own. I couldn't just walk out on the Yamaguchi-gumi, of course. I had to buy my way out. Yoshi looks and talks like an international banker but underneath all the charm and tailoring he's pure Yakuza."

Kay persisted. "Put me in touch with Hasegawa before you leave for Paris."

The countess slowly shook her head. "I've got a lot on my conscience, honey. But I won't do that. If you're smart you'll catch the next plane to New York. If not . . . at least I warned you."

Kay shrugged. "Well, thanks, and I really do appreciate your advice . . ."

The countess gave Kay one more close appraisal. "With those tits and that nice tight ass you could make a fortune in Tokyo. Good luck to you, honey."

Cricket Kimura had spent a frustrating morning and afternoon looking for his next victim.

Tak Saji had called each of the people involved in the Seisako lawsuit and warned them they were in danger. At least two of his possible victims had left Tokyo. One had flown to Rio de Janeiro, another to New York. Others on his list were probably making arrangements to do the same. But some, the stubborn ones, had to be still around. Kimura had found both the home and business office of a possible victim protected by heavily armed private security guards who weren't the usual old men in starched blue uniforms but tough young fellows who carried guns.

Yamato was doing a lousy job of keeping Saji out of his way, and Kimura intended to tell him so. Not that he was discouraged. Once Cricket Kimura began a job he finished it no matter what the odds against him might be. He hadn't risen to *oyabun* by backing down against anyone.

There was at least one person in particular on his list who would never take advice from the police, never leave town in fear, never hire private security guards: Jimmy Sato.

Kimura didn't like Jimmy Sato, and Jimmy didn't like him. He wanted to kill Jimmy. It would be easy to do so since he knew the inside of Jimmy's establishment so well. The only thing stopping him was Hasegawa's warning to leave Jimmy Sato alone.

Kimura considered Hasegawa's order and decided to ignore it. The principal goal, after all, was to kill enough people to kill the lawsuit. Hasegawa didn't care whether Jimmy Sato lived or died, he was only concerned because the *gaijin* woman from the sword shop would be calling on Jimmy and Countess Rostov.

The more Kimura thought about it, the more convinced he became that Jimmy should be his next target. If everything went right he could eliminate both Jimmy Sato *and* the only witness to Turo Kajima's murder in one afternoon.

Yes, the killing of both Jimmy *and* this *gaijin* would generate tremendous publicity. And wouldn't any additional public outcry serve Hasegawa's cause?

I'll do it, Kimura decided. Among other reasons, it will be a pleasure to wipe that perpetual smile off Jimmy Sato's face.

*   *   *

Once again Yoshi Hasegawa entered the exclusive bar in the Ginza through a private back door for a meeting with the Former Minister. This time Knuckles Yamato was also there.

As irritated as he was by being called to this meeting, Hasegawa bowed to Yamato and the Former Minister before letting out his annoyance. "I'm not accustomed to being *summoned* to meetings."

"I apologize," Yamato bowed in return. "I wouldn't have called you if I didn't have an emergency on my hands. I was afraid to use the telephone."

"What's the matter?"

The Former Minister, who loved to hold secrets, wanted to demonstrate that he was in possession of this one. "Hideki Kohno has escaped from Yamato-san's custody."

"What?" Hasegawa looked at Yamato's face and saw from the policeman's shame that this was true. "How did this *happen?*"

"Kohno-san's guards were in the habit of taking him for a walk every evening. Last night . . . during the walk . . . he escaped." Yamato provided the details even though reporting this failure was the worst humiliation of his career.

The Former Minister drank *sake* and listened with growing contempt. "Your people are incompetent."

"That's not the point." Hasegawa sat down and reached for a bottle of American bourbon, Wild Turkey, just to irritate the Former Minister. "The remarkable part is that Hideki Kohno has people who would take such a risk for him."

"He must have paid them," the Former Minister said.

"Perhaps. The guards didn't see these two people?"

"One was unconscious, the other blinded by headlights and knocked off his feet by the escape car."

Hasegawa flicked a piece of lint from the sleeve of his

Burberry jacket. "By now Kohno-san may have left Japan, but somehow I don't think so. This isn't all bad, you know."

Yamato looked outraged. "I've lost my prisoner! A prisoner who can ruin all of us!"

"He can't ruin us if he's left Japan and gone into hiding," Hasegawa pointed out. "And if he's still in Japan, I'm now free to kill him. Since he's no longer in your custody he's fair game."

"No!" Yamato blurted out.

"Hasegawa-san is right." The Former Minister gave Yamato a look. "We let Hideki Kohno live only because you would have been disgraced if he had died in your custody. Now that you have disgraced yourself by losing him there is no reason not to kill him."

"Only my most trusted men know that Kohno is gone. If I can find him before the trial nobody will know he was ever out of my custody." Yamato looked from Hasegawa to the Former Minister and saw he would get no help. "You're throwing me to the wolves. Leaving me to resign in disgrace."

"You have plenty of money in your Hong Kong bank," Hasegawa said. "Retire to the countryside. Or travel. I have a beautiful condominium in Hawaii, right on Waikiki Beach. I recommend the climate."

Yamato glared at them. "I shouldn't have let you know that Kohno-san had escaped. I won't make the mistake of trusting you two again." He moved slowly toward the door, more aged than when he had entered. "I'll recapture Hideki Kohno without your help. He'll go on trial as scheduled. And say *nothing*."

"I'll be satisfied if it works out that way," Hasegawa said. "Truly, I wish you no bad luck. But for my own peace of mind I must take advantage of your mistake and kill Kohno-san while I have the chance."

The Former Minister was seldom seen to smile, but this

situation did prompt a modest one to his lips. "I'd be willing to place a one million yen wager that Hasegawa-san's men find Hideki Kohno before you do."

Knuckles Yamato laughed. "Now I *know* I'll find him first. Any wager *you* make is lost at the start. Isn't that how we all got into this mess? Trying to help you make money to pay your gambling debts in Macau?"

The incipient smile disappeared from the Former Minister's face. "Don't overstep yourself, Yamato-san."

The police superintendent left, slamming the door behind him.

"I'm worried about that man," the Former Minister said. "He's not to be trusted."

"Of course not, he's a policeman." Hasegawa was silently agreeing with Yamato that the Former Minister's desperate need to pay off his gambling debts was a fatal weakness. The Former Minister was finished in Japanese politics. And in life.

"I wonder who Kohno-san's friends could be," the Former Minister said. "*Two* of them, no less."

"A man who has two real friends is lucky," Yoshi Hasegawa mused. "Until his luck runs out."

Chapter 19

IT WAS ALMOST NOON when Tak received a phone call from Patrol Officer Saguo Kagayama, who had taken a day's leave to help go through Dr. Wako's papers.

"We may have some evidence for you."

"What is it?"

"It would be better if you could come here and look at it."

"All right."

"Another thing, sir. You know the girl who was here last night? Kiki? The prostitute?"

"Yes."

"Kiki's coming here too. She claims to have some information. I told Kiki to telephone you but she won't call a police station. She says the Yakuza has people in our department who might learn she is doing a favor for you."

"She's probably right."

"Also, Kohno-san demands to speak with you. He's been complaining about his room. He says there are spiders and roaches in his futon, though I can't find any. He also wants a color television, a VCR and some porno movies. He doesn't like the food either; he demands a catered dinner tonight from Mitsukoshi."

All of which gave Tak his first laugh of the day. "I'll see you in fifteen minutes."

On his way out of police headquarters Tak encountered a dozen detectives leaving Yamato's office. One looked a bit startled when Tak passed him in the hallway. Tak didn't think anything of it until he was down in the garage and turning the ignition key in his car. He caught a glimpse of the detective who had passed him in the hallway running to his own car. When Tak pulled out onto Hibiya-dori, the detective's car was close behind him and stayed there all the way to Shimbashi station.

So I'm being followed, Tak thought. All right. There could be two reasons for that. First, Knuckles Yamato knows that I'm an old friend of Hideki Kohno. He must be wondering if I had a hand in getting Hideki out of Lion Mansion last night. This detective is assigned to follow me. Another reason for the tail could be Yamato making sure I don't succeed in finding the killer and linking him with the Seisa-ko swindle.

Either way, he had to lose this fellow without letting him know he had been spotted. Otherwise Yamato would know he had something to hide.

The bus traffic near Shimbashi station was clamorous. Tak moved behind a number six bus and stayed there, waiting to spot another number six coming in the opposite direction.

He got lucky when a number six *and* a number eighty-six came toward him, one right behind the other. Tak noticed bus stops for the number six coming up on either side of the street. As the two number sixes began to pull over, the eighty-six passed by. All Tak had to do was tap his foot on the accelerator to slide in front of the eighty-six.

With that bus behind him, and the two others pulled over to pick up passengers, the street was temporarily blocked.

Tak made a hard right and cut over to Gaein-higashi-dori, then after a few blocks headed for Tokyo Bay and the Shinagawa district with one eye on the rearview mirror.

By the time he arrived at the warehouse, he was certain no one had followed him. He took the steps two at a time and hurried into the second floor loft calling out his apologies. "Sorry to be late."

"Thank you for coming, sir." Patrol Officer Kagayama and Oto, the bank auditor who had volunteered to search through Dr. Wako's papers, both bowed.

Tak bowed in turn. "Looks like you've gone through everything. What did you find?"

Oto waved a diffident hand at the scattered papers. "Dr. Wako kept records going back to his first days as a cosmetic surgeon. We found hundreds of medical records. Many files of x-rays. Thousands of photographs."

"Photos?"

"Dr. Wako photographed his patients before altering them, then photographed them again after their surgery healed."

"I see." Actually Tak couldn't see where this was leading.

"We also found his records related to Seisa-ko," Kagayama put in. "How much he invested. What his losses were. Papers related to the lawsuit."

"So that's the evidence you found?"

"No, sir." Oto, with a bank auditor's punctilious way of revealing his findings, led Tak over to a table piled high with photographs. "The evidence . . . at least we *think* it is evidence . . . has to do with some of these photos."

The photographs were astounding. Breasts. Noses. Chins. Buttocks. Necks. Ears. Every body part.

Oto said, "Dr. Wako was a good photographer. I would guess he took his own pictures to save patients the embarrassment of having a photographer look at parts of their bodies they felt were inferior."

Tak hoped this was leading somewhere.

"He used a Nikon 35-mm camera. All the photos were of parts of bodies shot in color. Except for one series of photos in black and white."

Oto showed Tak a set of prints in which three men were coming out of what appeared to be the rear door of a restaurant. The photos had been taken, apparently, in the early dawn hours after a typical Japanese all-night party of heavy drinking. The key photo was grainy . . . probably shot with fast film but clear enough to show the faces.

"We recognized Hideki Kohno, of course," Kagayama said.

"And then," Oto added, "we also recognized this second man as a former government minister. The third man neither of us knew. We thought you might be able to identify him."

Tak tilted the photo toward the window light. "The third man is Yoshi Hasegawa, a Yakuza boss."

Kagayama allowed himself a satisfied smile. "Then this picture really *is* evidence. It ties together Hideki Kohno, the Yakuza and the government."

"Dr. Wako must have followed Hideki Kohno in his spare time, hoping to find out who his partners were." Tak could imagine the obsessed doctor waiting in an alley, camera in hand, for Hideki to emerge from a restaurant with Hasegawa and the Former Minister. "He was a good photographer. He got the picture he wanted. He showed it to Turo Kajima. This is the evidence of government corruption they were going to present in court."

"Would the photos win their case?" Oto asked.

"No," Tak said. "But they could have negotiated a settlement by threatening to give the pictures to the newspapers. We've had so many scandals involving government officials that no one wants to see another." Tak impulsively shook the hands of Patrol Officer Kagayama and auditor Oto. "You've done very good work. Kagayama-san, I'll ask you to hold the negatives and most of the photos. I'll take this one."

Suddenly the door to the room where they were holding Hideki began to shake as he pounded it from inside. "Let me out, let me out of here!" He was yelling in Japanese. "I need a real bathroom . . ."

Kagayama chuckled. "He's been saying that all day. I wouldn't worry about him, Saji-san. He's all right."

"I'm sure he is. I need to talk to him, though."

The door was unlocked and Tak slipped inside before Hideki could try to escape.

And Hideki had been poised to do just that, but the sight of Tak made him fall back a pace. "Tak, that chemical toilet . . . I've had headaches, chills. I'm *sick*. You've got to move me someplace else."

"Yamato-san is looking all over Tokyo for you. By now Hasegawa-san and his thugs are on your trail, too."

Hideki slumped. "What'll happen to me?"

"With more luck than you deserve you'll live to a ripe old age and probably spend your last years cheating elderly women out of their pensions." He showed the photo to Hideki. "When was this picture taken? And where?"

He drooped like a wilted flower. "It's all going to come out, isn't it? The whole story. Who took the picture?"

"One of the people you robbed—Dr. Wako."

"The tummy tucker?" Hideki pinched the bridge of his nose. "He made more trouble about his loss than all the others combined. You know how cheap doctors are. I look pretty good in this picture, don't I? That's a Ralph Lauren blazer."

"I'm more interested in the picture than in your wardrobe."

"It was taken the only time the three of us got together. About six months ago. We celebrated the success of Seisa-ko in the private room of a bar in Ginza called the Pink Door. Split up the money that night. I only got twenty percent. The Former Minister took forty percent and so did Hasegawa."

Hideki brightened. "Wait a minute. If this picture gets out, the heat will be on Hasegawa and the Former Minister instead of me. And I wouldn't even have to testify against them. The truth is right there in that photograph!"

"Now you've got the idea." About the only thing one

couldn't accuse Hideki of was being stupid. "Just sit tight for a few days and you may get out of this alive."

"Okay, but I need better food. This morning they gave me a bowl of rice and fish."

"Good Japanese breakfast."

"I'm used to bacon and eggs for breakfast, steak for dinner."

"We're on a limited budget," Tak said, and left.

Kiki was waiting for him in the warehouse. "Hi, policeman. You looking foxy today." During the day Kiki dressed in skin-tight gray slacks, spiked high heeled shoes and a red sweater molded to her body.

"Hello, Kiki." While the door was being locked, Tak asked Oto, "Can you give him a nice *bento* for dinner?"

"He told me he wants a Kobe steak."

"By tonight he'll be happy to eat a *bento.*"

Kiki snickered. "I know that guy, he rather eat pussy."

"Not on the menu. You have some information, Kiki?"

She slipped an arm through his and began walking him around the loft as if they were lovers on a stroll. "I practice my English with you. You tall for Japanese, you know that? I fit good on your arm. You want to go someplace and fuck? Make you good price. Police rate."

"Not today. You have information?"

The turndown didn't affect Kiki's good humor. "Got good stuff. Last night I see regular client. Hilton Chambers. *Gaijin* guy, you know? He sell antiques, call me two, three times a month. Do it his apartment. Anyway, before we start fuck he get a phone call. I don't listen at first. Then I hear names. Hasegawa-san on the phone. Lots of Hasegawa in Tokyo. But Kay Williams another name, so I figure this Hasegawa is maybe Yakuza boss."

"Why didn't you call me this morning?"

"Mornings I sleep. Work to five a.m. Need sleep."

"What did Hasegawa-san say about Kay Williams?"

"You hot for her, I can tell. Chambers-san tell Hasegawa-san she go see two people today. Jimmy Sato. Countess something. Chambers-san tell Hasegawa-san he sell sword for him, both of them make plenty money."

Countess Rostov, Tak thought. Kay had made a copy of the list of people involved in the lawsuit before meeting Hilton Chambers for a drink at the Imperial. Chambers steered her to the two people on the list who speak the best English. Afterwards he called Yoshi Hasegawa and told him where Kay would be today.

Chambers knew that Hasegawa could put his hands on the sword whenever he wanted . . . the killer was Hasegawa's man. Chambers was giving Kay to Hasegawa in return for the sword.

"She in trouble." Kiki was saying, as if reading his thoughts. "Those Yakuza guys don't like women mess in their business."

"Kiki, thank you, I'll talk to you later." He waved goodbye to the others as he ran across the loft and down the steps to his car.

The list of investors included Countess Rostov's name and phone number which he now called from the cellular phone in his car. The countess accepted the call and confirmed that Kay had stopped by her apartment that morning.

"No, I don't know where she was going from here," the countess said. "But I want to thank you for the warning call you gave me yesterday. I'm leaving for Paris tomorrow and I won't be back until this thing is settled."

Tak hung up and called Jimmy Sato's place—the White Heat Hotel in Shibuya.

"Jimmy busy," the girl on the hotel desk informed him.

"This is a police emergency. Go find him right now and tell him—"

"Jimmy busy." She hung up.

Tak threw his cellular phone on the floorboard and started his car. Thirty minutes to Shibuya, even with his siren on. He attached a red flashing light to the roof, hit the siren button and headed for the White Heat Hotel.

Chapter 20

THE JAPANESE, always intent on improving on other peoples' models, had turned their love hotels into sexual Disneylands.

A customer, for example, could rent a "theme room" of various accoutrements. A dungeon complete with a rack on which to tie down the willing victim . . . A heaven with fluffy clouds and winged angels on the walls, religious music over a sound system, everything in white including the see-through robe covering the prostitute's body . . . A hard-rock room with music blaring, photos of Mick Jagger and other rock stars on the walls, and a *karaoke* system at the foot of the bed so one could sing to one's girl of the evening before, or after, making love.

Customers did not have to slink into a love hotel in the dark of night with their coat collars turned up. Respectable businessmen entered love hotels at high noon without worrying about who might see them. Sometimes two businessmen would take a room and a girl together for a couple of hours of relaxation, finishing with a business meeting in the hotel bar. It was said that more Japanese business deals were concluded in love-hotel bars than in boardrooms.

The White Heat Hotel in Shibuya was just such a place, and Jimmy Sato was the proprietor.

Kay's taxi driver knew exactly where the White Heat was, off a side street a few blocks from Shibuya station. From the outside it looked like a mideast palace, all turrets and spires painted a shrieking pink. No one passing this way could miss it, which, of course, was the point.

Kay felt a trifle self-conscious entering, though no one else seemed to take special notice of her. Behind the desk stood a beautiful girl with straight black hair down to her waist and enormous almond eyes.

"You want room with guy or girl? Thirty thousand yen either way."

"I don't want a room. I want to talk to Jimmy Sato."

"Jimmy busy."

Kay put a pair of ten thousand yen notes on the counter. "I'll pay twenty thousand yen for a twenty-minute conversation with Mr. Sato. A thousand yen per minute."

The girl's hand scooped up the banknotes. "Wait in bar, I find Jimmy for you."

Kay expected the bar to be as garish as the rest of the establishment. Its comfortable leather chairs, soft lighting and the tasteful art on the walls were a pleasant surprise. She ordered *sake* on ice. Several girls lounged in the bar, each one slim and pretty and well dressed, some with men but most sitting in groups of twos and threes waiting for customers. Always suspicious that other good-looking women might be competition, they gave Kay wary glances.

The cold *sake* took her breath away. Kay was wishing she had ordered white wine when a little Japanese man came into the bar. Immediately the girls sat up straight and preened.

This, Kay thought, is the proprietor.

He stopped in front of Kay. "American?"

"Yes."

"Great! I'm Jimmy Sato."

"My name is Kay Williams."

He sat down and leaned forward so that his knees were almost touching Kay's. "I understand you paid twenty thousand yen just to gab with me, Miss Williams. I'm honored. And you're in luck. For twenty thousand yen you get more than just Jimmy Sato. You get Jimmy Cagney!"

And suddenly he was back on his feet, hands braced at his waist, feet planted wide, torso ducking and weaving, Jimmy Cagney imitation . . . "You . . . dirty . . . rat."

Kay dutifully applauded, seeing little more than a grotesque effort to imitate the great and unique Cagney. Jimmy Sato had a compact tough guy's body, small head, raspy voice, ears laid back flat against his head, but that didn't make him Jimmy Cagney.

Sato sat back down, and this time his knees did touch Kay's. "I love old Cagney movies," Sato said. "That's how I learned English, watching American flicks. Cagney was always my favorite."

"He was special." Kay moved her knees back from Sato's.

"Remember *White Heat*? That last scene? Where Cagney's on top of a huge tank filled with gas? His mom was a gangster too, always urging him on. She wanted him to be the *top* gangster. The best. Now he's surrounded by police. Wounded. Standing on top of a tank that's about to explode. Cagney yells: *Made it, Ma! Top of the World!* Then . . . boom! Wow, what a scene. That's where I got the name for my hotel, it's the title from the Cagney movie."

Kay could almost like Jimmy Sato. He did have a kind of charm of his own. But when his knees touched hers again she decided his charm was a little too pushy.

"Mr. Sato, I'd like to ask you a few questions about Seisako Securities. You're one of those suing the government, I'm told."

"I lost plenty in that deal. Of course, I've got plenty. This place does okay."

"Did Detective Saji warn you there's a man using a sword to terrorize those suing the government?"

"Saji-san called me yesterday. I appreciated the warning but this sword freak doesn't worry me."

"Why not?"

"Because he's Yakuza and I pay protection money to those guys. In my business you can't operate without paying off the Yakuza. They're worse than those spaghetti eaters in the Mafia."

"You've obviously spent a lot of time in the U.S."

"I lived in Nevada for six years. Spent most of the time as assistant manager of a whorehouse outside Reno. That was what you might call my apprenticeship."

Kay tried to steer the conversation back to her own subject. "The sword the killer is using belongs to me. I bought it just before it was stolen. If you know these people, maybe you can put me in touch with someone who can help me recover the sword. I've been told a man named Yoshi Hasegawa might be able to help."

"You want me to send you to the Yakuza? To Yoshi Hasegawa? Those people are dangerous. Hasn't anybody told you that?"

"Everyone has told me that."

"Either you're hard to scare or that sword is worth a hell of a lot of money."

"Some of both, I guess."

Sato regarded her with admiration. "I love American women. Japanese girls, I dunno, they're beautiful, gorgeous, but they don't have the spirt of American girls. You know what I mean? I'm talking about girls like Virginia Mayo from that same movie, *White Heat*. The one who played Cagney's wife. Now *that* was a woman. Remember the scene where she modeled her new fur coat for him? Dynamite!"

"You're avoiding my question, Mr. Sato. Will you put me in touch with someone who can help me or not?"

"Let me think it over. Meanwhile I'll buy you another drink. You like *sake*? Try my private stock."

He raised his hand and a waitress came on the run. The drinks he ordered followed immediately.

Sato lifted his glass. *"Kanpai."*

The powerful *sake* produced a mellow glow. "Lovely," Kay said.

"Hey, I got an idea. How'd you like to see the rest of this place? I mean, there's nothing like the White Heat Hotel in the States."

Kay looked doubtful.

"Don't worry, you won't see anything crude. I'll show you a couple of empty suites, that's all. Take you on the Jimmy Sato guided tour, just like Universal Studios in Hollywood. I do that for American tourists all the time. Some of them don't want the sex, they just want to see what a love hotel looks like. Crazy, huh?"

Jimmy Sato, with his goofy Cagney impressions and light-bulb grin, seemed about as threatening as a Saturday-morning cartoon. "Okay, I guess I'm as curious as the next person."

"Swell. Let's go."

Kay finished her *sake* and let Sato guide her out of the bar and past the lobby to a wide staircase leading to the second floor.

"These banisters are Italian marble," Sato said proudly. I brought a special guy over from Milan to install them."

Kay was both impressed and appalled by the lavishness. Marble banisters. Genuine Persian rugs. Massive sculptures in numerous styles lining the wide corridor of the second floor. Overdone, bizarre, garish, expensive—bad taste. The opposite of the traditional Japanese goal of simplicity, understatement. Evidently Japanese men liked their sexual adventures to have a circus atmosphere.

Sato produced a set of keys. "We call this the Wild West suite."

Kay preceded him into a room equipped with a horseshoe-shaped bed, crystal chandelier, red velvet drapes, all the appointments of a Wild West bordello. In the center of the room stood a mechanical bull with a velvet-covered saddle big enough to accommodate two.

Sato flipped a switch on the side of the mechanical bull and it began to rock gently. "Three speeds. This is the slowest. You notice the big saddle? Guy gets up here with a girl, they sit facing each other, no clothes. The rocking motion of the bull brings them together. *Facilitates sex.* Hey, that's the way the manufacturer put it. The horseshoe bed was made in Austin, Texas. I had it shipped to Tokyo by air freight. Cost me a fortune but worth every yen. Guys feel real macho when they climb onto this thing."

Kay began to feel soiled. "Thanks for the tour. Shall we go back to the bar now? I'd enjoy another *sake*."

"You haven't seen the best part." Sato moved over to a wall on which a large cabinet was mounted. He unlocked the cabinet and pushed back the sliding door. Inside, a compact video camera stood mounted on a short tripod. In front of the camera was a one-way mirror that made it possible to look into the next room without being seen.

Despite herself, Kay drew close enough to the cabinet to look through the glass. In the next room a naked Japanese girl was providing oral sex to a salaryman, his briefcase on the floor beside the bed, pants and shoes tossed aside. The room resembled a child's playroom, stuffed animals everywhere, a big hobbyhorse, the bed a playpen.

"You're *spying* on them." Kay noticed a blinking red light on the videotape recorder. "Wait a minute, that camera's running. You're *videotaping* those people."

"Automated system. A sideline business. I string together

fifteen, twenty scenes. Make dupes. Sell them for fifteen thousand yen per."

She moved to shut it off but Sato blocked her way. "Hey, don't be so quick to look down that pretty nose. Remember, I learned this business in the good old U.S.A."

"You're a creep." Kay hurried to the door and found it locked. She wheeled around. "Let me out of here before you get into more trouble than you can handle."

Sato swiveled the video camera around so that it pointed at Kay. He came toward her with his Jimmy Cagney swagger, chin jerking and mouth twitching. "Relax, sweetheart."

The mechanical bull continued its bucking motion behind him.

"You're not going to feel so good," Kay said as Sato advanced and she slipped off her shoe . . . "with this heel embedded in your skull."

Sato stopped and planted his feet wide apart. "Don't count on it, sweetheart. In this business you learn how to make women do what you want. I haven't had a *gaijin* girl in a long time, and never one as good-looking as you."

His voice was still imitation Cagney, but now with a pure . . . and nasty . . . Sato undertone.

Cricket Kimura parked his Porsche on a Shibuya backstreet and took a series of narrow alleys to the White Heat Hotel, the sword at his side in its paper wrapping.

The last dreary alley brought him to the rear exit of the hotel. He tested the door and found it locked, considered forcing it open and entering the hotel from the rear but rejected the idea. This quiet alley would make a better escape route than an entrance point.

Kimura knew the layout of the White Heat. He had been inside several times on business. Not for a couple of years, though, which was good. He doubted anyone inside would know his face except for Jimmy Sato and his wife, Suzuki, who ran the front desk. The girls who worked here were changed frequently so that customers always had new talent to choose from. Kimura did the same with his own strings. His visits to the White Heat had been to negotiate deals with Jimmy Sato to swap groups of girls.

Now he walked around the block and noticed in an alley across from the White Heat an ancient truck equipped with a woodstove for cooking sweet potatoes. The old man who owned the truck and sold hot slices of sweet potato from it had parked against a wall to take a midday nap in the front seat.

Kimura crossed the street and sat down on the truck's running board. He thought it unlikely anyone would notice him in the narrow space between the truck and the wall.

At midday the hotel catered to salarymen who partook of lunchtime sex. Kimura was in no hurry. He elected to wait until at least two o'clock, when the hotel would be less crowded. There was also the possibility the *gaijin* woman would appear if he waited.

He felt around the base of the stove and found a big sweet potato being kept warm on coals. Kimura loved sweet potatoes. He left three hundred yen for the old man and munched on the potato while he waited.

His patience was rewarded. Not long after he finished the potato, the *gaijin* woman was dropped off in front of the White Heat by a taxi. The woman and Jimmy Sato together. Perfect.

Kimura looked at his Rolex and decided to wait fifteen minutes. Let the girl introduce herself to Jimmy Sato and settle down to talk to him. She would have to sit through Jimmy's impression of some American movie actor. Kimura didn't know the actor and didn't care to hear Jimmy's impressions, but he knew there was no way a visitor to the White Heat could avoid them.

When fifteen minutes had passed Kimura walked across the street with head lowered and the sword carried in one hand against his leg. A man passed him coming out of the hotel and Kimura averted his face. Once inside, he went straight to the desk.

Suzuki Sato's usually bored eyes showed pinpoints of surprise at Kimura's appearance.

"Hello, Suzuki-san, how have you been?" Kimura went around the desk and took her arm.

"What do you want? You have no appointment with Jimmy, he would have mentioned that to me—"

"We *do* have an appointment. Jimmy just doesn't know it."

"Take your hand off my arm." She tried to pull away. "Jimmy will be angry when I tell him how you've treated me."

"Then let's go tell him. Where is he?"

She hesitated. "Room eleven."

"Is he with the *gaijin* woman?"

"How did you know? Is she a friend of yours?"

"I don't make friends with women. All right, get the key for room eleven."

"What do you want, Kimura-san?"

"I want to see your husband. Get the key and take me to him."

"I can't leave the desk . . . you're hurting me . . ."

Kimura had put enough pressure on her arm to cut off the circulation. He wanted to get her out from behind the desk before anyone came out of the bar or through the front door. "Let's *go*."

She took a key from one of the slots beneath the desk and Kimura pulled her roughly along with him. He took the steps to the second floor two at a time, literally dragging Suzuki Sato behind him. Her eyes were wild now. This was no business call and she knew it.

"We're under Yakuza protection—"

"You aren't protected by the Yamaguchi-gumi," he reminded her. "You chose the Inagawa-kai . . . rat people."

"If you hurt Jimmy the Inagawa-kai will kill you."

"They've tried it before and paid for it. These days they back away when I'm in their territory." He tightened his grip. "Quiet now."

A couple was leaving one of the rooms and Kimura kept his face turned and a strong grip on Suzuki Sato. It wasn't necessary . . . the man and woman had eyes only for each other.

When they reached room eleven Kimura told her to open the door. Suzuki Sato's hand was shaking when she put the key in the lock. The moment he heard the lock click Kimura pushed open the door with his foot and hustled Suzuki into the room, closing the door behind him.

Jimmy Sato and the *gaijin* woman were struggling on the floor. And Jimmy seemed to be getting the worst of it. He was on top of her, straddling her body, but she was hitting him with a shoe and had drawn blood over his right ear.

Now Sato hit her with his fist, a blow to her jaw. She dropped the shoe and her head lolled back.

Which was when Sato noticed his wife and Cricket Kimura.

"What is this? Suzuki, why have you brought this man up here? Kimura-san?" He looked furiously at the Yakuza gangster. "What the hell do you want?" Sato stood up and smoothed his clothes, leaving a dazed Kay on the floor. "This woman is crazy. Looking for some sword . . ."

Kimura let the brown paper wrapping drop away from the sword. "I know, this is the sword she's looking for."

He put the point against Suzuki Sato's back and ran it through her body with a single thrust. A strangled gasp, her knees buckled, she slipped to the floor.

Kimura pulled the sword free.

Jimmy Sato stared openmouthed, disbelieving. Then, find-

ing his voice . . . "Goddamn you, I'm protected, the Inagawa-kai—"

"They can't help you."

"Why? What have I done? . . ."

"You joined the Seisa-ko lawsuit."

"I'll drop out of it, I promise—"

"Too late, Jimmy."

Kimura came forward. The *gaijin* woman was still on the
floor, beginning to move, though obviously still groggy. He
had time to dispose of Jimmy Sato before dealing with her.

Sato backed away. His right hand went into a pocket and
came out with a large roll of ten thousand yen notes. "I'll pay
whatever you want . . ."

When he held the money out Kimura swung the sword.
Sato's arm separated from his body in a spray of blood. When
the arm hit the floor the fingers opened convulsively, money
scattered.

Sato managed to stay on his feet, but his face had lost all its
color. "You . . . you cut off my arm—"

"That's right." Kimura decided to finish this before the
man collapsed. "And now you're going to lose your head."
Kimura swung the sword with all his considerable power,
decapitating Jimmy Sato in a single stroke.

Kimura's focus on Sato had been so intense that he had not
noticed Kay Williams getting to her feet. Her cry when Sato
was beheaded made Kimura quickly turn to her and cut her
off as she went for the door. This time there was no window
for her to escape through. The White Heat was built for privacy, no windows above the first floor.

With escape blocked, Kay retreated behind the mechanical
bull, still going through its gentle bucking motions in the
center of the room. She flicked the switch to its highest level
and the bull began making more violent motions, spinning
now as well as bucking up and down.

Kimura had to jump back to avoid being hit by the contraption. It infuriated him that a *gaijin* woman could make him look foolish even for an instant. He would make her pay for that.

Kay dodged, feinted. Kimura kept pressing forward, keeping himself between her and the door.

I'm going to die, Kay thought. I'm going to die in a Japanese whorehouse. The thought was so preposterous it almost made her giddy.

As he moved past the mechanical bull, Kimura groped for the switch and turned it off. Abruptly, without the sound of machinery bucking and spinning, the room became as silent as . . . silent as death, Kay thought. Her back was against the wall now, she had nowhere else to go. Kimura loomed over her.

As he brought the sword up to shoulder level he became aware of a blinking red light above the woman's shoulder. He was looking into the lens of a video camera. The camera was running! He had just been videotaped killing Jimmy and Suzuki Sato!

Kay took advantage of the moment's diversion, ducked under Kimura's arm and ran for the door.

Kimura lashed out with the sword but Kay was moving fast. Even so, the blade made a clean slice across her back, like a surgeon's scalpel, a few millimeters deep. She screamed but reached the door and tried for the knob, found it, got the door open and was out of the room.

Kimura, still shaken by the video camera and its recording him, yanked it off its tripod, ran into the hallway, the camera in one hand, the sword in the other. He saw the girl stop a few yards down the hallway . . .

Kay had spotted a small red box on the wall. She broke the glass with her hand, pulled down the lever inside the box. The fire alarm began to shriek, which had the effect she wanted. People came running out of rooms into the hallway, most partly undressed, pulling on clothes as they ran.

Before Kimura could reach her, the hallway between them was clogged with people. Kay moved with them for the main staircase, hearing Kimura cursing in Japanese and trying to elbow his way past others to get to her. She glanced over her shoulder and felt a rush of panic as he lifted the sword.

But now she was on the staircase and moving faster than Kimura, pushing people out of the way. She got to the first floor and within seconds reached the street, where a crowd had already begun to gather.

Another panicky glance over her shoulder showed Kimura standing uncertainly in the doorway . . . he could not come out onto the street where everyone would clearly see the sword, and his face.

Reluctantly he withdrew into the hotel. Kay dropped to her knees and, finally, tears of relief came.

A minute later the fire trucks arrived, adding their sirens to that of the fire alarm still shrieking inside the building.

"Kay, are you all right?" someone was saying. Tak scooped her up.

She threw her arms around him. "He was here, again, killed Jimmy Sato and some woman . . . he tried to kill me again . . ."

"You're bleeding. He cut you across the back."

She tried to tell him what had happened but mostly it was gibberish that came out as Tak lifted and carried her to an ambulance that arrived with the fire trucks. "Which hospital are you from?" he asked an attendant.

"Keio."

"I'm Detective Inspector Saji, Metropolitan Police. Get this woman to the emergency room at Keio immediately. She's cut and in shock. Tell the doctor I want a police guard standing over her. Someone just tried to kill her. Do you understand that?"

The attendant had been nodding along with Tak's words.

"Kay, I'll come to the hospital as soon as possible." He put her down on a gurney the attendant had pulled out of the ambulance and watched the attendant close the door and drive away.

Tak then showed his identification to the fire inspector and was allowed to enter the hotel. He didn't expect to find a fire. Several firemen searching for a blaze were coming to the same conclusion. There was no smoke or any other indication of a fire.

Someone called for help from the second floor and Tak ran up the steps with his hand near his pistol.

In a suite two bodies lay on the floor—a woman sprawled in a lake of blood, and Jimmy Sato in hacked-up pieces on the other side of the room.

Once again, the killer was nowhere to be found.

Chapter 21

Kɪᴍᴜʀᴀ ᴡᴀs ᴡᴀᴛᴄʜɪɴɢ the tape of himself killing the Satos. He had already watched it eight times and would gladly have watched it all day.

He fast-forwarded past the section where one of Sato's girls was giving oral sex to a salaryman, lingered briefly on the struggle between Sato and the *gaijin* woman, then went to slow play as he entered the room with Suzuki Sato.

The way the camera had been positioned he was able to watch the sword come out of the front of Suzuki Sato's rib cage. Saw her face register shock. Pain. The approach of death. Saw his own face over her shoulder and noted how professional he was, not like somebody killing wildly for no reason at all.

Now came the sequence in which he faced Jimmy Sato, cutting off his arm before beheading him with a magnificent sweep. He replayed that scene several times.

Kimura knew he should erase the tape. It was evidence that could send him to prison for the rest of his life, or get him killed by the Yakuza, who did not favor public scrutiny or having one of theirs publicly identified in the act of murder. But he could not bring himself to destroy the images . . .

He saw his own face up close, registering surprise at the camera's existence. The woman duck under his arm and run for the door. The sword slice through the air, giving her a cut across the back.

Kimura hit the stop button and then the rewind. Grudgingly he had to concede that setting off the fire alarm had been a smart ploy. In one move she had saved her own life and almost caused him to be captured. If he had not known exactly where to find the rear exit he might have been trapped inside the hotel by a bunch of stupid firemen.

His cellular phone rang and he answered it cautiously.

"Kimura-san?"

He recognized the voice. "Yes, Hasegawa-san."

"What have you done? I ordered you to stay away from Jimmy Sato."

"I apologize, *Oyabun.* So many others on the list have left town or hired private security guards, my options became limited."

"I told you the American woman would be there."

"Yes, she was . . ."

"And you tried to kill her too? As well as Jimmy Sato's wife."

Kimura wished Hasegawa had not learned he had tried to kill the *gaijin* and failed. "The hotel fire alarm went off, she got lost in a crowd—"

"In other words you let her get a second look at you and then failed to at least solve that problem by disposing of her."

Kimura said nothing.

"Why did the alarm go off?"

"I don't know." He hated to lie to his *oyabun.*

"I've already had a phone call from the Inagawa-kai. They want your blood for killing the Satos."

"I'm not afraid of them—"

"Did you know that Suzuki Sato was the daughter of an Inagawa-kai boss in Osaka?"

"No, I didn't . . . I'm sorry, *Oyabun*, I pledge to make an atonement."

"I don't need any more parts of your fingers," Hasegawa snapped. "It's going to cost me *millions of yen* to avoid a war between the Yamaguchi-gumi and the Inagawa-kai. How could you disobey an order? You've never done that before."

"With respect, *Oyabun*, I obeyed your most important order. I disposed of another name on your list. You can be sure that the others are now thoroughly intimidated. If they haven't flown off to some other country they're hiding behind their doors. Your plan is working to perfection—"

"Not quite. Hideki Kohno escaped from police custody. He is at large and very dangerous to us."

That made Kimura feel a little better. It meant that Knuckles Yamato had made a mess of his end of things. "Can I help you with that situation?"

"You have enough on your hands." Hasegawa's anger seemed to have moderated.

"Should I proceed with another name?"

"Yes. One more example will be necessary to be certain people have gotten our message."

"I'll do another quickly, maybe tomorrow."

"Be more careful this time. No fire trucks. No husband and wife combinations. Just one victim disposed of neatly and quickly."

"As you say, *Oyabun*. I won't fail you."

"Good . . . the sword is still with you?"

Kimura thought that a strange question. "Yes, I've been using the sword, it's right here with me."

"Very well. We'll talk again soon. If you decide to go after another name tomorrow, let me know in advance who it will be."

And a strange request, too. "I will. Again, a thousand pardons for my haste in dealing with Sato-san."

"We will discuss the matter at a later time." Hasegawa hung up without saying goodbye.

For a few moments Kimura considered the unusual aspects of the conversation, then dismissed them from his mind and sat back to watch another replay of his day's work.

"I'm not staying in this bed," Kay declared. "And I'm not staying in this hospital. Bring my clothes or I'll walk out of here buck-naked, I swear I will."

"You've got an ugly cut on your back and your nerves are still shaky. At least stay the night."

Kay shook her head. "That lunatic could easily find me here. He'd only have to find out which hospital sent an ambulance to the White Heat."

"There are two armed policemen outside your door."

Kay had to laugh. "You haven't seen this guy, Tak. He's the terminator on steroids. You should have seen what he did to Jimmy Sato . . . what he did . . . when Sato held out money . . . it was horrible. Even worse than what he did to Turo Kajima." Tears began. "I was so damn scared . . ."

He sat next to her, and she put her face into his shoulder. He felt less awkward than he had expected. A nurse put her head in the door and Tak waved her away. For the few moments the door was open the sounds of voices could be heard. Kay stiffened. "What's that?"

"The press and television people are waiting to talk to me. Knuckles Yamato issued a statement that the death of the Satos was my fault. I didn't give them proper protection."

"He wouldn't give you the men. You only have Simple and Dim working for you, and they're useless!"

"Don't get excited." He tried to make her lie down. "Yamato-san is, as usual, protecting himself. What is it you say? CY something. I've forgotten that one."

"CYA. Cover Your Ass."

"Japanese officials are very adept at CYA. Yamato-san set me up to take the blame for not stopping these murders, and his plan has worked."

Kay realized she'd been sniveling like a frightened child and became disgusted with herself. "Well, you're going to find this Yakuza bum. And I'm going to help you. Someone has to . . ."

"No more going off on your own," Tak said.

"I'm cured of that. But I'm not going to spend any more time looking at mug shots. Tak, have you thought about my idea that someone in your department might be working with the Yakuza?"

"Yes . . . I'm sure Knuckles Yamato has Yakuza connections. I should have seen it when he showed up at the crime scene when Turo Kajima was killed. The Yakuza sent him to make sure the investigation wouldn't go anywhere."

Kay had been wondering how the killer happened to arrive at the White Heat while she was there. And how Tak had gotten there only a minute or two after the first fire trucks.

"You had a drink at the Imperial late yesterday afternoon with a man named Hilton Chambers."

"Hilton's an antique dealer too, and an old friend."

"Was it Chambers who sent you to Countess Rostov and Jimmy Sato?"

"Yes . . ."

"Your friend phoned Yoshi Hasegawa and told him where you'd be today."

"That's ridiculous! Why would Hilton do such a thing?"

"I asked a few questions about your so-called friend. His business has been very slow. He's deep in debt to the Yakuza, who supply him with expensive girls three or four times a week. Do you remember Kiki? The girl you met last night at the warehouse? She was in Chambers's bed when he talked to Yoshi Hasegawa. Kiki heard him make a deal to sell the sword to some other collector when the killer's finished with it. The two of them probably plan to split the profits from the sword."

Kay settled her head back against the outsized hospital pillow. "I can't believe it, Hilton wouldn't do that to me—"

"The man is desperate for money."

"Hilton is my *friend*. We compete against each other but we're friends . . ."

Tak went to the closet and took out Kay's clothes. One shoe was missing and the back of her dress had a long gash where the sword had cut it; otherwise her things were intact. He wheeled a screen in front of her bed and draped her clothes over it. "After I talk to the press I'll sign you out of here and take you somewhere for the night."

Kay couldn't quite handle it. The revelation about Hilton Chambers was, on top of everything else, more than she could take. Didn't friendship mean *anything*? Obviously, not in the case of Hilton Chambers.

"Put your clothes on, I'll be right back," Tak said, and went out to face the press.

"This is really nice," Kay said. "Cozy."

"You mean it's small." Tak looked around the interior of his house. "When I was a child I thought this place was *huge*. A *castle*. When I came back from the States I could see how tiny my parents' house really was." He looked around as if seeing it again in his twenty-first year, acutely aware of its humbleness. "One room plus a kitchen and bathroom, three hundred square feet."

"You grew up here?"

"I slept in that corner. My parents slept where you are now."

Kay was curled up inside a futon that Tak had laid out on the *tatami* mat. She had on a pair of his pajamas. She was warm and comfortable now and not afraid for the first time since escaping from Jimmy Sato's hotel. "What part of Tokyo is this?"

"Setagaya."

The house was about the size of a one-car garage and located on a street so narrow it could be called an alley. Every eight or ten minutes a train screamed by on tracks a hundred yards away. Next door was a rice-cookie bakery from which delicious smells emanated even at this late hour.

"You and your parents slept in the same room?"

"That's fairly common in Japan." Tak smiled. "I know what you're thinking. How did they make love with their son sleeping only a few feet away?"

Kay felt mildly embarrassed. "That's exactly what went through my mind."

"They used to go into the bathroom. When my parents thought I was asleep they'd sneak into the bathroom to make love. My father took a blanket with him. They'd spread the blanket in the tub and make love there. I doubt they ever knew I knew what they were doing."

"Do you still have the same tub?"

"Sure. Nothing's changed in this house in thirty years."

"I've been told that even small houses like this one are worth a lot of money in Tokyo."

"Kay, there are eleven million people in Tokyo. Land is *scarce*. Last year a developer offered me the yen equivalent of about a million U.S. dollars for this place. It wasn't the house he wanted, of course, it was the property."

"A million dollars! Why didn't you sell?"

"In Japan we don't sell our family homes."

"But think of the possibilities. You wouldn't have to work for someone like Knuckles Yamato."

"If I quit working I'd drink more."

The idea of Tak Saji as a millionaire took some getting used to. "This is the first time I've ever gone to bed in a futon." Kay snuggled down.

"Do you like it?" Tak thought she looked especially attractive in his pajamas.

"I love it," Kay said. "Feels big enough for two."

Was it an invitation? He hoped so, was afraid so. "I like a big futon," he said lamely.

"Where are you going to sleep?"

"I have a spare."

"Seems like a waste, this one is so roomy."

Definitely an invitation. "Do you want a cup of tea? A rice cookie from next door?"

"No, Tak, I don't want a cup of tea and I don't want a rice cookie or a bowl of soup. What I really want is for you to climb into this futon with me."

Tak froze.

After several moments Kay said, "What do I have to do, come out and *drag* you in here?"

"No! I mean . . . of course not." He flipped off the light switch and got out of his clothes. A train rumbled through the neighborhood, causing the little house to tremble.

Tak was trembling himself as he slipped into the futon.

Kay's arms snaked out as he leaned down to kiss her. Despite the constricting folds of the futon, he got her out of the pajamas and began devouring her, and was being devoured in return.

"Yumm," Kay murmured. "You're hard all over."

"And you're beautiful even in the dark." He ran his hands over her. "I've wanted to put my hands on you for two days."

"What other things have you wanted to do to me?"

In slow stages, he showed her.

Chapter 22

CRICKET KIMURA, dressed in a new Armani suit, planned to complete his assignment this day.

Before leaving his apartment he slipped the videotape of the killings into the inside pocket of his jacket. He didn't like to carry it around but he hadn't yet thought of an appropriate place to hide it. Overnight he had decided not to erase the tape. It was something he would want to look at over and over for the rest of his life.

He drove more sedately than usual to Torigako's cricket shop and went inside.

"Good morning, Torigako-san." He looked more closely at the bent old man. "What's wrong? You don't look well."

"I slept badly last night." Torigako smiled weakly. "Old age."

"You must take care of yourself."

"I have a beauty for you today." Torigako shuffled off a few paces and returned with a cage that held a very large cricket with a strange blue marking on its back.

"What's that blue mark?"

"I don't know how or where this cricket got that marking

but it is distinctive. And lucky, I'm sure. Do you like the cage? I took a lot of time with this one."

"You did your usual excellent job." Kimura was still staring at the unusual mark. "I hope he's as lucky as he looks." Kimura peeled three ten-thousand-yen notes off a roll that held more money than Torigako had earned in the last five years. "I'm giving you extra today so you can see a doctor. Your color is bad."

"I will do that, thanks to your generosity."

Kimura picked up the cricket cage and jiggled it. "Big handsome fellow, just the kind of cricket I like. And that blue spot is special. But can he sing, Torigako-san?"

"He sings sweet and loud, you will see."

"Remember—take care of yourself." Kimura walked out of the shop whistling.

As soon as Kimura was gone Torigako flopped down on the stool behind the counter. He felt torn apart. Yesterday's double murder at the White Heat Hotel had been the final straw. He could no longer keep silent.

He had looked up the phone number of the Tokyo Metropolitan Police Department and knew from the newspapers that the name of the officer in charge of the case was a Detective Takeo Saji. But when he reached for the phone Torigako instead dialed the number of his daughter's home in Kyoto.

"Maki? This is your father. Yes . . . I am fine, Maki. But I can no longer carry on in the shop. It's a shame . . . yes . . . I love my little crickets . . . and the children are wonderful, as always. Maki, may I come and stay with you? Not forever. Just a month or two, then I'll find a room of my own in Kyoto so I can be close to you . . ."

He listened while his daughter spoke.

"Thank you . . . thank you . . . I'll take the *shinkansen* to Kyoto this afternoon, as soon as I close down the shop and pack my few things." He put down the phone feeling much relieved. Now he had a bolt-hole.

"It's time anyway," he muttered to himself. Time to retire. Sit in the sun. Play with his grandchildren.

Now that he had talked with Maki he was feeling better about his decision. In quick order he called his landlord and told him he was giving up the shop, then called to have the telephone and electricity canceled. He told them he would send his final payment but refused to give a new address.

The hardest part was setting his crickets free. He had about twenty of them in the shop. He put them all into one cage, then walked slowly to a nearby park and set them free in the tallest grass he could find.

His stock of cages was left outside the shop. Sooner or later the children in the neighborhood would realize he was gone and take them. His tools fitted into a single satchel with room for his business records and personal papers, such as they were. He slept in the rear of his shop. His few clothes went into a second suitcase. The rest of his things were put out with the trash.

When the tiny shop was clean and empty he called the police and asked to be put through to Detective Takeo Saji.

"*Moshi-moshi.* This is Senior Superintendent Tadashi Ueno speaking."

"Oh. I was calling Detective Saji."

"Saji-san is not here at the moment. I was just passing his phone."

Torigako bit his lip. Now that he was ready to leave, he was in a hurry to catch the next *shinkansen* to Kyoto. "Do you work with Detective Saji?"

"I am his superior."

"Ah . . . good . . . I have information for you."

"What kind of information?"

"The killer with the sword, I know who he is."

"What? Speak up, I can't hear you very well."

"Masao Kimura." Having spoken the name, Torigako instantly put down the phone. He had done his duty, his conscience was clear at last. His last act was to pull the plug on the telephone. When that was done he picked up his two valises and went out into the street to look for a taxi to take him to Tokyo Station.

The vision of the white Rolls-Royce kept interfering with Kimura's concentration. He had one more death to arrange among a shrinking list of possibilities. Countess Rostov had flown to Paris. Asare Hoto, the industrialist, was at a business conference in New York. And so it went. There were only four he might get to on a tight time schedule.

But the Rolls continued to intrude on his thinking.

Before he realized what he was doing he found himself driving toward the Rolls agency where Hasegawa did all his personal business. He wanted to see the car and the crest Hasegawa was having designed for him. He imagined something with a crown in the center, surrounded by garlands.

The Rolls-Royce agency occupied a large showroom in Azabudai near the Russian embassy. In the days when they were communists the Russians had often complained to the Japanese government about the types of establishments located in their neighborhood. The Rolls-Royce agency for one. Plus all the decadent Roppongi night clubs. And it especially galled the Soviets that the lavish American Club of Tokyo was right next door. But those days were gone. Now the Russians were delighted to be in a neighborhood of sex and capitalism.

Kimura did not want Hasegawa to know how anxious he was to have the Rolls so he strolled into the agency like any other well-off businessman looking for a car to match his status. The Rolls-Royce agency did not employ salesmen. Instead, there was a so-called consultant who gave Kimura time to feel at ease before speaking to him.

"I am Sohasu Toto." The consultant presented Kimura with his *meishi*. "May I offer you some green tea?"

"That would be very pleasant," Kimura said in his most polite voice.

When they were seated in comfortable chairs and the tea had been tasted by Kimura and complimented on, he came gradually to his point.

"Toto-san, I have a close business associate who buys all of his cars here. I'm sure you know him. He is Yoshi Hasegawa, a man of some importance."

The consultant sat up a bit straighter. "Ah, yes. Hasegawa-san is a very good customer." He could not keep his eyes from straying to Kimura's hands, looking for a telltale finger with missing sections. Which he found. "You are also in the market for a new car then?"

"Not exactly. I'm aware that Hasegawa-san recently purchased a white Rolls-Royce as a gift for another of his associates. A *mutual* associate. Hasegawa-san told me you are putting a crest on the doors of that car. I would like to see the car for a moment."

A frown crossed Toto's face. "I'm sorry. The last time we had the honor of providing Hasegawa-san with a new automobile was two years ago."

"I'm sure that was for himself. This is a new car he has purchased as a gift for a colleague."

"Excuse me, let me check our order file."

Kimura had another cup of green tea while the consultant went into an office to look at his records. While waiting, he peered around the showroom. No white Rolls in sight. It must be in the back. Yes, they would be doing the detail work and putting on the crest back there.

Toto returned. "I am sorry, sir, there is no current order on our books from Hasegawa-san."

Kimura wondered if Hasegawa might have ordered the car from another agency. No, Hasegawa was not a man to change his coachmaker, tailor or barber. "There's some mistake. I'm *positive* Hasegawa-san ordered a car from you. A white Rolls, I don't know which model."

"I am very sorry I cannot find the order. I'm sure it's my mistake."

The apology was just the Japanese way of telling him there was no order. "You have cars in a garage behind the showroom? I'd like to see them. Please."

"If you wish." Toto did not want to bring a customer into the garage, that was very irregular. But this man was Yakuza, which gave him license to bend the rules.

Kimura followed Toto through an office into a high-ceilinged garage at the rear of the building. As might be expected in a luxury-car agency, there were not many autos in stock. Only six. Two were older models receiving their regular servicing. Another was a vintage black Bentley. Three new Rolls-Royces being prepared for customers sat in pristine splendor. None was white. Each had been ordered by someone other than Yoshi Hasegawa.

Still thinking, hoping, that Toto had made some sort of error, Kimura said, "Have you been asked to put a special crest on any of those new cars?"

"No."

Kimura couldn't avoid it. There was no Rolls-Royce for him. Why . . . ?

And then in swift insight he did understand. There would be no white Rolls-Royce. No crest on the doors. No reward for his work. No seat on the *sanro-kai.* Just a bullet in the head after he finished his job.

"Are you all right, sir?"

Somehow Kimura managed a smile. "I can see I was in error. Hasegawa-san hasn't yet placed that order." He was thinking that he had better cover his tracks. "Please don't mention to him that I have been here. It would be an embarrassment to me and to Hasegawa-san."

"Of course."

Kimura almost offered money to assure the man's silence, then realized that would be out of place in a Rolls-Royce agency. "I do intend to purchase one of your fine cars in the near future, after Hasegawa-san has placed his order. I will keep your *meishi* for that purpose."

With a bow Toto said, "I will be delighted to serve you."

When Kimura got to the street and was well out of sight of the agency's windows he gave vent to all his suppressed rage by kicking a garbage can halfway down Sakurada-dori. Betrayed! By my own *oyabun*! He wanted to cry, but this was no time for weakness or despair.

He got into his car and began driving aimlessly through the streets of Roppongi. The pleasure he had felt just a few days ago in sitting behind the wheel of his new Porsche had soured. Luxury cars now seemed a symbol of treachery.

That was the wrong frame of mind. Don't panic, he told himself sternly. You've survived gang wars and other acts of betrayal. If Yoshi Hasegawa has sold you out, he's the one who should worry.

Chapter 23

"How did it feel?" Kay asked.

Tak started to knot his tie. "How did what feel?"

"How did it feel to sleep with an American girl again. Is it different with a Japanese girl?"

"You ask more questions than a squad of policemen."

"Here, let me do that, you're not getting it straight." Kay pushed his hands away from the tie and finished knotting it. "That's better."

"You're bossy, too. You think you know how to do everything better than the other person."

She raised an eyebrow. "If I'm such a bitch, how come you went to bed with me last night?"

"Strictly speaking, we didn't go to bed." Tak was pleased to correct Kay for a change. "We went to futon."

"You Japanese men love to lord it over women. What you need is a course in feminist rights."

"Just as I said—bossy."

As they finished dressing, Kay told him she would like to stop at the Imperial for a quick change of clothes before they went anywhere else. "When I was taking my bath I couldn't help thinking about your parents making love in that same

225

tub. It's wonderfully roomy for bathing, it must be fine for making love. Can we try it?"

"We'll have to be careful not to hurt ourselves. I never did find out what position they used."

"We'll experiment."

"Tonight," he promised. "This morning we have to see Hideki and then make some progress on this case."

"I'd almost succeeded in putting the sword and that gangster out of my mind. Can you catch him, Tak? I just want him caught and to hell with the sword." She laughed nervously. "Did I really say that? I take it back."

"We'll get him," Tak promised. "Whether he realizes it or not, I think he's cut himself off even from his own kind."

After Kay changed to fresh clothes at the Imperial they drove toward the Shinegawa warehouse. Once again a police car was following Tak, and again he lost it in traffic.

At the warehouse Kay used a first-floor pay phone and her credit card to call Walter Emerson in Philadelphia while Tak went upstairs to talk to Hideki. It was a little after 7:00 A.M. in Tokyo. In Philadelphia it was 7:00 P.M. the night before.

"Walter? Kay Williams. I'm still in Tokyo. There's been a—"

"You don't have to tell me, the story made CNN and the New York *Times*. My sword is more famous than ever. But where the hell *is* it?"

"We're getting closer."

"Closer isn't close enough. Did you know that someone is offering *my* sword to other collectors?"

Hilton Chambers, Kay thought. "No one is getting that sword except you."

"You are damned right there. Or you better be. I'm the one who *paid* for the sword and I intend to hold it in my hands within the week or you will find yourself facing my lawyers in *court*."

"You already told me that, Walter. Frankly, I'm getting pretty goddamn tired of hearing it."

"Listen to me—"

"*Twice* I've almost been *killed* trying to get that sword back for you. I've seen three people die." Kay felt herself revving up to say something she would regret. "I still intend to recover your sword. But you had better hope, Walter, that when I see you I don't take the damned thing and shove it up your big fat *ass*."

So saying, she slammed down the receiver and stormed up the steps into the warehouse.

Tak had let Hideki out of the room for some exercise and they were walking around the warehouse floor while the butcher who had been on guard outside the door all night was out buying breakfast for himself and Hideki.

As Kay approached, Hideki began wiping his eyes. He was unshaven and his fine clothes were now badly wrinkled.

"What's wrong?"

"I can't take this place anymore." Hideki appealed to Kay with the insistent whine of a small boy complaining to his mother. "I can't sleep in a place where you can hear rats crawling in the walls."

"They're probably only mice," Kay said.

"They're rats! And the food is bad, the chemical toilet smells, and look at me, I'm wearing *wrinkled* clothes. Hideki Kohno does not wear *wrinkled* clothes." He turned from Kay to Tak. "I usually change my clothes three, four times a day, you know that.

Again, Tak almost regretted the way he'd been treating Hideki, almost felt sorry for him, despite what he'd done. "I'll have someone go to Daiei and pick up fresh clothes for you."

"Daiei!" Hideki drew himself up to his full height. Which

wasn't much, though the gesture did lend him some badly needed dignity. "I don't wear cheap clothes from Daiei."

"All right, how about Issey Miyake's? Just stay here for two more days. If I don't have this case under control by then I'll let you go. You can even leave the country if you want."

"You mean it?"

"I don't want to see you murdered, Hideki. Your father was always very good to my father, and to me."

"Isn't your life worth a few days' discomfort?" Kay was still angry at Walter Emerson and happy to transfer some of that anger to the self-indulgent Hideki Kohno. "A couple of days ago you were a prisoner waiting for the Yakuza to kill you. Tak's the only one in this world who gives a damn what happens to you and all you can do is complain about wrinkled clothes and bad food. If he let you walk out on that street right now you wouldn't last the day."

A slow wise-guy smile spread across Hideki's face. "I get it, you two are sleeping together. Am I right?"

Tak gave Hideki a shove. "Back into your room. Breakfast has arrived."

Oto-san had arrived carrying a bowl of *soba*.

"*Soba*? For breakfast?" Hideki rolled his eyes. "You see what I'm talking about?"

"Very healthy." Tak wouldn't personally care to eat *soba* for breakfast but it wouldn't do Hideki any harm. "I'll be back later."

"What about the VCR and the movies I asked for?"

"I'll have some good books sent in with the new clothes. About time you learned something."

On the way to police headquarters they discussed Hilton Chambers. Kay was in favor of going to Hilton's antique shop in the Ginza and working him over with a brass candlestick or whatever other blunt object came to hand.

"Tempting," Tak agreed. "But we've got other things to do . . ."

At headquarters the chill against Tak appeared even deeper and more widespread. Simple and Dim were gone, "reassigned to more urgent duties." The other detectives in the squad room had been temporarily moved to other quarters. Tak was physically and administratively isolated.

"Gee, it's nice to have such a big office to yourself," Kay said. "Does this mean you've been promoted?"

"Hardly." Tak looked at a note left on his desk. The childish scrawl was Senior Superintendent Ueno's. A name was written down, impossible to decipher.

Tak called Ueno's office and asked him what the note meant.

"An anonymous caller," Ueno said importantly. "He claimed he knew who the killer with the sword was. He gave me a name but I couldn't exactly make out what he said. I wrote it down as best I could. The first name began with an M and an A. The second name began K-I-M. That's all I can say."

"I don't suppose you thought to turn on the phone's tape-recording system."

"Ah . . . no . . . I don't believe I did turn it on."

"Thank you, Ueno-san. You've been as helpful as ever."

"It was probably a false tip anyway," Ueno said. "You know how these crimes bring out crazy people."

"We haven't had a single crank call on this one," Tak reminded him. "We seldom get them when the Yakuza is involved. People are too frightened of gangsters. Which means this call might have been legitimate."

"Your theories are always interesting, Saji-san." Ueno spoke with his usual air of maddening superiority. "But so far your results are few."

"The results would come faster if I had some help."

"Get on with your work and don't try to blame others for your failure." Ueno broke the connection.

Kay was no longer surprised by Senior Superintendent Ueno's incompetence. In some ways it was comforting to know that all Japanese weren't models of efficiency. "You do think the call was genuine?"

"Possibly." Tak wrote the letters M-A and K-I-M on a notepad. "Let's try the computer."

"It won't be there," Kay predicted.

She was right. There were a few Yakuza whose first names began with M-A and last names with K-I-M, but they looked nothing like the killer.

"Told you so."

"I knew you'd say that." He began tapping the enter key on the computer over and over again. "Computers. They puzzle me."

"You agree the killer's file was erased?"

"Yes." Tak shifted around uncomfortably. "I missed some of the computer courses, they were too early in the day for me. That's when I was drinking heavily. And then, I wasn't really interested in computers to begin with. So I don't know this system as well as I should."

"I hate computers," Kay said. "No soul. Too damn impersonal. I flat out hate them."

"Well, you're an antique dealer. Computers are new, you like things that are old."

"Maybe. I also get backaches when I have to sit at one."

"Next time I'll rub it for you—your back, not the computer. Sorry, bad joke. Right now I have to go down to the computer center. I may have been drunk or hung over at the time but I seem to recall our system center manager saying everything put into the system is backed up somewhere on a permanent high-capacity disk file. Maybe somebody in the computer center can find the backup of the file that was erased. If someone really did erase one of the files."

"Good idea."

"Wait here for me. *Don't* go off and interview any Seisa-ko investors today."

Tak was gone about thirty minutes.

He returned smiling and sat down again at the computer. "Two files were erased from the computer this week. I was right, the deleted files were still on a backup disk. One was the file on a Yakuza gangster named Ari Hirada who died in prison. The other was a Yamaguchi-gumi gang member named Masao Kimura who generally fits the description you gave me. I had Masao Kimura's file restored to the system. I'll do a call-up so you can look at him."

It took about a minute for Tak to bring up the system and go through the prompts that led him to Masao Kimura's file.

When Kimura's face appeared on the screen, Kay grabbed hold of Tak's arm. "That's *him*. God, it makes my skin crawl just to look at his face."

Tak gave Kay a hug. "We've got him. Let's look at Kimura-san's record."

The text under the photo was in Japanese, so Tak had to translate and explain.

" 'Masao Kimura, also known as Cricket Kimura. Thirty-eight years old. Mid-level *oyabun* in the Yamaguchi-gumi.' Yoshi Hasegawa is the Yamaguchi-gumi boss for all of Tokyo," Tak said. "So Cricket Kimura works for him. It says Kimura-san has been a gang member since he was seventeen. Arrests for extortion, running a prostitution ring, suspicion of murder, dealing in guns. No convictions."

"Ugly damn eyes," Kay remarked.

"He's Yakuza at its worst. I wish I could see Yamato-san's face when he hears I've put out an arrest warrant for Cricket

Kimura. I'll bring in the press and television reporters for a news conference. Give them photos of the killer. We'll have his face all over the media by six o'clock tonight.''

Kimura was still driving aimlessly around the city when his car phone rang. He answered it with a sullen *"Hai!"*

"Kimura-san? Do you know who this is?''

He recognized Knuckles Yamato's voice. Before he could hang up Yamato said, "I know you don't want to talk to me but it would be to your advantage.''

"Why should I believe you?''

"Have you discovered yet that Yoshi Hasegawa plans to betray you?''

"Yes," Kimura said savagely.

"That saves us time. We can be of use to each other, Kimura-san.''

"How?''

"Your patron has betrayed me, too. Or he would, if I allowed it. Meet me at 11:00 A.M. at the Doutor coffee shop in Kichijoji.''

"Why should I go all the way out there?''

"So that no one who knows us will see us together.''

"Yes, it would damage my reputation to be seen with a crooked policeman.''

"Eleven o'clock. The Doutor coffee shop. Kichijoji.'' Yamato broke the connection.

Kimura's first instinct was to suspect a trap. Knuckles Yamato couldn't be trusted any more than Yoshi Hasegawa. He was glad to hear that Hasegawa was trying to double-cross the policeman too. Let them go at each other like wolves.

Presently, though, he found himself driving in the direction of Kichijoji. Although Yamato would sell him out in a minute, Kimura sensed that the policeman really did need his help right now. And Kimura was forced to admit that he needed help too.

Of the hundreds of Doutor coffee shops in Tokyo, the Kichijoji is one of the largest. Kimura found Knuckles Yamato smoking a cigarette over a cup of coffee. In an unsuccessful attempt to look less like a policeman, Yamato was wearing a hat with a bright red feather in the band.

"Take that thing off, you look ridiculous," Kimura said by way of greeting.

"So nice of you to come," Yamato replied, but he did remove the hat.

Kimura ordered coffee. As soon as it came he said, "Let's make this quick. What do you want?"

"You realize that Hasegawa-san is going to betray you, but you don't know exactly how. Correct?"

Kimura shrugged, unwilling to give Yamato the satisfaction of a direct answer.

"You've heard of the Former Minister?"

"Of course." The Former Minister, he knew, was a high-level fixer, though he didn't know the man's name.

"The Former Minister told me that a trusted colleague of yours, a man named Matsuka-san, has been instructed to kill you as soon as you finish your job."

"Matsuka-san! That's impossible. He's my—" Kimura was able to stop himself from making the inane comment that Matsuka was his best friend. "So Matsuka-san has been bought."

"I don't know what sort of deal Hasegawa-san made. I suppose he'll give your territory to Matsuka-san after you're gone."

Kimura fought not to show how hard hit he was by this news. He lifted his coffee cup with a controlled hand and sipped. "You aren't telling me this out of charity."

"No, I want something."

"What do you want?"

"Hideki Kohno."

"I don't have him."

Yamato added sugar to his coffee and stirred. "Detective Saji has Kohno-san. When that little viper was taken from my custody I suspected Saji-san. Twice I sent detectives to follow him and twice they lost him in traffic, or so they think. I think Saji-san realized he was being followed and lost them. He has Hideki Kohno hidden somewhere."

"What's that to do with me?"

"I have a plan for making Detective Saji return Kohno-san to my custody. The plan requires your help."

"I have problems of my own."

Yamato smiled. "You have more problems than you realize. Detective Saji has identified you."

That gave Kimura such a jolt he almost spilled his coffee.

"He's obtained a warrant for your arrest from the public prosecutor. At two o'clock . . . just three hours from now . . . he'll hold a news conference and pass out your photo." Yamato took out a copy of the warrant and showed it to Kimura.

"He has no proof—"

"He's got the *gaijin* woman. She saw you murder Turo Kajima and Jimmy Sato and his wife. She had no trouble identifying you from your photo."

"You told me you'd erased my photo from your computer!"

"I did. I have no idea where he got a picture of you. I once warned you that he's very resourceful."

"The woman is the only one who could have identified me. I can't allow her to live."

"You're right. And Hideki Kohno must die, too. I'm sure he's already talked to Detective Saji. First I have to get him back into police custody so that my record isn't compromised. Then I'll arrange for him to commit *sepuku* by hanging himself."

Kimura was impatient to be on the move. He had a good deal to do over the next three hours. "I still don't see why you're telling me all this."

"I sent a man to watch Detective Saji's house last night. My man tells me Saji-san is now sleeping with the *gaijin* woman. I'll arrange to have the woman taken from him. Then you contact Saji-san and offer to trade her for Hideki Kohno. Saji-san will make that deal, believe me. You can do what you want with the woman, I'm interested only in Kohno-san."

"You're sure Saji-san will give Hideki Kohno to me if he thinks he's getting the woman?"

"Detective Saji is tainted with western romanticism. Last night the *gaijin* woman stayed overnight at his house. He probably thinks he's in love with her, or some such idiotic thing."

Kimura's mind was moving at great speed. "We'll have to be in constant touch the rest of the day. Is your cellular phone line clear?"

"It's state-of-the-art, equipped with antibugging software." Yamato stood and put down a thousand-yen note to pay for the coffee. "Allow me."

Despite his troubles, Kimura laughed. "Are you trying to bribe me? What a turnaround *that* would be."

Chapter 24

Tʜᴇ ᴀᴋ ʜᴀᴅ ꜱᴜʙᴍɪᴛᴛᴇᴅ a formal request for an arrest warrant in
the name of Masao Kimura for the murders of Turo Kajima,
Jimmy Sato and Suzuki Sato.

The prosecutor's office approved the warrant within an
hour. They were pleased that Tak was bringing a case against
a known Yakuza gangster. It was always good politics to go
after the Yakuza. The warrant for Kimura's arrest would help
deflate the public hysteria about an unknown killer running
around Tokyo with a lethal sword.

Within the Tokyo Metropolitan Police the reaction to
Tak's case was considerably less enthusiastic. No one was
willing to believe that Tak could make the charge stick. After
all, the only known witness to the crimes was a *gaijin*
woman. Kimura would have to be captured with the sword in
his hand to assure a conviction.

There were no congratulations offered to Tak except from
Patrol Officer Kagayama, who called as soon as he heard the
news.

"I knew you'd get him," Kagayama said.

"We don't have him yet," Tak told him. "And we don't
have the sword either. We need both to make a case."

236

"You'll do it," Kagayama said. "And it will be a great day for us *burakumin*. People will see from your example that we're as good as anyone else."

Tak didn't want to talk about being *burakumin* and changed the subject. "Did you get my message about the fresh clothes and books for Kohno-san?"

"I'm having one of our people deliver them this afternoon. I'm off duty for the rest of the day. If you need me for anything else you know where to reach me."

The conversation with Patrol Officer Kagayama left Tak feeling down. He didn't *want* to be an example for other *burakumin*. He mentioned his feelings to Kay . . . "You have to understand that it's very un-Japanese to stand out from everyone else. Being a leader of outcasts is a nightmare for any Japanese."

"It looks to me," Kay said, "like you're a leader of these people whether you want to be or not."

"I'm not up to being their leader."

"Then don't think of it that way. You're just trying to *survive*, right? Do something you want to do and make a decent living at the same time, right? That's what Kagayama and the other *burakumin* want, too. Just set the example, they'll do the rest."

"I'm nobody's example."

A clerk came in from the prosecutor's office delivering multiple copies of the arrest warrant for distribution to other prefectures. After signing all the warrants Tak began work on the statement he would make to the press.

Kay went down the hall to the coffee machine and came back amazed all over again at how good the coffee was in Japan, even from a vending machine.

"Anything I can do to help?"

"Not right now. But this might be a good time to give Hilton Chambers a scare, even the score a little."

"Love it. You know what that bastard is up to? When I

talked to my client this morning I found out that Hilton has been offering the sword to other collectors in the U.S. Yes, let's yank his chain. But how?"

He offered a suggestion that Kay readily accepted. The next minute she was dialing Hilton Chambers's phone number.

"*Moshi-moshi.*"

"Hilton? It's me, Kay."

"Kay! I tried to call you at the Imperial. The newspapers are full of what happened to you yesterday. My dear, are you all right?"

"I'm just *fine,* Hilton." The scummy son-of-a-bitch. "Still shook up, of course. But otherwise okay." She wished he were in the room so she could show him just how fine she was—with a kick in the balls.

"Glad to hear it. Can I do anything for you?"

"Yes, as a matter of fact, you can." Kay looked over at Tak. "I'm finally getting my sword back and I need a little information from you."

". . . You're getting the sword back? Well, well, that's great news. I'm glad for you." A pause. "Ah, how are you getting it? I didn't see anything in the papers about the sword being recovered."

"I made a deal with the local Yakuza boss, Yoshi Hasegawa. Somehow he managed to get hold of the sword and he's willing to return it to me. He wants a fat finder's fee, of course, but even with that I'll net a nice profit."

"Wonderful," Hilton said in a flat voice.

"I'm supposed to meet Hasegawa tonight at eight o'clock at the entrance to Shibuya station. I insisted on a busy public place. Just thought I'd check with you. Does Shibuya station sound safe? I don't expect trouble, but I've had too many close calls in Tokyo already."

"The entrance to Shibuya station is one of the busiest places in Tokyo. Thousands of people."

"Well, that's *just* what I wanted. Hilton, can we have another drink together before I leave?"

"Love to," Hilton said, his mind obviously elsewhere.

"Call you later." Kay put down the phone with a delighted smile. "He's really seething! You can bet he'll be at Shibuya station tonight at eight o'clock to see if I collect the sword. I'm going to be there too."

"Why?"

"I want to look him in the face and tell him what a malicious double-crossing little pissant he is."

Tak didn't much like the gleam in Kay's eyes. "I'll go with you, just to make sure that's all you do."

"All right," she said, and smiled. "But you can be a real killjoy, detective."

Hilton Chambers was pacing the narrow aisle of his Ginza shop wondering why Yoshi Hasegawa was giving the sword to Kay.

He decided politics must lay behind the decision. Perhaps the Former Minister told Hasegawa to get the sword out of the country as fast as possible. Giving it back to Kay would accomplish that; she'd be on the next flight to New York.

But I can't afford to lose that sword, he told himself. He gazed around his shop. The carpet was threadbare and he couldn't afford to replace it. Nothing special about any of the antiques currently in stock. Mostly they were indifferent pieces like the Korean-made reproductions of Japanese *tonsu* chests, antique *sake* jugs that weren't that old, lithos of Hiroshige wood-block cuts rather than the real things, a hodgepodge of even more inferior merchandise. Business had been so bad lately that his cash reserves, never substantial, had melted away.

I must have that sword . . .

After a time he stopped pacing. If Hasegawa gave the sword to Kay tonight, he would just have to take it away from her.

A glass display case near his desk held a potpourri of objects, from old inkwells to silver cigarette cases and a collection of ivory butterflies. He opened the case and removed a two-shot derringer pistol. The Japanese were very tough about gun ownership. Getting a permit to carry a pistol was almost impossible, especially for a *gaijin*. But fortunately this old derringer, manufactured in the 1930s, was legally an antique, not a firearm. However, Hilton had been assured by the Dutch gentleman who sold it to him that the derringer was in perfect working order. The Dutchman had even provided Hilton with a box of proper cartridges that Hilton found at the back of a shelf. He broke open the pistol and loaded a cartridge into each of the two over-under barrels and snapped the weapon closed.

It seemed easy enough to operate. Just aim, cock the hammer, pull the trigger. After the first shot, aim, cock the hammer, pull the trigger again to fire the second round.

He slipped the derringer into his coat pocket.

Chapter 25

Kᴉᴍᴜʀᴀ'ꜱ ᴍᴇɴ ᴀʟᴡᴀʏꜱ ᴄᴀʀʀɪᴇᴅ cellular phones so he had no trouble reaching Nobuo Matsuka from his own car phone as he drove toward Yurakucho.

"Big Matsuka-san," he said. "I have a job for you."

"Yes, *Oyabun.*"

"I want you to meet me on the roof of the Seibu department store in Yurakucho in exactly one hour."

"The roof of a department store?"

"All will be explained. Just be there on time. Matsuka-san, one more thing. You still have that sword hanging on the wall of your apartment, don't you?"

"Yes, Kimura-san. You've seen it there."

"Bring the sword with you."

"To the roof of the Seibu department store?"

"Wrap your sword in a sheet or brown paper. Make certain no one sees you going up on the roof. Use the back stairway. And one more thing." Kimura glanced down at his own clothes. "Wear a dark blue suit, light blue shirt, red tie."

"Kimura-san, what's going on?"

"No questions. Just do as I say." He pushed the off button and returned the car phone to its receiver.

241

He drove leisurely to Yurakucho and circled through the neighborhood until he found a parking place on the street.

Before leaving his car he stuffed into his coat pocket the black hood he had used to disguise himself when he killed Dr. Wako. When he climbed out of the Porsche he was carrying a golf bag built to hold just a single club.

He didn't know why he hadn't thought of the golf bag before. All over Tokyo you saw businessmen carrying golf bags built to hold a single driver. The city was full of rooftop ranges where you could spend a half hour driving golf balls into green netting.

His sword fit perfectly into the golf bag.

Kimura walked slowly, as if he had not much to do this afternoon, toward the Kata Building a few blocks from Sukiyabashi crossing, the golf bag swinging from his hand.

He went through the back door of the Kata Building and took an elevator to the fourth floor.

The Kata Building housed the corporate offices of the Homare Kata Software Corporation. Homare Kata was one of the investors suing the government for allowing Seisa-ko Securities to sell registered shares in a nonexistent country club. He was a wise businessman, a cautious man in most endeavors. When he had learned that a killer was doing away with investors in Seisa-ko he had hired bodyguards to protect him.

The previous day Kimura had surveyed this building and decided he would never be able to reach Homare Kata. The executive was well protected by a team of professionals. He did not expect to get through to Kata today either. What he wanted to accomplish was the *appearance* of an attack on Kata.

On the fourth floor he stepped into the stairwell and slipped the black hood over his head. He walked down to the third floor and removed the sword from the golf bag.

He cracked the door to the third floor just far enough to see two bodyguards in neat dark business suits standing in the corridor. There would be two armed men in the reception area of Kata Software Corporation and another two in Homare Kata's private office.

Kimura gripped the sword tightly and stepped through the door into the corridor.

One of the bodyguards turned toward him. Kimura swept the sword in a long arc that took off the man's right arm with a bone-breaking crack. The guard went down calling for help.

The second bodyguard reached quickly for the pistol under his coat. Kimura sliced the guard's shoulder muscles so that his gun hand sagged uselessly. The guard staggered against the wall and slid down to the floor, leaving a stain of blood on the wall.

Kimura could have killed both bodyguards easily. Instead he rushed into the stairwell and slid the sword into its scabbard inside the golf bag, ripped off the hood, stuffed it into his pocket and walked down to the first floor with the golf bag in hand.

As he exited the building the screams of women who had discovered the two bodyguards in the corridor carried all the way down to the street.

With unusual restraint Kimura strolled back to his Porsche and stowed the golf bag in the trunk, then ambled on through Yurakucho to the Seibu department store.

By the time he reached Seibu, police cars were racing past him toward the Kata Building. Kimura took the elevator to the cinemas on the top floor of the Seibu Building, then went up the steps to the roof, from which he had a clear view of Yurakucho station just one block away, Hibiya park and the Imperial Hotel a few blocks in the other direction, as well as the Kata Building two blocks farther on. By now police cars and ambulances had parked in a helter-skelter pattern in front of the Kata Building.

Matsuka had not yet arrived so Kimura sat down on an air-conditioning unit and smoked a cigarette while he took in the view. A beautiful day in Tokyo. Kimura was a man who appreciated the pleasures of nature.

The only annoying aspect to the day was the cloud of huge black crows circling Hibiya park. When he was a youngster there were lots of small birds in Tokyo. Gradually the big crows from the countryside moved into the city and started driving away the smaller birds. Now one hardly ever saw small birds in Tokyo, just those big ugly crows. There was a lesson to be learned from that, Kimura thought. The big and strong always prevailed over the small and weak. A very simple rule of life.

A few minutes later Matsuka came huffing and puffing onto the roof, having walked all the way up the back stairway from the first floor to avoid being seen. The sword from his living-room wall was in one hand, wrapped in a beach towel. Matsuka, as directed by Kimura, wore a blue suit, light blue shirt and red tie. The tie was slightly askew.

"You're early, Matsuka-san. That's good. I appreciate punctuality."

Matsuka sat down heavily on the air-conditioning unit opposite Kimura and began wiping his sweaty face with a handkerchief. "Long climb up from the first floor."

"Good for the lungs." Kimura threw his cigarette over the side of the building. "Let me see your sword."

After a couple more deep breaths and another swipe across his brow with the handkerchief, Matsuka unwrapped the sword.

Kimura took it from him, unsheathed it and inspected the blade. "A piece of junk."

"Well, it's only for decoration. Not like your sword."

"There is no sword like mine. Not thirty minutes ago I cut off a man's arm and sliced up another's shoulder." Kimura snapped his fingers. "Just like that."

Matsuka was gradually becoming aware of the unpleasant

glint in Kimura's eyes. "Where did this happen?" Matsuka asked cautiously.

"Right over there." Kimura pointed to the Kata Building.

"A shoulder and an arm. You left them alive?"

"I wanted those two men to live."

"Who were they?" Matsuka was having serious misgivings about coming up to this rooftop.

"Bodyguards for an important executive. Do you know why I let them live?"

Matsuka remained silent, sensing that any answer he gave would only irritate Kimura.

"I wanted them to be able to tell the police they were attacked by a man in a dark suit, light blue shirt and red tie, with a hood over his head." Kimura took the black hood from his pocket. "This hood. Scary looking, isn't it?"

Though not brilliant, Matsuka was smart enough to see where this conversation was leading. He was also smart enough to come to this meeting armed. His hand snaked out from under his coat holding a Spanish Star automatic.

Kimura quickly kicked Matsuka in the chest, sending him toppling from the air-conditioning unit onto the weatherized surface of the roof. He stomped on Matsuka's wrist. The gun jumped out of Matsuka's hand and Kimura kicked it away.

"Get up." Kimura dragged Matsuka to his feet and hit him twice, in the face and stomach. "Traitor." He brought his knee up into Matsuka's groin. "False friend." He punched Matsuka in the face, breaking his nose. Then he let him drop.

Matsuka lay gasping for breath and trying to clear his nose of blood. "You're crazy, I've done nothing—"

"Don't lie to me, Matsuka-san. Not with your dying breath."

"No . . ." Matsuka struggled to his feet. "I'm not lying—"

"Look me in the eye and tell me that Yoshi Hasegawa hasn't ordered you to kill me."

Matsuka tried but couldn't do it.

"Put on the hood."

"No . . . I—"

"Put it *on*."

Slowly Matsuka covered his head and adjusted the hood so that he could see through the eyeholes. "I don't understand," he said in a muffled voice. "You're wrong, I've done nothing."

Kimura picked up Matsuka's sword and handed it to him. With trembling fingers Matsuka accepted it.

For a moment they stood facing each other, wordless, then Kimura dove into Matsuka with his right shoulder. Matsuka staggered back two steps. Kimura hit him again. This time the backs of Matsuka's legs met the ledge of the roof.

Matsuka went off the roof with his arms waving and his cries of terror lost in the folds of the hood. He never let go of the cheap sword. He held it all the way down past the twelve stories of the Seibu department store. Even when he hit the concrete alley at the rear of the store, his hand never loosened its grip on the sword.

Kimura looked down at Matsuka's broken body. Now, finally, the police would have their mad killer.

Chapter 26

"THAT'S NOT HIM." Kay forced herself to take a second look at the body. "I'm sure that's not the man who killed Turo Kajima and the Satos. And that certainly isn't my sword in his hand. This is just one of those cheap things you find in a souvenir shop."

Tak turned the black hood over in his hands. The hood, he felt, was the real thing. The same one worn by the man who killed Dr. Wako. Everything else, though, was faked. A driver's license and other items in the dead man's wallet identified him as Nobuo Matsuka. Like other Yakuza he had proudly carried the membership card of his gang in his wallet. Matsuka had been a member of the Yamaguchi-gumi . . . "This man was killed to draw suspicion away from Cricket Kimura." Tak covered the body. "The idea just might work, too."

"No one's going to believe this is the killer." Kay said. "He doesn't look at all like him."

"You're the only person who can say he's the wrong man," Tak told her. "A *gaijin* witness. And a woman at that."

Tak had been about to hold a news conference announcing that Masao "Cricket" Kimura was being sought for the three

247

sword killings when Tadashi Ueno came running into the
squad room with news of the attempt on Homare Kata's life.

In Yurakucho two bodyguards working for Homare Kata
had been hacked up. Not more than twenty minutes later,
and only a few blocks away, the killer fell or jumped from the
top of Seibu department store.

The news conference was postponed and Tak had rushed to
Yurakucho, bringing Kay with him. He left her in his car,
under guard, while he looked at the two bodyguards who
were being put into ambulances. Their wounds were savage
enough to have been inflicted by the same man, though at
the time Tak was surprised the killer had left both victims
alive.

One of the bodyguards was still conscious. Tak had time to
ask a single question: "What did the killer look like?"

Straining to get the words out, the bodyguard answered,
"Suit . . . red tie . . . hood . . ."

Tak called Patrol Officer Kagayama on his car phone, told
him what had happened and to get to the Yurakucho Seibu
fast.

Standing over the body of Nobuo Matsuka now, he felt the
case against Cricket Kimura slipping away. He called headquarters to put a rush on information about Matsuka from
the Yakuza files. A courier arrived within ten minutes with
the file.

Patrol Officer Kagayama arrived at the same time.

"Take a radio up on the roof and tell me what you see,"
Tak said. "You'll find other investigators up there. Yamato-
san's people. If they try to send you away, tell them I detailed
you to look for physical evidence. I'm still in charge of this
case."

"*Hai.*" Kagayama ran off toward the elevators.

Tak slid behind the wheel of his car, opened the envelope
and looked at Matsuka's file.

"Who is he?" Kay asked.

"Yakuza pimp and thug. Another Yamaguchi-gumi man. Background like Cricket Kimura's. In fact, it looks like they're part of the same team. Younger than Kimura. Clothes and watch are cheap, he's obviously not an *oyabun*."

"He's obviously not the man we're looking for either."

"No, but this complicates the case against Kimura."

"This is the wrong man. I *swear* it."

A plain black car with police plates pulled into the alley and the driver got out and opened the door. Knuckles Yamato and Tadashi Ueno emerged from the car. Yamato walked to the body with his heavy stride and stood there until Ueno threw back the sheet. Yamato grunted and smiled.

Tak got out of his car as they approached.

Yamato bowed with false deference to Kay, who lowered her head in a gesture of equally counterfeit respect. She couldn't understand their conversation, she could only tell that Tak looked grim.

". . . evidence is clear," Yamato was saying in Japanese. "This is the man we've been looking for."

"Definitely the man," Ueno parroted.

"Williams-san says he isn't the man," Tak countered. "And she has seen the killer *twice*."

Yamato shrugged it away. *"Gaijins* think all Asians look alike. She could easily be mistaken."

"Easily mistaken . . ." Ueno repeated.

"The sword in the dead man's hand isn't the one stolen from Williams-san," Tak pointed out.

"The killer might have used two different swords," Yamato countered.

"Two swords . . ." Ueno insisted.

Tak pressed on. "Williams-san insists that the killer had sections missing from two fingers. This man has only one missing section and the wound is not more than a day old."

"We will never know the truth of that. A bent finger can easily look like a severed part of a finger."

"Very easily . . ." from Ueno.

Yamato turned on Tadashi Ueno. "Stop repeating my words. Go, do something useful."

Yamato watched Ueno run off, then said, "Look here, this corpse is dressed in a dark suit and red tie. He had a black hood over his head. I am told one of the bodyguards outside Kata-san's office gave the same description."

Tak couldn't contradict that one.

Yamato pressed his advantage. "And Kata-san was also one of the Seisa-ko investors who is suing, which supports your own theory that these killings were designed to frighten people away from the lawsuit. You should be happy, Saji-san. You warned the investors. You saved lives. Kata-san is an important businessman, he's very pleased that you called to warn him about this maniac. Now, I want you to go to the prosecutor's office and have the arrest warrant for Masao Kimura withdrawn. As far as the department is concerned, the case is closed. I am sure the prosecutor will agree when I report what happened this afternoon."

"We should at least bring in Cricket Kimura for questioning—"

"We no longer have any grounds for bringing him in. The only evidence against the man was that *gaijin's* identification, which is no doubt spurious."

Tak had one more card to play. "There's another piece of evidence. The day Turo Kajima was killed, Cricket Kimura's file was erased from the Yakuza database. Someone in the department didn't want Miss Williams to see his face on our computer."

Yamato was startled but quickly recovered his poise. "That's a serious charge. Who would do such a thing?"

"I don't know . . . sir."

"I'll look into the matter myself. Meanwhile, withdraw the warrant on Kimura-san."

Yamato walked back to his car. Ueno, seeing that his chief was about to leave, ran forward to open the car door and climb in behind him.

By the time Tak was getting back into his car, Kagayama was on the radio to him from the rooftop. Tak doubted there'd be any evidence up there. This killer was too smart to leave evidence behind. He asked anyway. "Kagayama-san? What did you find?"

"A nine-millimeter pistol and a large towel. The pistol is a Star, made in Spain. I suspect the towel was used as a wrapping for the sword so it could be carried on the street without drawing attention."

"No signs of a struggle?"

"No evidence the victim was thrown off the roof. No blood. No scuff marks. Nothing." Kagayama lowered his voice. "Yamato-san's men are saying it was clearly a suicide. The killer was remorseful after hacking up those two bodyguards at the Kata Building."

"Have you ever seen a remorseful Yakuza?"

"No, sir."

"Neither have I. Thank you, Kagayama-san. I'll talk to you later."

Tak explained the situation to Kay, who was angry but not surprised. Knuckles Yamato's expression and body language had said it all.

"As far as the department is concerned, the case is closed. The killer took his own life."

"What do we do now?"

"First I have to follow Yamato-san's orders and have the arrest warrant for Cricket Kimura withdrawn." Tak started the engine and drove out of the alley. "Then I'll go find this Yakuza pimp."

* * *

As soon as he was alone in his office Yamato used his personal cellular phone, which did not go through the police department switching system, to call Kimura.

"You did well," Yamato told him. "Everyone is convinced Matsuka-san was the one running around Tokyo cutting off heads. The case is closed. The arrest warrant will be dismissed within the hour."

"Good," Kimura said. Then, grudgingly, "Thank you."

"I make a better ally than an enemy. Remember that in our future dealings. Now we have to get Hideki Kohno back. I have a man watching Detective Saji and the woman. As soon as the woman is alone, my man will call me. You'll need two men to pick her up. Men who can impersonate police officers. I'll provide police identification cards for each of them. They should drive a plain black Toyota like the ones used by our police."

"I'll steal one." Kimura was amused by that. "Yes, that's it, I'll steal a *real* police car. I know where I can get one on five minutes' notice."

"This isn't a game, Kimura-san. You get no points for humor. The police identification cards will be left for you in an envelope on top of the cigarette vending machine at Meguro station. Have your men ready to move."

Yoshi Hasegawa had received a telephone call from the sales manager at the Rolls-Royce agency where he bought his cars saying that a man came into the showroom that morning asking questions about him.

In the most delicate language possible the sales manager let Hasegawa know the visitor was Yakuza. "An apparent business associate of yours," was the way the sales manager put it.

From the description, Hasegawa suspected the visitor had been Cricket Kimura.

Hasegawa was in the back seat of his Rolls now, returning from a pleasant morning of watching sumo wrestlers train for the summer *basho,* when he received another call, this one from the Former Minister.

"You've heard the news?" the Former Minister asked.

"Exactly which news are you talking about?"

"The television reporters are saying that the man who has been cutting off heads committed *sepuku* after failing to kill Homare Kata."

"That's ridiculous," Hasegawa snapped. "Cricket Kimura isn't the type to kill himself."

"It wasn't Cricket Kimura who was found dead. It was your man Matsuka-san."

Hasegawa shifted uncomfortably against the Rolls's luxurious cushions. "I see. Kimura-san must have discovered I set up his friend to kill him. How did he find out? Did you mention that plan to anyone?"

The Former Minister paused just a moment before giving an indignant reply. "Of course not."

"I don't believe you. You told Yamato." Hasegawa was furious. "You can't even keep secrets anymore. Pathetic old fool. Giving you a secret is like handing a child a hundred yen coin, it's spent in ten minutes."

"You can't speak to me that way." The Former Minister's aged voice was reduced to a quaver.

"You'd better go to your summer home right now. It's going to take a strong hand to clear up these matters. I don't want you around to mess things up."

"I won't be ordered around like some—"

"Leave Tokyo this afternoon. Otherwise I won't be responsible for your safety."

"Don't threaten me, Hasegawa-san. I have too many friends."

"Your friends in the Diet have deserted you. The Seisa-ko scandal has made them anxious for their own skins."

"They made millions of yen out of that deal . . ."

Hasegawa was tired of arguing with a relic. "I don't really care what you do. Stay in Tokyo. Go to Monte Carlo and gamble away the last of your money. Either way, you are finished."

Hasegawa put down the phone. The Former Minister was exactly that. *Former.* He poured a pony of brandy from the portable bar, inhaled its sharp aroma and considered this new problem . . . Kimura and Yamato were now aligned against him. But it was too late for Yamato to save Kimura. Tak Saji had identified Kimura and would take him within twenty-four hours. This Saji, it now was clear, was a man to be reckoned with. No one had foreseen that.

Hasegawa had always known how to turn adversity to his advantage. It was the basis of his power. If Yamato and Kimura were allied against him, he would simply form a new alliance . . . with Tak Saji, who would take care of Kimura for him.

Chapter 27

Aт нек suggestion they ended up in her room at the Imperial Hotel. Tak was miserable over having been forced to cancel the arrest warrant. She thought she could change his mood.

"In the States some people would call this a nooner." She put the chain on the door, always aware that Cricket Kimura was out there somewhere. "Do you remember?"

"Nooner. No, but I understand. Sex in the afternoon . . . English is, as they say, such a rich language." He drew her toward the Imperial's luxurious bed.

"I hope this doesn't mean we won't do it later tonight too," she said, keeping a straight face.

"There is no later, there is just now. We live by discrete moments." His hands were at work on her blouse.

"Is that *haiku*?"

"No, that is Saji."

Tak's innate sadness lent a gentle touch to his lovemaking. But Kay brought out another side of him, too. A whimsical side he had suppressed for a very long time. They fell onto the bed, laughing, working at each other's clothes as if there were a prize for the one who got the other undressed first. And if there had been a prize, Tak would have won . . .

* * *

Afterward, lying in a bed rich with the aroma of sex, holding hands, titillating each other's toes, they had a rambling discussion that wandered over the terrain of both of their lives. After taking a shower together, they dressed.

"If I leave you alone for a while will you keep your door locked and promise not to go out anywhere?" Tak asked.

"Where are you going?"

"You often answer a question with a question, did you know that?"

"You just did that yourself. So what?"

"There you go again."

"That wasn't a real question, that was just a so what."

She'd returned to her old obstinacy . . . she would call it independence. Tak told her he had some Yakuza contacts in Shinjuku who might tell him where to find Cricket Kimura. "I can't call them on the phone. They know their phones are tapped. I'll have to go see them in person."

"Why can't I come with you? He *does* have my sword—"

"They won't talk at all if a *gaijin* is with me. Especially a woman."

"Sexist jerks. Why would they say anything to a policeman?"

"These people are Inagawa-kai. Jimmy Sato was tied into that gang through his wife. Her father is an Inagawa-kai *oyabun* in Osaka. They'll want to see Cricket Kimura dead."

Kay looked at herself. "I guess I'm all dressed up with no place to go."

"I'll be back soon. Here, take this." He removed a five-shot .32-caliber revolver from an ankle holster. "Keep my backup gun."

Kay accepted it with a brittle smile. "How nice. I love Smith and Wessons. Don't you have a bazooka you could give me? Or a flamethrower?" She was angry at being left behind, left out, and was not about to hide her feelings just because Tak was great in bed.

"I'll be back soon. Lock the door behind me." Tak left before she could fire another broadside.

At five minutes after four Yamato phoned Kimura. "Detective Saji just left the Imperial. The woman is in her room alone."

"I'll have her picked up. My men are ready to go and I got hold of a genuine police car."

"I don't want to know about that."

"Then don't count your cars at the Azabu police station."

She considered herself a good businesswoman as well as an excellent judge of antiques. Left alone in her room, Kay began totting up travel expenses on her calculator. This trip was costing Walter Emerson . . . or her . . . a great deal of money. After her unfortunate remark about where she planned to stick the sword when it was recovered, she had to hope he would still pay her expenses.

A knock on the door and Kay quickly picked up Tak's pistol.

"Who is it?"

"Ono-san, hotel staff."

She looked through the peephole and saw the Japanese in the swallowtail coat who had helped her several times in the lobby. Definitely a member of the Imperial staff. Behind him stood two wider, more stolid-looking Japanese in plain dark suits.

"Who's that with you?"

"I'm sorry to disturb you. These are detectives from Tokyo

Metropolitan Police. They speak no English. They ask me to interpret."

Ono spoke to the two men in Japanese and they held their police identification cards up to the peephole for Kay's inspection. Their credentials looked identical to the laminated card Tak had shown her the first time they met at the police *koban* in Shinjuku. "What do they want?"

"They wish you to come with them to Keio hospital."

"Hospital? What for?" She took a grip on the pistol.

There was a rapid exchange of Japanese between Ono and the detectives. Kay recognized only a few words, Tak's name among them.

"They tell me a detective has been shot . . . Detective Saji."

"Shot! Tak's been shot?"

One of the detectives was pointing at his abdomen and talking excitedly to Ono.

"In the stomach," the hotel man translated. "Saji-san is asking you to come to Keio hospital. Bad wound, officer says. I'm so sorry to hear this."

Kay put down the gun. "Tell them I'll be right out." She got into a pair of shoes, shoved the pistol in her purse and went out into the hallway.

They escorted her down to the lobby and across the deep red carpeting to the front entrance of the Imperial on Hibiya-dori. A black police car exactly like Tak's was waiting. One of the policemen got in front behind the wheel. The other opened a back door for Kay and helped her into the car, then slid in next to her.

Ono leaned in the window. "On behalf of the Imperial Hotel, I hope your friend Detective Saji recovers quickly. Please call if we can assist you."

The police car pulled out onto Hibiya-dori and Kay settled back. Now that she had a moment to think, she felt more upset than when she had first learned the news. At times like this the language barrier was terribly frustrating. She wanted to know what had happened to Tak. Who shot him? How serious was the wound? If Tak was able to send men to the hotel for her he must at least be conscious . . . And something about the demeanor of the two policemen was vaguely disturbing. She couldn't pin it down. Couldn't quantify it. Until her attention strayed to the hands of the detective driving the car—a section was missing from one of the detective's left-hand fingers.

She sat perfectly still, afraid even to turn her head, thinking about the gun in her purse. Well, at least if these men were Yakuza, then Tak hadn't been shot. He was safe.

Safer than I am, she thought.

Her cheeks reddened. I let myself be conned by two thugs . . . She unzipped her shoulder bag and darted her hand inside, groping for the pistol.

The man next to her grabbed her wrist and pulled her hand out of the purse. He said something in Japanese that caused the driver to swerve to the curb and stop. A hand was clamped on her mouth. The driver reached back and ripped the purse from her hands, then pressed a foul-smelling rag to her mouth and nostrils.

She struggled, kicked, shook her head, tried to flail her arms.

It took both of them to pin her to the seat and hold her while the chemical on the rag did its work.

Her resistance began to ebb. She felt increasingly weary, nauseous. She was in a sinking ship. A crashing plane. Every sensation was headed downward. Galaxies of light exploded in the blackness.

She made one last attempt at struggle, and almost did pull free.

Her left arm came loose and she began punching with it, striking out into the darkness, wild for a target. Her fist connected with skin and bone and she heard a curse. She was punched in the face, which ended her will to struggle.

After that she slipped into the dark land behind the galaxies of light.

Chapter 28

THE INAGAWA-KAI PEOPLE in Shinjuku had much to say about Cricket Kimura but they could not or would not tell Tak where to find him. They claimed they were going to take care of the cricket man themselves. "Kimura-san is the same as dead, do not worry about it."

Which at least in part was bluster. Admit it or not, they had a well-founded fear of Kimura. He had always been a tough competitor. Now, with the sword he was wielding with such lethal effect, he was almost as formidable as Yoshi Hasegawa.

The Inagawa-kai scoffed at the idea of Nobuo Matsuka as the hooded killer. Matsuka did not have the *chikara* for such violence. Matsuka was set up by Kimura to take the blame for the killings. Any fool could see that.

One of the Inagawa-kai said to Tak, "Kimura-san has always been a little crazy. He finally went over the edge. That doesn't mean he is easier to stop. Even crazy, he is very smart. This week is the turning point of his life, and he knows it. He either will push Yoshi Hasegawa aside and become the Yamaguchi-gumi *oyabun* for all of Tokyo, or he will die."

261

Tak still believed in *ummei*, the Japanese concept of destiny coupled with personal will. He had to admit, grudgingly, that Cricket Kimura was more than an ordinary Yakuza thug. Kimura had the brains and drive to reach the top ranks of the Yamaguchi-gumi.

His car phone rang and he answered with his call number.

"Detective Saji? This is Masao Kimura. How are you this afternoon?"

Tak wondered where Kimura had gotten his confidential police phone number. Probably from Yamato. "I've been chasing you for three days. You're a hard man to locate."

"I'm always available to my friends."

"I doubt you would include me in that group."

"A shame. A man can always use a friend in the police."

"I thought Yamato-san was the only friend you needed in the department."

"Ah so."

"What do you want?"

"As long as we're speaking of Yamato-san, you should know he is very upset with you for helping Hideki Kohno escape his custody. If the news got out that he had lost an important prisoner, Yamato-san's reputation would be damaged. He can't tolerate that."

"I don't know anything about Hideki Kohno. And the superintendent supervisor's reputation isn't my concern."

"Disloyalty." Kimura sighed theatrically. "We sometimes have the problem of disloyalty in the Yakuza too. *We* know how to deal with it."

"Was Matsuka-san disloyal?"

Kimura dropped his playfulness. "I want Hideki Kohno delivered to me this evening at an agreed upon location."

"I don't have him."

"Of course you do. You have Hideki Kohno . . . and *I* have the *gaijin* who calls herself Williams-san. We will make a player trade, just like in baseball. Think of it this way: I'm the Yomiuri Giants trading you a pitcher. You're the Seibu Lions trading me a catcher."

Tak pulled his car onto the apron of a gas station. "I don't believe you. Prove it." But he did believe it; Kimura wouldn't be stupid enough to lie now. Too much was at stake for him. He should never have left her alone . . .

"I'll call you again in five minutes. That should give you time to contact the Imperial. They will tell you that Williams-san left the hotel with two police detectives. My men. We told her you had been shot by one of those terrible Yakuza. She was *very* concerned about you."

The connection was broken.

Tak called the Imperial Hotel. No one answered the phone in Kay's room. He reached the concierge. Eventually one of the staff confirmed that Kay had left the hotel in the company of two detectives to visit a wounded policeman at Keio hospital.

When the phone began to ring he took ten seconds to answer, not wanting Kimura to think he was eager for a deal.

"All right, you've got her. What will you do if I can't deliver Kohno-san?"

"Kill her."

"But then everyone will know Matsuka-san didn't do your crimes . . . And how do I know she's alive?"

"You must trust me. We must trust each other."

"No. I do have Kohno, but there's no trade on that basis—"

"All right, you can see your precious *gaijin* before the trade."

"I won't deal until I see her alive *and* in good condition. I know how you work. If she's been raped or beaten I'll kill you where you stand." Exactly how, he had no idea. He added another condition. "And the trade must be made in a public place."

"You're in no position to dictate terms."

"Neither are you."

A silent stalemate went on for almost a minute.

Kimura spoke first. "Where?"

Tak thought about the date Kay had made to meet Hilton Chambers at Shibuya station. Of all the busy places in Tokyo, Shibuya was the busiest, loudest, most crowded. "Entrance to Shibuya station. Eight o'clock tonight."

"Shibuya station is a madhouse at that hour."

"You should feel right at home."

"Don't push your luck, detective. You'll deliver Kohno-san in exchange for the girl?"

"The girl means more to me than Hideki Kohno."

"So I've been told. All right, the Yomiuri Giants and Seibu Lions have a trade. Shibuya station at eight o'clock."

Kay drifted into consciousness with as much pain and fear as when she was blacking out. She wanted to sit up but her head was a pumpkin filled with lead.

Double vision was a by-product of whatever they'd given her. It took forever for the multiple images to come together, and then she wished they hadn't. She found herself alone in a room with grimy brick walls, oil stains on the floor, cobwebs in most of the corners, the smell of gasoline. A garage. Parked on the other side of the garage was the police car she'd been taken away in.

The place also smelled of metalworking and somewhere in the neighborhood one or more lathes could be heard running. No use trying to stand. Her wrist was manacled to a water pipe. She was on a mattress.

"Help me!" Yelling made her head ache but she kept it up. "Help! Someone help me . . ."

And then it dawned on her that no one within earshot would speak English. There was a Japanese word for help, she'd heard it once . . . *"Tasukete."*

Either that wasn't the right word or she was mispronouncing it. Whatever, no one came running.

She sank to the mattress and nursed her headache. Now and then her vision blurred, then cleared.

Eventually a door at the back of the garage opened and Cricket Kimura came striding in, dressed as always in a smartly cut suit. He looked shorter without the sword in his hand. An errant thought. He was talking and laughing, chiding her about something, bragging, making threats, all of which Kay had to gather from his tone and body language.

Now he took a videocassette from his coat pocket and waved it in her face. Kay guessed it was the cassette taken from Jimmy Sato's place. She was amazed he had kept a videotape that must show him committing a double murder.

Kimura continued haranguing her in Japanese as he paced back and forth. In a way he reminded her of Benito Mussolini, seen in old newsreel clips strutting with his chin out, making speeches about how he had made the trains run on time in Italy.

The sword was nowhere to be seen. Under the circumstances, just as well. If Kimura did produce it, Kay was sure she would not leave this garage alive . . .

Kimura began taking off his clothes, still talking, coat first, necktie, shirt.

Certain she was about to be raped, Kay tried to send her mind to some distant place. But rape didn't seem to be on Kimura's mind, at least not at the moment. When he was stripped to the waist he pointed to various parts of an elaborate tattoo that covered his body, a tattoo of a dragon, all red and blue. The head of the dragon descended from his chest to below the waist. As he spoke, Kimura unzipped his pants and lowered the trousers and underwear to just above the knees. He took his penis in hand and waved it. Kay cringed, then recognized that the dragon's open mouth descended below waist level and the tongue was tattooed onto Kimura's penis.

Out of sheer self-preservation, she heard herself saying inanely, "Interesting . . . *yoi.*" This man was crazy. Which was hardly a surprise.

Kimura, still talking, dressed and left the garage, then returned immediately with a blue and white wooden cage a bit smaller than a birdcage. Dried grass lay at the bottom of the cage. A cricket sat among the withering blades of grass, still and quiet.

Kimura put the cage a few inches in front of Kay's face and began talking about the cricket. Once he even imitated the call of a cricket with a high-pitched whistle. Kay was astounded when Kimura put his lips close to the cage and pantomimed a kiss. Good god . . .

"*Un ga,*" he said over and over again, then put aside the cage and came closer to Kay, reached down and slid a hand inside her dress. He cupped her breast in his other hand and pinched the nipple between thumb and forefinger. His eyes glittered in a spacey manner. Kay, straining to remain immobile, wondered if he was on drugs. He said something, probably about her breast, because he gave the nipple a vicious final pinch before removing his hand.

Then, abruptly, he picked up the cricket cage and walked out of the garage.

Tak stopped at an ATM and drew out two hundred thousand yen, most of what he had in the account.

Then he went home and rummaged about until he found the little .25 caliber Browning he had owned for years but never carried. He didn't like automatics, they jammed too easily. Besides, the Browning looked too much like the pistols Shinjuku pimps carried when they wanted to impress their girls.

He proceeded to clean and load the weapon. Although his

ankle holster was made to carry the pistol he had given Kay, the little Browning fit into it tolerably well.

He then drove slowly in the general direction of Shina-gawa, frequently checking the rearview mirror and also watching for cars that might be trying to shadow him from in front. There were, it seemed, no detectives trying to follow him this time. Yamato had found another way to get to Hideki.

When he did arrive at the warehouse, his feet seemed to drag up the steps like lead ingots.

Ono was still on guard outside the door, and Tak told him he could go on home to his family.

He found Hideki asleep on the cot and snoring. At rest he looked like an innocent boy. Tak knew Hideki better than that, knew him to be dishonest to the bone. Still, he felt a certain closeness to him, felt he owed Hideki some loyalty. Even if Hideki didn't deserve it. He wouldn't sink to his level. And there was *giri*. Kay would never understand *giri*, the Japanese concept of moral obligation. Sometimes Tak didn't understand it himself. He just knew it existed as surely as the sun and moon.

He shook Hideki. "Get up, I'm taking you out of here."

The welcome words brought Hideki to his feet with his usual litany of complaints. ". . . about time, another day in this dump and I'd be crazier than you. And look, your friends didn't get me clothes from Issey Miyake. My gardener dresses better than this."

"Your gardener isn't running for his life." Tak handed Hideki a wad of ten thousand yen notes. "Here's money to get you to wherever you're going."

Hideki grabbed the bills and quickly sorted through them. "This is only a couple hundred thousand yen."

"That's *all* I had."

"I guess it'll have to do. Let's go, you can drop me at Tokyo station."

Tak waited until they were in the car to tell him where they were headed. "We'll have to go to Shibuya station. The sword killer turned out to be a Yakuza *oyabun* named Cricket Kimura. He's kidnapped Kay Williams and he wants me to trade you for Kay. The trade takes place at eight o'clock in Shibuya."

"*What?*"

Tak allowed himself to enjoy seeing Hideki squirm, then told him, "I'll show Kimura that I've brought you. When I make my move to get Kay away from him, you take off."

Hideki swiveled around. "I'm not going anywhere near the Yakuza. Not with you or anyone else."

"You can lose yourself in the crowd very quickly in Shibuya—"

"Don't tell me that! You're one man. You have no friends, no one to help you. You're a drunk who keeps his job only because you once saved a member of the imperial family. Not even an important member, just some fucking fourth cousin or something."

"I'm not drunk tonight." Tak had to restrain himself from hitting Hideki. He had to get him to the station.

Hideki pushed down the door handle and tried to jump out. Tak grabbed his shirt and yanked him back into his seat. The door slammed shut as they made a turn. Keeping his eyes on the road, Tak took hold of the back of Hideki's neck and slammed his face straight into the dashboard. No more restraint.

"Stay where you are. I need you, and *you* need *me.*"

Hideki moaned and felt his nose to make sure it wasn't broken. "You don't have a chance against the Yakuza." He buried his bruised face in his hands. "Not a chance."

"You had better hope I do."

Chapter 29

At DARK Kimura came for her, along with the two who had so convincingly played their roles as detectives. Kimura was still loud and jovial in contrast to his men, who seemed tense.

At Kimura's order they each brought out pistols and checked their loads. He was like the battlefield commander and a word clicked in Kay's mind—*samurai.*

Yes, that was it. Kimura was playing the *samurai.* The harsh, guttural orders. The joking with his troops. His personality had been redefined in a weird reaction to the sword.

Her impression that Kimura had gone over the edge was reinforced by the way his two men were acting. When their boss wasn't looking, they exchanged worried looks and quick shrugs. Which didn't keep them from obeying his orders. They moved quickly when Kimura pointed at Kay and issued an order.

Immediately they unlocked the handcuffs that manacled Kay to the water pipe and bundled her into the back seat of the police car. The car, built to transport prisoners, had a ringbolt attached to the floor. From the ringbolt ran a stout three-foot length of chain to which Kay's wrists were handcuffed. One of the guards then slapped a wide piece of flesh-colored adhesive tape across her mouth. At night, from any distance of more than three feet, no one would notice she was gagged.

Kay had gotten the idea by now that they were on their way to exchange her for Hideki Kohno . . . she had heard Kohno's name mentioned several times . . . and as the lone witness to his murders, she was convinced that Kimura would never allow her to live through the exchange.

The two fake detectives got into the front seat and Kimura moved in next to Kay. The driver hit a button on a control wand and the garage door began to open. As it rolled upward, Kimura showed Kay a thin-bladed knife about eight inches long and said something to her in Japanese. She figured he was saying that the knife was for her.

He put a piece of the adhesive tape on the knife and slid it up his forearm under his shirt and coat, then pressed a thumb against his underarm to hold the blade in place. When he needed the knife he could make it slide out of his sleeve into his hand with a flick of his wrist.

Kay imagined him putting the point of the knife against her spine and driving it into her back . . .

They were out of the garage and driving through Tokyo's dark backstreets, and Kimura had still another surprise for her. From beneath the seat he brought out a golf bag designed to carry a single driver. He unzipped the bag and drew out the sword. Her sword.

He began speaking to her in an intimate tone, as if he believed she could understand Japanese and appreciate what he was saying. He clearly was speaking about the sword, kissing the blade as he carried on. At times he actually *cooed* to it. Weird. Terrifying.

Abruptly Kimura stopped talking. His face was sweaty, flushed. He put the sword back into the golf bag and stowed it under the seat, then tapped the driver on the shoulder, directing him to turn up a narrow street on the left.

In this section of Tokyo the streets were a maze of shack-like structures, none higher than two stories or newer than thirty years. Kimura gave directions to the driver. Obviously this was a place he often visited. Kimura told the driver to stop in front of a tiny shop no more than twelve feet wide. He climbed out while issuing orders to his men at a fast clip. They nodded and uttered placating sounds to keep their boss happy.

Kimura pounded on the shop door like a landlord calling for eviction. He noticed a stack of cricket cages in front of the shop and said something with a question mark at the end. Obviously upset, he picked up one of the cages and peered inside, dropped it and began pounding on the door again. *"Torigako-san! Torigako-san!"*

No answer. The shop was dark both at street level and upstairs.

Kimura reared back and drove his right foot into the door. The wood cracked noisily. The door sagged and fell from its hinges. He charged inside, pulled the string for the bare ceiling lightbulb and bellowed as though in pain when the light did not go on. The power had been turned off.

Kimura came back out to the car and snapped an order to one of his men who frantically searched the glove compartment for a flashlight. Kimura grabbed it from him and roamed through both floors of the little shop, shining the light into every corner. The shop's owner apparently had moved out. No electricity. No clothes or other personal belongings left behind. Stock of cages abandoned.

Wherever he went in the shop, Kimura left destruction. A shelf ripped from the wall. Lightbulbs broken. Holes kicked or punched in walls. An old lamp thrown through the front window, showering the police car with glass.

His sounds were like those of a jilted lover.

Suddenly, the two in the front seat, having seen enough, opened their doors and disappeared on the run into a narrow footpath between two shacks, their leather heels clacking until they were too far away to be heard.

It seemed Tak was right, Kimura had cut himself off even from his own kind. He was alone. Which maybe meant the odds had shifted a click or two in her favor.

She wrapped her hands around the chain attached to her handcuffs, braced her feet against the floor and pulled with all her might for almost a full minute. The only result that brought her was a sharp pain in her midsection. She eased off, panting, unable to take advantage of this opportunity.

Moments later Kimura reappeared, saw that his men had deserted him and began calling their names. The names became curses. He pounded the roof of the police car and shook his head, then came around the car to take the wheel, changed his mind, went back to the front of the shop, where he picked among the cages until he apparently found one that pleased him and put it under his arm. When he entered the car tears actually glistened in the corners of his eyes and his hands were unsteady.

He looked over his shoulder, shamed that a *gaijin* woman had been a witness to the desertion of his men. He delivered a backhand slap to Kay's face that was so hard she cried out through the tape over her mouth.

The ability to deliver a blow seemed to restore some of his self-esteem. He put the cricket cage gently on the seat next to him, saw that his driver had left the key in the ignition, turned over the engine and drove the police car in the direction of Shibuya station.

Yamato was insulted by the place Hasegawa had chosen for their meeting, a dingy noodle shop under the railroad tracks a block from Yurakucho station.

Smelly place. Terrible food. Though safe enough, Yamato had to admit. But still an inappropriate setting even for a quick confidential meeting. You couldn't hear yourself think in here. The cook was shouting at his regular customers, carrying on a conversation with them at the top of his voice.

Yamato tilted his stool, smoked his cigarette, looked at his watch. Hasegawa was ten minutes late. Yamato would have left except that he was looking forward to seeing Hasegawa's face when the Yakuza boss learned that Kohno would soon be back in police custody.

Yamato did wonder, though, why Hasegawa had asked for this meeting. It was not like him to choose a public place, even one as nondescript as this. Sniffing at the aroma of noodles, Yamato wondered if maybe they weren't all right after all. As a patrol officer he had eaten in worse places. Three-stool huts east of Shinjuku station. Sushi bars where the fish wasn't quite fresh. All kinds of cheap spots. But not these days, Yamato thought with satisfaction.

Hasegawa was now *twenty* minutes late. That was definitely an insult. To wait any longer would be humiliating.

Yamato lurched to his feet and marched out of the shop to the disappointed cries of the cook, who thought this fine gentleman in a good suit would buy the full *seto*.

It was almost seven o'clock. The streets were crowded, bustling, noisy, disorderly. The Tokyo that Yamato loved. He crossed the street, angling toward his car about half a block away.

Tires squealed behind him. He glanced back, saw a Toyota Crown coming at him with only its parking lights on.

He dodged left, then cut right. One of the green steel support beams for the railroad tracks offered the nearest cover. He ran hard, closing on the beam, angry at himself for putting on so much weight.

Two more steps and he would be safe.

But he was one step too slow. The grill of the heavy Toyota

smashed into his back, the left front tire clipped his leg. He did reach the steel beam, the car driving him into the beam and crushing him between the two masses of metal.

Yamato slid down the beam onto the pavement.

The driver reversed the Toyota, ignoring the outraged cries of bypassers, and rammed his car forward so that the right front tire drove over Yamato's body as he sped away.

Yamato's arms and legs were useless. *Hasegawa . . . trap . . . accident . . .* Those were the last thoughts that rolled through Yamato's mind as the curtain fell.

Chapter 30

THE NEWS THAT YAMATO had been killed in a traffic accident came to Tak over the radio in his police car. Hideki heard the report, too.

"Didn't I warn you, Tak? Don't mess with the Yakuza. Even a top cop isn't safe from those guys."

Tak wished he could say the Yakuza wouldn't dare kill a high-ranking police officer, that Japan wasn't the kind of country where that happened, Yamato's death really was accidental. But he knew better. "Yoshi Hasegawa's cleaning house. Every link between him and Seisa-ko is being destroyed."

"And *I'm* one of those links," Hideki said. "You can't do this, Tak. They'll kill *both* of us."

"You should have thought about that before you went into business with the Yakuza."

"You won't be such a tough guy when you've got that damned sword at your throat."

Occasionally Hideki regarded the door as a possible means of escape, but he was unwilling to have his head bounced off the dashboard again. "I've got almost a million dollars on deposit in three banks, Tak. Bahamas. Switzerland. Canada.

You can have one of those accounts if you'll stop the car and let me out right now."

"And if I let you go how would I collect?"

"I'll send you the money as soon as I'm out of the country."

"You've become a comedian, my friend."

Hideki contrived to look hurt. "I wouldn't stiff you."

"Yes, you would. And if you admit to having almost a million dollars put away, that means you have three million. I don't even care about your money, Hideki. What I want is to get Kay away from Kimura."

"She's just another piece of ass, Tak. You can buy a lot of ass with half a million dollars."

"Your father would be ashamed to hear you talk like that."

Hideki's face flushed. "Don't talk to me about my father! You were always trying to come between us, always happy to show me up in front of him."

"You showed yourself up. And I never tried to come between you. That's just your excuse for disappointing him again and again."

They lapsed into silence as the rambling green facade of Shibuya station came into view, along with the mob converging there for drink, sex, music and companionship.

Shibuya Crossing was a giant green anthill. Whenever the traffic lights changed, at least a thousand people rushed across the intersection from multiple directions. They met in the center, creating a gridlock of human bodies, gradually working their way past each other to reach the opposite sides of the street.

After dark Shibuya became especially bizarre with the five-story television screen on the 109 Building blasting out music videos, television sets built into lampposts to show the latest sports news, and the night clubs and *karaoke* bars swinging into action.

Tak crawled through the traffic, glad to be in a police car that could be parked wherever he wanted.

"Stop thinking about it," he told Hideki, whose desire to escape into the sidewalk crowds was written across his face.

He pulled his car up onto the sidewalk and parked next to a Hanzomen-line subway entrance. Before Hideki could try to bolt, Tak took him by the arm and pulled him out the door on the driver's side. He pulled a handkerchief out of his pocket, wrapped it once around his wrist, then wrapped the rest of its length tightly around Hideki's wrist and took a hard grip on the loose end. "When I was a new patrol officer I couldn't afford handcuffs. Still don't use them. This works just as well."

As he talked Tak was scanning the crowd for Kimura or Kay. "When I'm ready to let you go I'll drop my end of the handkerchief and you can run like the thief you are."

Hideki was afraid the Yakuza were already close by. "These people work in groups. They'll come at us from all sides . . ."

Tak moved into the crowd and let himself and Hideki be carried along toward the intersection in front of Shibuya station. The lamppost televisions were showing the quarterly sumo *basho*, the most recently promoted stamping his feet in preparation for a match.

Out of two or three thousand faces Tak had little hope of spotting Kimura quickly. With luck, Kimura and his men would have a hard time spotting him, too. They'd have an even more difficult job getting next to him in this crowd. Tak glanced at his watch. Right on time. He wondered if Hilton Chambers was somewhere around, too. He hoped so. Anything . . . anyone . . . that distracted Kimura would be a help. That was one reason for choosing Shibuya, that and the rowdy crowds into which Tak planned to disappear if he could separate Kay from Kimura.

"We'll wait across the street."

"What's the difference? One corner's the same as another."

"I'd rather not have this department store at my back. Too many doors behind us."

"You're right about that." The AIAI store suddenly seemed a threat to Hideki. "Let's go."

They crossed slowly, taking care to stay lost in the mass of people. When they reached the opposite side of the street they put their backs against the wall of a *yakitori* and began scanning the crowds for familiar, and dangerous, faces.

Suddenly a face did jump out of the crowd. Not Kimura's or Kay's but a *gaijin* who moved nervously, darting in and out of the throngs. Tak had never met Hilton Chambers but he knew the type. Thin face. Good clothes. Weak chin. Nose as straight as a ruler.

"Hideki, do you see that westerner across the street? The one in the poplin suit? Do you know him?"

Hideki gave the man a searching look. "Yes, he once tried to sell me a fake Hiroshige print. I don't remember his name."

"Hilton Chambers?"

"Might be, I'm not certain. Where's Kimura? Why doesn't he come?"

"He'll be here soon enough."

Kimura took the stolen police car through the Shibuya crowds as if driving a tank into enemy territory. He went over a curb and stopped directly in front of a camera shop, partially blocking the entrance. The owner came out to complain, quickly saw that Kimura wasn't a policeman, probably a Yakuza. He also saw a *gaijin* woman with her mouth covered by tape, which sent him scuttling back into his shop, shutting the door, putting up his CLOSED sign.

Meanwhile, Kimura detached the handcuffs from the chain and put one cuff around his own wrist. The cuff snapped shut and Kay was manacled to him, which literally made her flesh crawl.

But finally, a free hand . . . She reached up and ripped the tape from her mouth without caring how much it hurt. Kimura hardly noticed. He had been preoccupied since their stop at the cricket shop, which Kay interpreted as good for her. Or at least so she hoped. She watched Kimura without appearing to do so, and saw what she wanted—the key to the handcuffs being dropped into a pocket of his coat.

When he put the golf bag holding the sword over his shoulder and pulled her along, she went almost willingly. One way or another, this was going to be over. And soon.

Kimura didn't care about the *gaijin* woman anymore. His store of luck may have been depleted, that was all he could think about.

Why had Torigako disappeared? When this business of Hideki Kohno was over he would find the old man and ask him in person. Torigako couldn't hide. Wherever the old man had gone, he'd find him. And when he had Torigako in his hands, he would show him what a sharp sword could do to an old man's flesh.

Nishida and Yamaoka . . . the two who had deserted him at Torigako's shop . . . they would go into Tokyo Bay in pieces, like the whores he had killed at the apartment.

A bubble of panic. Did Torigako take all his luck with him?

He tried to calm himself by concentrating on the job ahead. Get Kohno. Dispatch the girl. Melt into the crowd. If he killed a hundred people at Shibuya Crossing it wouldn't matter. Yamato would protect him so long as he brought Kohno to him.

It also occurred to Kimura that he was now as good as indentured to the fat policeman. How had he let that happen?

Do a favor for a policeman and he thinks you're his slave. He would have to change that.

They came now to Shibuya Crossing, the corner near the 109 department store. Kimura held the *gaijin* woman's arm in a steady grip. No trouble, she was probably in shock.

He cursed Nishida and Yamaoka again for deserting him. It would have been much easier to cuff this troublesome woman to one of them.

A mob of people were poised at the converging corners of Shibuya Crossing, waiting for the green light.

Suddenly Kimura spotted Tak Saji on the opposite side of the intersection.

Kohno wasn't with him . . . no, there he was. Kohno was so short he just hadn't seen the little swindler at first. Saji and Kohno were standing with their backs to the wall of a *yakitori.*

He felt the woman stir next to him. She saw Tak Saji too and her hopes obviously were on the rise. Keep her docile, Kimura thought. Let her think she might survive.

Across the street Saji lifted his hand to show Kimura he had Kohno bound to him. And Kohno was squirming with fear, a lovely sight to Kimura.

As the light turned green and pedestrians rushed across Shibuya Crossing under a canopy of gaudy lights and loud music, Kimura pulled the girl closer and joined them. They walked slowly, bumping shoulders with passersby, toward Saji and Kohno, who stayed where they were.

"I want that sword," said a voice in *gaijin*-accented Japanese. "It's in the golf bag, isn't it? Give it to me. *Now.*"

Kimura glanced over his shoulder at a thin-faced *gaijin* he had never seen before. The man was actually pushing a gun in his ribs. Trying to *frighten* him.

"Hilton, for God's sake, get away from here," Kay told him.

"No . . ." Chambers switched to English. "I want that

sword, Kay. I need it, don't . . ." His face registered shock as he looked down at a slim, shiny piece of metal lodged in his chest just above his ribs. He began to sink as he walked, and blood appeared on his lips.

Kay couldn't stop to try to help him, Kimura was pulling her along. The knife, previously taped to the underside of Kimura's arm, was now protruding from Hilton Chambers's chest. Chambers was on the ground . . . And then she couldn't see him anymore. The crowd had enveloped him, just another Shibuya drunk for all anyone could tell. And a *gaijin* at that.

They reached the sidewalk, and Kimura stopped ten yards from Saji and Kohno. He was off balance . . . the *gaijin* who had wanted the sword was not in his plan. At this point he couldn't afford the time to wonder who the man had been. He had left his knife in the man but he still had the gun under his coat. And the sword.

Kay saw her one chance . . . Kimura was watching Tak so intently that he took notice too late as she reached into his coat pocket and grabbed the key to the handcuffs.

Kimura snatched at her hand.

She leaned away from him and threw the key as far as she could.

Kimura stared at her. Stupid woman! Now she couldn't be separated from him. But *he* couldn't be separated from her either.

He brought out his pistol.

Tak let go of his end of the handkerchief and bumped Hideki aside. "Go, get out of here!"

Hideki dodged into the crowd and ran down a flight of subway steps as Tak drew his gun.

Kimura pulled Kay in front of him, challenged Tak to shoot.

The lights on Shibuya Crossing had turned red, the intersection was clear of people. Cars beginning to cross were held up amid a clamor of honking horns by the presence in the street of a sprawled body.

Just before Kimura fired at him, Tak dodged into the stairwell of the subway entrance that Hideki had escaped into. Kimura's bullet chipped the wall. When Tak peered around the entranceway he saw that Kimura had picked Kay up under his arm and was carrying her at a run toward a side alley. He had to keep the woman alive for the moment. If he killed her she would literally become dead weight. He needed someplace where he could get a few moments to free himself from this damned woman. Cut her loose.

The policeman was right behind him. Kimura stopped long enough to turn and fire another shot. It went wide, thanks to the woman thrashing around.

Kimura went through the nearest door in a rush to get off the busy street. The interior was quiet. He saw a row of lockers and realized he had entered the dressing room of an *onsen*, a public bath.

A man wearing bathing sandals, a large towel wrapped around his waist and a smaller folded towel resting on the top of his head, came into the dressing room. He stopped and blinked at the sight of Kimura with a swearing, struggling *gaijin* woman under his arm.

In a panic now, Kimura shot the man in the chest. He toppled over a bench and lay still on the tile floor, blood flowing into the drain.

Kay did what she could, raked Kimura's eyes with her fingernails. He promptly hit her with the gun barrel and ran up a flight of stairs, emerging into the public bath.

Women, men and children bathing together in mineral waters took one look at the wild-eyed intruder and began splashing away from him.

"Where's the exit?" Kimura waved his pistol and fired into the air. *"Which way?"*

The now screaming patrons were climbing from the heated

waters of the tub and running for the exit that Kimura was looking for. He ran in the same direction.

Kay, half-stunned by the blow to her head, was still under Kimura's arm, her head below waist level. In front of her was Kimura's right hand, the one that held his pistol.

She grabbed the hand and sank her teeth into his wrist, and the gun clattered to the floor before bouncing into the heated bath.

"*Enough!*" Kimura was carrying this woman no farther. He dumped her on the walkway next to the bath, shrugged off the carrying case and pulled out the sword. He lifted his own left hand in order to bring Kay's handcuffed wrist to eye level and raised the sword.

Kay fought him, understanding too well that he intended to cut off her hand to be free of her. Her efforts bought a few precious seconds as Tak came up the steps and fired a shot that echoed through the now empty space of the public bath.

Kimura shuddered only slightly as the bullet struck. He ran straight for Tak, the sword still raised over his head, Kay dragged in his wake.

"*Tomare,*" Tak commanded.

Kimura would not stop. He would have Tak Saji's head for a doorstop, there weren't enough bullets in the policeman's gun to stop him, he was *samurai* . . . He ran directly at Tak, screaming obscenities.

Tak took aim directly between Kimura's red eyes. When Kimura was only yards away he fired a single bullet into the Yakuza's brain.

Kimura's head snapped backward as if jerked by a leash. He toppled into the mineral bath, sending up sprays of water.

Kay went into the water with him. Fortunately it was only chest deep so she quickly surfaced. Next to her, Kimura floated on his back, dead eyes fixed on the ceiling, a twist of residual anger on his mouth.

Tak knelt at the edge of the bath and pulled Kay toward

him. Now it was Kimura's turn to follow in Kay's wake. Tak eased both of them out of the bath and laid Kimura out on his back. It would take a locksmith to open the cuffs. Until then Kay would remain attached to Kimura, who looked terrifying even in death.

"There's a videotape in his pocket," she managed to say. "I think it's the tape from the White Heat Hotel that shows him killing the Satos."

Tak felt around in Kimura's clothing and pulled out the tape, which he hoped was in good condition even though wet. "At least I should be able to prove I shot the right Yakuza."

Tak also retrieved the sword and put it, finally, into Kay's hands. "You were right, this is an extraordinary weapon."

Kay stared at it numbly. "The first time I saw this sword I thought it was beautiful. Now I hate the sight of it."

Tak noticed a cricket thrashing in the water next to Kimura's body. The cricket was trying desperately to stay afloat, to avoid drowning. Tak reached down, scooped it up in the palm of his hand, and set it down on the bath house floor.

"Lucky cricket," he said.

Chapter 31

It WAS ALMOST 1:00 A.M. before Tak was able to bring Kay back to her room at the Imperial. Over a period of four hours they had repeated their stories several times to different teams of investigators. Interpreters had been brought in to interrogate Kay. The only thing Tak and Kay left out of their stories was that they had helped Hideki Kohno break out of police custody, and that Hideki had been at Shibuya Crossing this night.

Eventually the senior officials of the Tokyo Metropolitan Police accepted Tak's evidence that Cricket Kimura was the killer who had been terrorizing Tokyo with a stolen sword. The videotape of Kimura killing the Satos . . . still in good enough condition . . . was irrefutable evidence.

What the police department would not accept was Tak's belief that the Yakuza had killed Superintendent Supervisor Tetsuo Yamato. His suggestion that Yamato may have been doing business with gangsters was met with chilly disbelief.

At one point during their interviews a police inspector from the central crimes unit had wanted to impound the sword as evidence. Which brought Kay out of her chair bran-

285

dishing her bill of sale and threatening to call her "good friend the American ambassador."

After much discussion among the bureaucrats, Kay was allowed to keep the sword.

"So you've got your sword back." Tak took two Asahi Gold beers out of the hotel minibar and handed one to Kay.

"Walter Emerson's sword, actually." Kay drank some of the Asahi. "I like drinking beer from the bottle. Phil always said that showed a low-class upbringing."

"Did I ever tell you that Phil is what you Americans used to call a flaming asshole."

She laughed. "We still use the term and it fits Phil like a glove." She smiled at her mixed metaphor. "I was so scared, Tak. First I was afraid he'd kill me, and that was bad enough. But when he was about to cut off my hand . . . *God* . . ."

"Cricket Kimura was one tough Yakuza, and smarter than most, I'll admit. But in the end he was alone. That's why he couldn't hold onto that sword, why you and I were able to beat him."

"For once *you* weren't all alone."

"No, I wasn't. I had some *burakumin* behind me. Ono-san. Kiki. Patrol Officer Kagayama. I had more support than I've ever known in my life."

"You had me, too."

"Yes, I had you . . . When are you leaving with the sword?"

"I'm sending it to Walter Emerson in the morning by a bonded personal-courier service. That way I can stay in Japan for a while. Would you like that?"

"I would. The brass want me out of the way for a while, I've been ordered to take two weeks' leave. We'll go to Hakone, it's near Mount Fuji. Spectacular country, especially this time of year."

"Can we climb Mount Fuji?"

"It's a little early in the season. They haven't opened the

mountain to climbers yet." Tak looked at his watch. "Kay, would you do something for me? And what are you grinning about?"

"It took you forever to call me Kay. Now the way you say it sounds just right. What? What do you want me to do?"

"Lend me the sword." He reacted to her surprise. "Just for tonight. I'll have it back to you by eight tomorrow morning."

"But why?"

"Call it official business." He went to the closet where she had put the sword when they came in. Before taking it he said, "May I?"

"Yes." She would not press him for an answer. She absolutely trusted him. How could she not?

"What time is the courier supposed to be here?"

"Ten o'clock."

"You'll have your sword back by then, and in good condition. Now, see you in the morning. Get some rest."

He kissed her good night and was gone.

Kay lay back against her pillow with the uneasy feeling that this game wasn't over, it was only going into extra innings.

Chapter 32

Yoshi Hasegawa usually slept soundly, and so he was surprised to come awake in the middle of the night with a sharp sense of unease. As he came more fully awake he realized his sleep had been disturbed by more than just vague feelings. Downstairs people were talking.

He got out of bed, put on slippers and a silk *yukata* and padded down the steps to the first floor.

"Kenshi-san!" He called for his bodyguard several times and was puzzled by the lack of response. *If the fool has fallen asleep again I'll send him back to the Yokohama docks to collect loans.*

The voices he had heard came from the television set in the living room. An old black-and-white Kurosawa movie was being shown to his empty, darkened living room on ASAHI TV. He switched off the set and went to find Kenshi.

Kenshi lay on the kitchen floor, bound and gagged and unconscious. "Kenshi-san . . ." Hasegawa knew the bodyguard carried his gun in a holster on his hip. When he lifted the back of Kenshi's coat, the holster was empty.

"I have his gun. I'm keeping it safe for him."

Hasegawa turned to find Tak Saji standing in the doorway

288

with a Czech 9-mm pistol aimed at his midsection and the Meiji sword slung over his shoulder.

"Ah . . . Saji-san, I believe." Hasegawa dipped his head in a half bow. "So nice of you to visit my humble house. May I offer you a drink?"

"I'll have *sake*."

"Let's go into my study."

Tak followed Hasegawa into the handsomely decorated study and allowed him to pour out two glasses of *sake* from a bottle stored in a small fridge.

"*Kanpai,*" Hasegawa said before he drank.

"Put mine on the corner of the desk," Tak said. "Then go around and sit down."

Exactly what Hasegawa wanted to do. His own pistol was in the top right-hand drawer of the desk. He settled himself as if he had not a care and raised his glass to Tak.

While they drank, Hasegawa appraised Tak carefully. His observations were somewhat unsettling. Most policemen had stolid faces that exposed their lack of brains and imagination. Tak had both to spare, and nerve too, breaking into this house.

"You've been busy, Saji-san. I applaud your industry."

"Most of the week I've been a step or two behind you."

"You made up for it tonight. I understand the cricket man is no more." He let the corners of his mouth sag in a mock sadness. "I imagine you had to pry that sword from Kimura-san's hand. He was attached to it in an unhealthy way."

"He killed a salaryman tonight. No one important, just a poor fellow who happened to be in the wrong place at the wrong time. The dressing room of an *onsen*."

"That's too bad. Believe me, Kimura-san was not given license to commit wholesale murder. When he became crazed by the sword I tried to have him stopped."

"Yes, Kimura-san was too good at his work. He attracted

even more attention than you had intended. You sent a friend to kill him, but Kimura-san was too quick."

"Things became complicated," Hasegawa admitted. "I only intended to frighten the people who were trying to sue Seisa-ko, not the entire population of Tokyo. By the way, it was clever of you to steal Hideki Kohno away from Yamato-san. Not that the act did him . . . or you . . . any good."

"What are you telling me?"

Hasegawa decided it would be wise to let Tak know what had become of Hideki Kohno, just to remind the policeman of his power. "My people were watching all the train stations. They spotted Kohno-san a few hours ago at Shinjuku station buying a ticket to Osaka on the *shinkansen*. I'm afraid Kohno-san had an accident. Fell to the tracks in front of an incoming train. He didn't suffer. Died instantly."

Tak wilted. "I wanted to save his life if I could, his father was good to me . . ."

"*Giri*. I understand. Do not blame yourself, Hideki Kohno was going to die anyway. Do you know what he did? He tried to cheat me. I discovered he had held out some of the proceeds from our Seisa-ko venture. Wasn't satisfied with his end of it so he stole from the Yakuza. Have you ever heard of anything so foolish?"

"Foolish," Tak agreed.

"So you see, the things that happened were for the most part Hideki Kohno's fault. He was too greedy. Steal some, but leave some. That has always been my rule. Kohno-san wanted too much, which upset many people."

"You make yourself sound like a *victim*."

"I am. In this case, at least."

"What about Yamato-san's death? Are you going to claim you had nothing to do with that?"

"A crooked policeman? Believe me, the city is safer without him. Do you know how he came to work with us? He killed a whore during a night of rough sex and we covered up for him."

"Blackmailed him, you mean."

"Yamato-san had already taken money from us. His indiscretion only underscored his need for my protection."

"You didn't protect him too well this evening."

"I deny that my people had anything to do with Yamato-san's accident." Hasegawa spoke as if testifying in court. "Now get to the point. Why are you here?"

Tak transferred the pistol to his left hand and drew the sword with his right. "There is no chance you will be arrested, let alone convicted, for killing Yamato-san."

"I certainly hope not." Hasegawa laughed to take some tension out of the moment. "You don't expect me to believe you care what happened to Yamato-san. He despised you as a *burakumin*. He wanted you off the police force."

"I didn't like Yamato-san any more than I like you. But he was an inspector supervisor of the Tokyo Metropolitan Police. You can't murder one of ours and get away with it."

"One of ours? You're as mad as Cricket Kimura. You aren't one of them. You're an outcast. A *burakumin*."

"I know what I am," Tak said quietly.

Hasegawa took a drink. He now understood why Tak Saji was in his house. "You haven't touched your *sake*. I'm hurt. It's the very best, you know."

"I'm sure it is."

A brilliant lie came to Hasegawa. "Look here, I understand your feelings better than you realize. Do you know why? Because *I* am *burakumin* myself." He was gratified to see Tak look unsure of himself, exactly the reaction he had hoped for. "It's true. That's why I went into the Yakuza as a boy. What else was there for me? You know what it's like. No one will give you a job, let you marry their daughter."

Tak had raised the sword to shoulder level. Now he let it drop lower. "I don't believe you."

"I can prove I'm *burakumin*. When I finally got some money I paid an official to change my page in the family register. I kept the original. Let me show you." He opened the drawer that held his pistol, scooped it out with a smooth movement and fired twice into Tak's chest.

Strangely, the shots made no sound even in the small confines of his study.

Hasegawa pulled the trigger again.

No sound. Neither did the heavy pistol do its usual buck and jump in his hand. Tak Saji continued to stand in front of him, feet planted, looking at him.

"You couldn't be *burakumin*," Tak said. "You have no humility."

Hasegawa could not understand why the gun didn't fire. He kept on pulling the trigger but his fingers had lost their feeling. He looked down on a remarkable sight, his own hand lying on the desk with the gun gripping it.

He stared stupidly at the end of the arm where his hand should be. Not there. *Nothing* there. Pulling the trigger had been in his mind only.

The sword was stained with blood. Hasegawa could not understand that either. He had not even seen Tak swing the blade. Had not felt it sever his hand. So sharp. So fast. A thing of beauty . . .

Weakness overcame Hasegawa. With a great sigh he slipped from the chair.

"Call a doctor," he said from the floor. "I'm bleeding to death."

"The last victim of Tokyo's mad sword killer," Tak said as he wiped the sword clean with a handkerchief and returned it to the scabbard.

"You're . . ." Hasegawa was having a difficult time forming words. ". . . police."

"Not tonight."

The Yakuza boss watched his blood pump out onto the

carpet. His legs felt chilled, immobile. He could not move either of his arms. The room lights were fading.

Tak drank down his *sake*. As Hasegawa had promised, it was the very finest. He then wiped off the glass and the Czech 9-mm pistol, the only two items he had touched in the house, put them on the desk, and let himself out.

Chapter 33

"BEST WEEK I'VE HAD in years." Kay nestled in closer to Tak. "I always thought the crowds and the twenty-four-hour hustle of Tokyo was Japan. Hakone is so different."

"Mount Fuji is the heart of this country. Not Tokyo. Look, there it is."

They were crossing Lake Ashi on a steamer. The clouds parted to reveal the snowcapped mountain directly in front of them. They strolled to the bow and enjoyed the view until the clouds again closed in on the mountain.

"What shall we do tonight? The usual?"

Tak ran a hand up Kay's arm. "I don't see a reason to make any changes."

"Neither do I. I like our evenings just the way they are."

They had fallen into a relaxed ritual of going to the hotel's *onsen* every evening about seven o'clock for a communal bath, then to the dining room for a leisurely dinner.

The steamer deposited them at the landing in front of the Lake Ashi Prince Hotel and for the rest of the afternoon they hiked in the hills, going high enough to see the village of Hakonemachi at one end of the lake and the town of Togendai at the other. The scenery surprised Kay. Mountains

294

as green as Ireland's surrounded Lake Ashi, with the lake picking up their emerald sheen.

They returned to the hotel about six-thirty. As they passed the newsstand in the lobby, Kay noticed the photo on the front page of the *Daily Yomiuri*. It was the picture of Hideki Kohno, Yoshi Hasegawa, and the Former Minister that the *burakumin* auditor had found among Dr. Wako's papers. She guessed that Tak had given the photo to the newspaper.

"What's the story say?" she asked him.

"The Former Minister is facing indictment for fraud in the Seisa-ko case and for accepting bribes from the Yakuza."

Kay thought she knew how Yoshi Hasegawa died, and risked a question. "What about Hasegawa's killer?"

"The official theory is that Cricket Kimura killed Hasegawa-san just before he went to Shibuya. Although the time of death doesn't jibe with that theory."

"Do you think the official theory is correct?"

"As a policeman it's my duty to support the official theory."

By then they had reached their room and Kay made up her mind to say no more about the death of Yoshi Hasegawa.

They had changed into bathing robes before either noticed the red message light blinking on the phone.

Kay called the desk and told Tak, "One of my clients left a message for me. Billy Sturgis. He's as rich as Croesus and a rabid collector of antique chess sets." She looked at her watch. "Seven P.M. in Japan, five A.M. in New York. His message says to call him any time of the day or night."

"Guess you'd better call him," Tak said uneasily.

She dialed Billy Sturgis's townhouse and he answered on the second ring.

"Hello, Billy."

"Kay! I've been up all night waiting for your call. I need you desperately."

"What for?"

"When I heard you were in Japan it was like a sign from heaven. Darling, you must go to Beijing for me tomorrow."

"Beijing!" Kay raised her eyebrows to Tak as if to say this was a ridiculous request. "Why?"

"A member of the Communist Central Committee owns a chess set from the Manchu dynasty. Jade figures in a design similar to the terra-cotta warriors. The board is marble. This is the set you see in so many nineteenth-century picture books about China."

"Wait a minute." Kay had spent a couple of weeks researching Chinese chess sets for Sturgis. "Is that the set the empress dowager gave to her son? Turned out he wasn't interested in chess and passed it on to someone else?"

"Yes! The old bitch was so disappointed in her son that she never gave him a decent gift after that. Somehow the set ended up in the family of Lin Pao Wu, second secretary in the ministry of technology. He's owned it for thirty-five years. Never told anyone, of course. Bloody Communist Party doesn't want its officials owning things of real value or beauty. But times have changed in Beijing and Lin Pao Wu wants to sell his one treasure."

"How did he contact you?"

"By letter. Not just me, though. He sent sealed instructions to Earl Granham and Fox West. He's set up a secret auction, you see. Each of us is to send a representative to the auction. You'll be my rep."

Kay couldn't suppress the excitement that ran through her. "Why don't you go yourself? Won't Granham and West be there?"

"No. Lin Pao Wu doesn't want us in China. He's afraid his masters will sniff out what he's up to if three well-known collectors suddenly appear over there."

No false modesty in Billy Sturgis. She tugged at the belt of her robe. "Billy, I'm on vacation."

"You can go on vacation anytime. How often can you hold

in your hands a jade chess set commissioned by the dowager empress of China?"

She turned to Tak, who sat on the bed reading a book of *haiku* poetry with studied indifference. Kay had come to know him so well that she could read his disappointment a lot more easily than she could read *haiku*. "Yes . . . I'll do it." She watched Tak stiffen almost imperceptibly.

"When you arrive in Beijing go to the Bank of China and ask for Mr. Wang. On my authority he'll give you twenty bank drafts, each made out to the bearer for fifty thousand U.S. dollars."

"So the bids will be in fifty-thousand-dollar increments. How high am I authorized to go? The full million?"

"I don't even want the set unless it's in mint condition." He paused. *"Mint.* That's your job, Kay. Bid what the set is really worth. I mean, who knows whether a Communist would take proper care of something so special. I don't want it badly enough to overpay."

"I understand. What's my fee?"

"I've been thinking on that. I don't believe a flat fee works in an auction situation. There's no incentive for you to save me money. Let's do it this way. Thirty thousand for being my rep. Plus expenses, of course. Plus an additional five thousand for each fifty thousand less than one million that you get the set for. That way you have an incentive to bid skillfully on my behalf. All right?"

"Deal. But tell me something, why is Lin Pao Wu willing to part with the chess set after all these years?"

"An elegant reason." Sturgis began to laugh. "They've just started to build private housing in China. Lin Pao Wu wants to buy condominiums! In Beijing! Darling, the *whole world* is changing. By the way, while you're in Beijing have some Peking duck for me. My doctor forbids it, too much fat."

"I'll have a double portion."

Sturgis sighed. "You slim girls can eat anything. I hate all of you. Have a good trip."

Kay put down the phone and turned to Tak. "I'm sorry, Tak, this is just too big an opportunity to pass up. There's an auction coming up next week for an important piece, a Manchu dynasty chess set." She bit her lip. "I have to leave early tomorrow morning."

Tak forced a smile. "You can't stay in Hakone forever, I always knew that."

She slid into his lap and her arms encircled his neck. "I have an idea. Why don't you quit the police department. Sell your house in Tokyo, you said it's worth a lot of money, and come back to the U.S."

"What would I do there?"

"Whatever you want."

"I'm a policeman, Kay. A Japanese policeman. I'm proud of that. I belong here in Japan, doing my job. Just as you belong on a plane headed for a deal in some far-off place."

"You don't think we belong together?"

"Not permanently, it seems. And don't look crushed. You don't think so either or you wouldn't be on your way to Beijing."

"You may be right . . . but it's mean of you to say it straight out. I always heard Japanese men were so reticent. Are you certain you want to go on being a policeman? In Japan?"

"Yes, I am. Because I'd spent so much time outside of Japan, I wasn't even sure that I was truly Japanese. You helped me see that I'm as Japanese as the emperor. I can't fight that, don't even want to anymore. I thank you for that."

"You're welcome," she said. "You know, I feel just like I did when I was a little girl, all ugly and rejected."

"You're the one who's leaving tomorrow," Tak reminded her.

"True . . . dammit." She looked up at him. "Do you still

want to go to the *onsen* with me, now that you've seen what a calculating and ambitious businesswoman I am?"

"Will you let me scrub your back?"

"Of course."

"And soap your breasts?"

"If the other bathers don't mind, why should I?"

They looked at each other for a long time, aware that they would probably never be this way together again.

Tak got up and grabbed her hand. "Race you to the *onsen!*"